Love
Profound

KELLY ELLIOTT

piatkus

PIATKUS

First published in Great Britain in 2017 by Piatkus

1 3 5 7 9 10 8 6 4 2

A CIP catalogue record for this book
is available from the British Library.

ISBN 978-0-349-41842-1

Printed and bound in Great Britain by
Clays Ltd, St Ives plc

Cover photo and designer: Sara Eirew Photography
Editor: Cori McCarthy, Yellowbird Editing
Proofer: Amy Rose Capetta, Yellowbird Editing
Developmental/Proofer: Elaine York, Allusion Graphics
Interior Designer: JT Formatting

Papers used by Piatkus are from well-managed forests
and other responsible sources.

MIX
Paper from
responsible sources
FSC

A Note to Readers

Love Profound is book two in the Cowboys and Angels series. The books in this series are not stand-alone books. Stories intertwine between books and continued to grow within each book. If you have picked up this book and have not read *Lost Love*, I strongly suggest that you read them in order.

For a list of characters in the series as well as other fun extras, please visit the series website: www.cowboysandangelsseries.com

CHAPTER 1

Amelia

Early March

I stared at my computer screen with a goofy smile on my face. "Come on, April. I'm on a deadline, sweetie. I need you to push that calf on out."

"Who are you talking to?"

I glanced over my shoulder as my smile grew bigger. "April."

My brother, Mitchell, rolled his eyes. "The giraffe?"

With a chuckle, I replied, "The one and only. Come on, tell me you're not the least bit curious about her."

"I'm not the least bit curious about her."

I huffed, turning back to my laptop. I was on a deadline with this book and the last thing I really needed to be doing was staring at the ass of a giraffe.

"Where is everyone?" Mitchell asked.

"Well, Steed and Paxton are on their honeymoon, in case your forgot, and Mom and Dad took Chloe out for a ride."

My older brother sat down in the chair, sighing. "I knew about Steed and Paxton, smart ass. I meant Mom, Dad, and Chloe."

"Are you off work today? What brings you by?"

"I've got the week off," he said.

I raised my eyebrows. "And that's why you're here pouting?"

He frowned. "I'm not pouting."

"You're pouting."

"I'm bored. I thought taking spring break off was a good idea, but I'm too used to working."

"Want to come to New York with me? I leave tomorrow morning to hang out with Waylynn. Sister bonding trip and all."

His eyes lit up. "New York, huh?"

With an evil grin, I added, "We can get drunk and have fun. By fun, I mean have meaningless sex with good-looking, rich people."

Mitchell laughed. "Damn, I don't think I like the sound of my baby sister talking about fucking people."

"I said *meaningless sex*. I didn't say fucking."

His head pulled back in surprise. "Meli, isn't that the same thing?"

"No. When you say *fucking* it sounds vulgar. When I say have meaningless sex, it doesn't sound so bad."

"It's fucking, no matter how you spin it."

I let out a long groan. "Fine. You could go to New York and fuck a bunch of new women whom you haven't already fucked in the back of your truck before breaking their hearts when they quickly realized the only thing they're getting from you is your dick, and only long enough for them to call out your name a few times."

His brows rose. "Holy shit, do you always talk so filthy?"

My jaw fell while I stared at him, dumbfounded. "Are you serious right now?"

He shook his head. "Dad would wash your mouth out with soap if he heard his little angel talking that way."

With a chuckle, I shook my head. "Well, Dad would want to do a lot more to me if he knew all the things I've done. How do you think I write such hot sex? It's called on-the-job training." Flashing him another evil smile, I winked. "Matter of fact, your friend Rodney might have taught me a new position or two."

Mitchell's face turned red. He stood, nearly knocking over the barstool he was sitting on. "I'll fucking rip his dick off if he touched you."

I grinned. "He did a lot more than touch, big brother." Leaning back, I grabbed the table and started a pretend orgasm.

Balling his fists, Mitchell's eyes nearly popped out of his head while he paced. "I'll kill him. No. I'll lose my job if I kill him. I need to find someone who will kill him. But make him hurt first…for a long time."

With a roar of laughter, I got up and walked over to him. "Mitchell, do you honestly think one of your friends would ever touch me? Hell, half the guys in this town are afraid to even look at me, let alone sleep with me. Oh, wait, as you put it…fuck me."

"Don't say that." He covered his ears.

I rolled my eyes. "Sit back down, and don't put a hit out on Rodney. He's a nice guy. I tried hitting on him once. I used my best moves and he turned me down flat. Said he valued his life over his dick."

Mitchell's body relaxed and he let out a chuckle. "You realize you almost had me wanting to kill one of my closest friends, Amelia?"

I shrugged. "You do know I have had sex before and with some people you know."

He shuddered. "Why are we having this conversation?"

"You brought it up!"

"No, I didn't. I simply said I was on vacation. You brought up having sex!"

My father, mother, and Chloe walked into the kitchen and stopped. Mom looked at me and asked, "Who is having S-E-X?"

"That spells *sex*!" Chloe called out as she ran by all of us and headed into the game room.

"Lord Almighty, that child is a good speller," Mom said.

"Back to my original question, who is having S-E...oh, hell, sex?"

"Mitchell..." I said a little too quickly. He turned and glared at me.

With a serious look, my mother said, "I hope you're wearing a C-O-N—"

Standing, he held up his hands. "Mom, please."

Mitchell shot me the finger when my parents weren't looking, and I hid a smile behind my hands.

"Don't 'Mom, please' me, young man. Practicing safe... festivities...is never anything to shy away from."

My hands dropped to my lap as I stared at my mother.

"*Festivities*?" Mitchell and I said at once.

"Little ears around. Little ears," Mom said with a wink and a smile. "Amelia, the same goes for you."

A loud bang caused both my mother and me to let out a scream. Mitchell nearly jumped behind something to take cover.

My dad stood in the doorway, a large roasting pan at his feet with the contents of a roast and veggies scattered across the floor. His expression was horrified. "Amelia...what?"

Standing, I chuckled and said, "Well, I think this is the perfect time for me to go play with my niece. Later, y'all."

I made my way into my old room, and I couldn't help but smile when I found Chloe on the floor, playing with all of my old Breyer horses. As I slid to the ground, I spied my favorite one.

"Spirit," I said with a huge smile on my face.

"You named them all?" she asked with a tilt of her head.

Turning the plastic horse in my hand, I nodded. "If you look on their bellies, you'll see the name of that horse. Grammy couldn't remember them all, so she had to write them down."

Chloe giggled. "Is it okay that I'm playing with them, Aunt Meli?"

I reached for another horse. "Of course, Chloe. I got them down from my bedroom closet and gave them to your dad for you to play with."

Her grin reached from ear to ear. "Thank you! I hope Santa brings me my very own horse for Christmas. Like Stanley is your very own horse."

"Oh, he totally will!" It was out of my mouth before I could stop myself.

Chloe's eyes lit up with hope and excitement, while I cringed secretly. *Crap.* I basically told her she was getting a horse for Christmas. Steed was going to kill me.

"Do you think Daddy and Mommy are having fun on their honeymoon?"

With a grin, I replied, "I bet they are. Your mommy has always wanted to go to Ireland."

Chloe picked up a horse and stared at it.

"Why the sad face?" I brushed a piece of her blonde hair behind her ear.

"I wanted to go with them, but Daddy said I couldn't."

I let out a soft chuckle. "Oh, sweetie, I'm sure they are both missing you so much."

"Then why didn't they take me with them?"

Lord. How do I explain this?

"Well, when mommies and daddies get married, they always go on vacation by themselves. It's a way to celebrate becoming one."

"One?"

Those blue eyes were staring into mine. "It's just a phrase."

"Phrase?"

"A saying?"

"Huh?"

I rolled my eyes. "Never mind all of that. Okay, let's try this. Some day when you get married, you'll go on a honeymoon with your husband. All alone. It's a tradition."

She smiled. "I like traditions! Let's make a tradition, Meli! Like playing with horses."

Chloe grabbed another horse and fell right into a scene from one of her movies. Letting out a soft sigh, I mumbled, "I should have started with that first."

CHAPTER 2

Amelia

"Are you sure you've got everything?" Mom asked.

I stared at my phone in shock. "The live feed is down!"

"Live feed?"

"It's the damn giraffe, Mom. She is obsessed with it," Trevor said as he took my suitcase from my hand.

My mother *tsked*, like only a mom could. "Goodness, Amelia. Do you not have anything else to do besides watch a pregnant giraffe all day?"

After I had hit refresh and April reappeared on the screen, I dropped my phone into my purse. "Yes, I've got a book due in three weeks. I need inspiration to get me writing."

"And staring at a giraffe's ass is doing it for you?" Trevor asked.

I hit him on the arm. "Shut up. You know how much I love the anticipation of her birth. When I found out about April, I fell in love. Now I need to see her through to the very end. Like when you're reading a good series and you have to finish it so you make sure everyone gets their HEA!"

Both Mom and Trevor rolled their eyes.

With a slight chuckle, Trevor said, "Come on, let's get you to the airport. By the way, I'm picking up Wade a few hours after you take off."

Narrowing my brows, I asked, "Wade?"

Trevor shut the back door and faced me. "Yeah. I went to Texas A&M with him. He was a year ahead of me, has a degree in Agriculture."

"Why's he coming here?"

He smiled and winked. "I hired him for the ranch."

I could see the happiness in my brother's eyes. My father knew how much Trevor loved this ranch, not that my other brothers didn't, but Trevor lived for it. His goal was to take over the ranch from our father and run the day-to-day business.

Mom entwined her arm with mine. "He's proud of you, Trevor. The things you're doing for the ranch do not go unnoticed."

I smiled as my brother tipped his hat to our mother and leaned in to kiss her cheek. "We best get on the road if we want to get you there on time, Meli."

Nodding, I faced Mom. "I'll miss you."

Her hand landed softly on the side of my face. Sweet, loving eyes stared into mine. "I'll miss you, sweetheart. Tell Waylynn I miss her, and I can't wait to see her again."

My hand covered Mom's. "I will. I'll only be gone two weeks."

She smiled and stepped to the side as I climbed up into Trevor's truck. I rolled the window down and waved.

"Oh! If Steed asks, it wasn't me who gave Chloe the idea of a horse for Christmas."

Her grin faded, she closed her eyes, and shook her head while Trevor lost it laughing.

The two-hour drive to the San Antonio airport seemed to drag. Trevor was listening to some sports talk show on the radio, and I was about to pull my hair out from boredom.

"So, who is this Wade guy?" I asked.

Reaching over to turn the radio down, Trevor peered at me before looking straight ahead. "I already told you."

"No, you told me you went to school with him and that he was coming to work at the ranch. What made you want to hire him? You have a degree in ranch management."

He chuckled. "Yeah, well, his degree goes more into the science side of running a ranch. The land, food the cattle graze on, benefits of going organic. All of that."

"Organic? Y'all are switching over to organic?"

With a shrug, he replied, "I don't know. That's where Wade will come into play. The guy is smart as all get out when it comes to cattle. Hell, not just cattle. He's already working on a side gig with some girl in Fredericksburg who makes all natural products from goat's milk. She's looking to find someone to buy it from, and Wade's thinking we might be able to sell her some of our goat milk for her products."

"Wow. Wade sounds like a go-getter. Where has he been working?"

"His daddy's place in Colorado."

I turned to Trevor. "Colorado?"

"Yeah. Why do you sound so surprised?"

With a silent chuckle, I shook my head, staring back out the front window. "Not surprised, *tickled*, I guess you could say. My latest book is based in Colorado. I was actually thinking of taking a trip up there."

In my mind I pictured this Wade character as a skinny, nerdy cowboy who loved science, but not enough to give up his roots.

"Were y'all good friends in college?"

Trevor laughed. "Yeah. We were. He took me under his wing when I started partying a little too hard. He's more of a book guy over a partying guy."

Ding. Ding. Ding. Yep. Cowboy nerd.

"Well, maybe he can help me if I have any questions about Colorado."

Trevor laughed. "Oh, trust me, he'll help you with anything the moment he sees you."

I was about to ask what he meant, but Trevor pulled up to the curb and put his truck in park. "Alright. Have a safe flight, little sis, and kiss Waylynn for me."

I jumped out of his truck and waited for him to get my suitcase from the back seat. "I will, and be careful driving back home, okay?"

With a full-on smile, dimples to boot, Trevor wrapped me up in his arms. "I love you, Meli."

I hugged him back. "I love you more, Trev."

Standing on the curb, I watched as he drove off to kill time before Wade showed up.

I reached for my suitcase and headed into the airport where I checked in and made my way to the gate. As I sat waiting, I stared at the blank Word document in front of me. This was the worst case of writer's block I'd ever had.

Shit. Shit. Shit.

What was wrong with me? I chuckled. I knew what was wrong. I needed to get laid. It had been far too long. Pretty much ever since Ryan, my ex. The one guy I opened my heart for only to have him stomp on it, the cheating, rotten bastard. I'd been with a couple of guys since, but nothing serious.

After staring at the screen for ten minutes, I packed up my laptop and began one of my all-time favorite activities. Well, other than watching to see if April had given birth yet.

I people watched.

Unfortunately, all the happy couples around left me snarling. Ugh. The one sitting across from me seriously needed to get a hotel room. Rolling my eyes, I looked away. I didn't want to admit my heart ached to have a man look at me that way. I wrote about love, but it seemed I was destined to never find it.

Another couple caught my attention. The man gently placed his hand on the side of the woman's face, smiling at her with so much love I wasn't sure if I should cry or scream. Then he leaned in and gave her the sweetest kiss.

"Stupid freakin' love," I mumbled as I reached into my over-sized purse and pulled out my favorite go-to book. *The Lace Reader* by Brunonia Barry. I was soon lost in Towner's story and quickly forgot about my own real-world problems.

CHAPTER 3

Amelia

My sister's scream echoed through the airport and caused me to let out a wail of my own. The second I saw her I rushed to her open arms.

"Waylynn!" I cried as she wrapped me in a hug and held tight.

"I'm so glad you're here," she whispered in the saddest voice I'd ever heard.

Pulling back, I searched her face. "What's wrong?"

She shook her head. "Nothing. Everything is amazing now that we're together."

Something deep in my gut told me she was lying through her teeth. I could see it in her eyes. We might have been ten years apart in age, but we were closer than if we had been twins. It was Waylynn who got me drunk for the first time. Taught me the proper way to French kiss a guy, and even showed me how to give a hand job on an oversized cucumber. The things she and I got into... If my father ever found out, he would have put us both in a convent.

"What trouble are we after?" Waylynn asked as she hooked her arm with mine and guided me to the luggage area. Her forced smile wasn't lost on me.

"Well, if I don't manage to get laid in New York City, then we have a serious problem."

My older sister let out a chuckle. "First on our list of things to do: get you laid."

I dropped my head back and looked up to the heavens. "Thank God!"

"You know you don't have to stay in a hotel, Meli."

Dropping my computer bag in the desk chair, I faced my sister. "I know, but I'm more comfortable here. Besides, I know Jack doesn't care for me."

Waylynn sighed and sat on the edge of the bed. "Jack doesn't care for anyone but Jack."

I leaned against the desk. "We've been worried, Waylynn. Mom asked me to do some digging while I was here. Things aren't going good with y'all?"

She let out a fake chuckle. "I figured as much, especially with how often Mom texts, asking how things are going." Waylynn sighed heavily. "No, things aren't good. He's never home, always on business trips and when he *is* here there's always some damn function I need to attend to 'represent' him like I'm a window dressing at Macy's."

I huffed. "You realize you're nothing but his arm candy, Waylynn. Why do you put up with him?"

With a frown, she stood. "I love him. Or, at least, I used to love him. These days I'm not so sure how I feel anymore."

My heart broke for my sister as I walked over and held her tightly. "I'm so sorry, Waylynn. I know how much he's meant to you."

She let out a sniffle but then pulled back, her façade in place again. "Let's go cause some shit! You're in New York, after all."

I grinned and shook my head, letting it go for now. "Sounds like a plan!"

We spent the rest of the day exploring the West Village in New York City and eating everything we could get our hands on. By the time I got back to my hotel, I was feeling sick to my stomach. When Waylynn's text came through, I groaned in protest as I dragged my ass off the bed and over to my phone.

Waylynn: *I've got us an invite to the Electric Room!*

My heart jumped with excitement. I smiled and replied:

Me: *Are you shitting me? Waylynn, do you know how hard it is to get into that place?*

Waylynn: *LOL! Yes! I'll have Jack's driver get me at eleven and then we'll pick you up. Sound good?*

Me: *Yes! I'll be ready.*

The next text I sent off was to my best friend, Jen, back in Oak Springs.

Me: *You'll never guess what?!*

Jen: *I bet I can play this game better. But what?*

My curiosity piqued.

Me: *You think you've got something better than me?*

Jen: *Oh, I'm almost positive I've got something better. Book worthy.*

My brows lifted, and I hit her number.

"Hey," Jen panted.

"Are you running or something?"

"Yep. I needed to clear my head."

This had to be bad. Jen never ran. "What happened?"

"Are you sitting down?"

I sat on the edge of the bed. "Yeah."

"I had sex with Martin."

My eyes widened in shock. "Martin, as in the hot UPS guy?"

Jen groaned. "Oh, God. Amelia, I'm going to go to Hell."

Laughing, I dropped back on the bed and stared at the ceiling. "Why? 'Cause you had sex with a hot guy?"

"He delivered my latest BOB, and I might have slipped and told him what it was. He asked me about it, and I thought I was being cute by asking if he wanted to help me try it out."

I shot up to sitting. "You did not!"

"I did! And before I knew it, I was saying yes, and we were all over each other. Clothes flying. We didn't even make it to my bedroom. He fucked me with my brand new vibrator in the damn hall and then again with his rather large dick in the living room."

I covered my mouth to keep from laughing, and stood up. "I knew he was big! You could just tell."

Jen groaned again. This time louder. "I had sex with the UPS guy. I'm like one of those lonely housewives who ends up having an affair with the mailman or the pool boy!"

I chuckle. "It's kind of funny...and how can you have an affair when you're not even married!"

"Yeah, I guess so."

"Did you have fun?"

The silence on the other end of the phone was my answer. She had liked it, but was too embarrassed to admit it.

"Am I a slut if I say I did? And…that he's coming back over tonight."

"No, you're not a slut. You're a woman and he's a guy and y'all have flirted since high school. Hey, wait. Wasn't he engaged to Melanie Anne?"

"Yeah, but they split up. I keep thinking, how many other women does he fuck when he makes deliveries? Is he like the naughty Santa bringing the 'special' packages to only the good and bad women around town? Oh, my God, what have I done?"

I chewed my lip. The same thought had crossed my mind almost at the exact same time that Jen voiced it. "Not all men are pigs, Jen. Just the ones I date. I think you're pretty safe."

She laughed, and I could hear the shower turn on. "I better get into the shower. He'll be here soon. I'm making dinner and then we're heading over to Cord's Place."

"If you're worried about it, ask him. But for now, have fun."

"I will, on both accounts. And you, too! Hook up with some rich business guy who wants to bend you over his desk and take you from behind."

"Those things only happen in my books, Jen."

"Well, so does sleeping with the UPS driver, and look at me!"

We both laughed as we said our goodbyes.

After hanging up, I made my way onto the balcony of my suite. New York City was breathtaking, but it didn't hold a candle to the view from my parents' back porch. I'd take that over this any day. Sitting in a chair, I blew out a deep breath. I was happy for Jen. She deserved to find someone, whether it was an old, high school crush or some rich, oil tycoon. She longed for love. Like I had once, until my heart was shattered into a million pieces.

The memory hit me full force.

The knock on Ryan's door went unanswered. I was about to turn and leave, when I reached for the doorknob to try it.

Open.

Smiling, I made my way into his parents' house. We were both home on spring break. The last one of our senior year before we graduated from Texas A&M.

I made my way through the house, wondering where Ryan was. His truck was in the driveway so I knew he was here somewhere.

The loud bang from upstairs caused me to climb the stairs. I opened my mouth to call out Ryan's name when I heard a moan. A female-sounding moan. My heart seized tightly in my chest.

"Yes. Yes. That feels so good."

My hand covered my mouth as I slowly walked up the last of the steps. The moans grew louder—Ryan's mixed with what sounded like two other women.

A sickness rolled through my body and settled right in the pit of my stomach.

"Yes! Ryan, yes!"

I stopped outside his parents' room where the voices were coming from.

"Angelica, God, you feel amazing."

Who was Angelica?

Everything in me screamed that I should run. Instead, I reached for the door handle and turned. The door opened slowly, and I couldn't believe my eyes.

Ryan was in bed with not only one woman, but two. He was screwing one while the other watched and got herself off.

The girl sitting off to the side looked at me. "Sorry, honey, I'm next."

The room started to spin and the only thing I could do was stand there like an idiot and watch the man I'd given my heart to screw some woman while he sucked on the tit of another one.

"Having fun?" I finally managed.

Ryan quickly pulled out of the girl and jumped off the bed, not even bothering to cover himself. His floozies also didn't seem to care that they had been caught naked.

"Amelia! What are you doing here? I didn't think you were coming home until tomorrow."

Without answering, I slipped the engagement ring on my finger off and threw it as hard as I could at him.

"Don't even think of contacting me. If you do, I'll tell me father what I walked in on."

Spinning on my heel, I headed out of the bedroom, down the stairs, and out of the house. Never once letting the burning tears fall.

The knock on the hotel door pulled me out of the memory. I made my way through the room and opened the door. A bellman stood there holding a dress bag.

"Delivery for Amelia Parker."

"That's me," I said with a smile and took the bag and envelope from him. "One second."

After giving him a tip, I laid the bag on the bed and pulled it up to reveal a beautiful, black and white cocktail dress. Opening the envelope, I found a note from Waylynn.

Jack bought me this dress
a few weeks ago,
but I think it will
look beautiful on you.
See you after eleven

Smiling like a silly girl, I stripped out of my clothes and headed to the shower. Tonight I wasn't going to think about old boyfriends and broken hearts. I was going to drink and have fun.

CHAPTER 4

Amelia

"Amelia, are you even listening to me?"

I glanced up and smiled at my agent, Allysa. We'd met up at Café Bene near Times Square to talk shop while I was in town. "Sorry, I've got a massive headache. Waylynn and I went out last night. I might've had a little too much to drink."

Allysa smiled and nodded like she understood. I doubted that she did. She was thirty-three, married to a lawyer, and had two small kids. I bet she hadn't been to a club in ten years.

"I was mentioning the plan for shopping that series you pitched."

Nodding, I said, "Yes, I think that sounds perfect."

She frowned slightly, before grinning. "You know, they're recording your audiobook right down the road."

My body perked. "No kidding? Would we be able to take a sneak peek while it's happening?"

She pulled out her phone. "Let me see if I can make that happen."

It didn't take her long to complete the call and announce that we could go visit the studio. My heart started pounding as we quickly paid and hailed a cab.

Why am I so nervous?

Nervous as fuck was more like it.

Stepping into the room where one of my romance novels was being recorded for the audiobook version, the first thing I noticed was the drop-dead gorgeous guy in the booth who was bringing my words to life. His dark blond hair appeared disheveled, probably because he was one of those guys who had a habit of running his hands through it.

Well, hello there, James.

I had to wipe the drool from the sides of my mouth. James was the hero in my book, and this piece of hotness in front of the microphone fit my character's description almost perfectly. Purely a coincidence, I was sure, but nonetheless, it made my insides melt a little.

I could hear him talking through the speaker, and my pulse raced, my stomach dipping. *Jesus.* The man had a voice that could talk the panties off any woman. My readers were going to love this audiobook. Hell, *I* was sucked in, and it was my own book.

"We'll finish this chapter and then give you a chance to meet Liam," my agent said.

I quickly thought of Liam Hemsworth. *Yummy.*

A few minutes later, Liam walked into the control room. I swallowed hard while I took him in.

Tall. *Check.*

Built like a Greek god. *Check, check.*

Handsome as all get out. *Check-a-dee, check, check.*

Liam extended his hand. "Amelia, so nice to meet you."

Find your voice, for Christ's sake, Amelia. "Liam, the pleasure is all mine. You're Australian?"

He smiled, and I was pretty positive I heard angels singing. It should be illegal for a man to smile at a woman like that. "I am."

I nodded. "How long have you lived in the US?"

"Four years now."

I nodded again. All I seemed to be able to do was nod. This guy had my body aching to do some seriously naughty things.

"Well, thank you for bringing a voice to my James. From the sound of it, you're doing a great job."

Liam leaned in close and whispered, "He's a bit of a dirty bloke, isn't he?"

My cheeks heated instantly. "Yes. He is."

Drawing back, he winked. "You're from Texas?"

I nodded, trying to get his sexy voice out of my mind. "I am. Ever been there?"

He laughed. "No. I'd love to visit, though."

I didn't say anything to that…mostly because I was fighting the urge to tell him he could come home with me. *But only after he makes me come.*

After a few awkward moments of silence, I said, "You should visit some time."

Wait, what? Why in the hell did I say that?

His megawatt smile nearly had me stumbling backwards. "I'd love to…Amelia."

Oh. My. God.

Say my name again! Say it again!

My teeth sank into my lip, and I was pretty sure I was going to leave marks from how hard I was biting. I hadn't had a guy light my fire in a long time. Maybe it was because he was playing the part of James—my favorite character I'd written so far. He made me swoon in nearly every chapter.

Is Liam the swooning type? I wondered.

"We'd better let Liam get back to work. They're on a tight schedule," Allysa said while glancing between Liam and me.

"Oh, yes, right. Well, it was nice meeting you, Liam," I said, extending my hand toward him.

He took it and placed a soft kiss on the back of it. When I turned to follow Allysa out, I felt a hand on my arm, pulling me to a stop.

"Join me for bevvies this evening." His husky voice slid against my ear.

My eyes scanned the room. No one was paying attention to Liam and me. We had fallen behind everyone. Turning to him, I lifted a brow. "What in the heck is a bevvie?"

He chuckled. "Join me for a beer later?"

I chewed on the corner of my lip. Digging into my oversized purse, I found a card in the little pocket and handed it over. "I'd love to. Here's my card. It has my cell on it."

Spinning on my heel, I walked out the door with a huge smile.

Well, my trip just took a turn toward fun.

I see your UPS man, Jen, and raise you a hot Australian actor.

"What do you mean you're meeting a guy for dinner?" Waylynn asked as we strolled through the shoe department at Bergdorf Goodman.

"He's doing the voice recording for my audiobook. It's fine, Waylynn. I didn't pick the guy up on the side of the road and ask him to fuck me."

"You want him to fuck you?" she asked, surprise lacing her voice.

Laughing, I replied, "Well, now that you ask, I don't think I would mind trying out Aussie dick."

She slapped me on the shoulder and shook her head. "You're bad."

I gave her a wink. "Not yet."

"Ugh. Where did my baby sister go?"

"She grew up. And excuse me, wasn't it you who set me up with Doctor Hot Pants the last time I was here? If I remember correctly, he and I had a lot of fun together. Matter of fact, I think that was the last time I actually had real sex."

Waylynn stopped walking. "*Real* sex?"

"Yeah, sex with something other than a battery operated device."

Two older women walked by and huffed, shooting both of us dirty looks.

"Manny Tate was your last hook up?"

I snapped my fingers. "Manny! That's his name." I looked up in thought and smiled. "Yeah, he certainly knew what he was doing with his hands."

"TMI, Meli. T-M-I!"

I picked up a pair of Jimmy Choos and frowned at the price tag. I owned one pair, and I had spent weeks in despair over paying so much for them. Unlike my sister, standing next to me in her expensive-ass Manolo Blahnik pumps that must have cost her over a thousand dollars, I couldn't spend money that way. Or course, she was also married to one of the richest men in New York City and was told to dress the part. When she was at home she was in yoga pants, an old T-shirt, and a pair of Converse sneakers. Out in public she had to be dressed to the nines to fit in with the *Who's Who* of New York City socialites. I knew she hated it.

"So, how come you're not dating anyone?" she asked.

Letting out a gruff laugh, I said, "Hello? Do you not remember Ryan?"

She turned to me and frowned. "You're not still hung up on him, are you?"

"God, no. But I won't ever let myself be hurt like that again."

"What's that supposed to mean? You're never going to date again?"

I shrugged. "I'll date when I find a guy I connect with. One I can trust. It just hasn't happened yet. Pretty much all men are cheating pigs."

"Our brothers aren't."

Turning to her, I lifted my brow. "They're manwhores. They can't cheat on women because they won't date them seriously in the first place. I can't tell you how many women Trevor and Cord have slept with. Trevor's banged pretty much every single one of my friends. Three of whom have yet to talk to me since he broke their hearts."

Waylynn laughed. "Well, any woman in Oak Springs should know the Parker boys are not the settling-down type."

"Well, they all *thought* they could settle him down. Needless to say, he proved them wrong. Besides, I don't believe in love anymore."

Waylynn stopped walking. "What? You make your living writing about love and you say you don't believe in it?"

I shrugged. "I guess I believe in it. But I don't think it will happen for me. I thought I had it once, but spending so much time with Steed and Paxton, I see what Ryan and I had was nothing more than physical attraction. When it wore off for him, he moved on."

"Amelia, just because you had one bad apple doesn't mean the whole bunch was ruined."

Lifting a brow, I replied, "One bad apple spoils the rest, that's what I've always heard."

She frowned and shook her head. "Love will come when you least expect it, Meli. Just wait."

"What about you? Are you happy in love? I mean, you gave up your career as a dancer for Jack."

With a huff, Waylynn picked up a pair of Louis Vuitton pumps and looked at the price tag. I couldn't help but look myself. Over six hundred dollars. Waylynn lifted the shoe and nodded to the young sales lady. "Size six, please."

Waylynn turned to me, her eyes filled with sadness. "I can honestly tell you that Jack Monroe was the worst mistake of my life."

I was stunned to finally hear the full confession, but not surprised. "Oh, Waylynn. I'm so sorry. What can I do? Here you are telling me love will come when I least expect it, but when will it come for you?"

A fake laugh slipped from Waylynn as the sales lady took the sleek, black pump from a thin box. Waylynn sat down. "Don't be sorry. I'm the idiot who let it happen and nothing can be done to fix this mistake. Meli, this is my reality. I've fully accepted that love has already bypassed me."

After the second shoe slipped on, Waylynn stood and walked over to a mirror, staring at her reflection. She wasn't even looking at the shoes.

"How do they feel, ma'am?"

Slapping on her signature window-dressing smile, she said, "Fine. Everything is perfectly fine."

I studied my older sister, understanding just how unhappy she truly was.

"I'll take them," she finally said. When she turned back to face me, she gave me that same fake smile. "Might as well spend his money if that's the only thing he gives me. Right?"

Before I could offer words of comfort to my sister and best friend, my phone buzzed in my purse. Reaching in, I saw a local NYC number.

212-555-1212: *Hey, Amelia! It's Liam. We still on for bevvies tonight?*

I glanced over to my sister again who was sitting next to me. She had launched into a conversation with the sales lady, so I focused on the text.

Grinning like a silly teenager, I quickly stored his number in my phone.

Me: *Am I going to have to go buy a book...*How to Speak Australian...*just to go out with you?*

Liam: *No. I promise not to speak Australian.*

Me: *NO! Speak it! It's hot as hell.*

A few minutes passed, and I was worried I had scared him off.

Liam: *Then I'll be sure to lay it on thick and heavy tonight.*

"What's that smile?" Waylynn asked as we walked outside, waving for a cab like a madwoman.

I chuckled. "Liam is texting about tonight."

Waylynn wiggled her eyebrows. "Well, by the look on your face, I think we need to make one more stop before heading back to your hotel."

"Where?"

"The drugstore...for condoms."

CHAPTER 5

Liam

"You're going out on a date with the author of the book you're recording? Isn't that…against the rules or something?"

Fixing my hair one more time, I pulled my eyes from the mirror and turned to Nancy, my roommate and ex-girlfriend.

"No. At least, I don't think so."

"Huh. Well, you better be careful. You've got a good-paying job, and you don't need some woman messing it up for you." Nancy and I had dated for over two and half years before deciding we made better friends than lovers.

"I didn't mess things up with you," I said, and laughed. "You're just worried I won't make rent if I get tossed out on my can."

"Something like that," she said as she brushed past me. It didn't go unnoticed that she was dressed sexy as sin tonight. Sometimes I wondered if Nancy wanted me back in her bed. It seemed like every time I had a date, she dressed a little racier, making more than her normal, fair share of sexual comments.

"Just be careful, Liam. You've worked too hard to give it all up for some girl."

With a light-hearted chuckle, I replied, "I think I'm okay, Nancy. You a bit jealous?"

She leaned against the counter and stared. "If I wanted your cock, all I'd have to do is spread my legs and you'd be inside me."

"Is that right?"

Sitting on the counter, she lifted her skirt higher on her thighs and spread her legs open enough so I could see she wasn't wearing panties. But I couldn't be bothered any more with someone like Nancy and her jealous ways.

"Is this you saying you want me to fuck you?" I asked.

"Maybe. You interested?"

I reached for my wallet and pushed it into the back pocket of my jeans. It pissed me off that she thought she could flash her pussy and I'd jump. Fuck that. "Don't wait up for me. I'll be home late."

Shooting a dirty look, Nancy jumped off the counter and grunted. "Don't come looking for me tonight when she turns you down."

Not bothering to answer, I headed to the front door and made my way to the stairs. I hardly ever took the elevator. The seven floors to our apartment were a good form of exercise, a way to blow off steam. And after what Nancy had just pulled, I definitely had some steam to blow off.

I waited for the Uber driver to show up. Once he did, I told him to take me to the Ritz. I was meeting Amelia in the lobby before dinner.

The moment I walked in, I sought her out. She was sitting at the bar laughing at something another woman had said. Both of them were knock-out gorgeous, but the other one seemed to be a few years older.

I made my way to the bar and smiled when Amelia glanced up. Damn, those blue eyes were fucking breathtaking. The other girl looked at me, her eyes the same piercing color.

Sisters. They had to be. One had dark blonde hair, the other red, but those eyes and the smile were the same. The blonde leaned in and said something to Amelia, causing Amelia to push her away.

"Ladies," I purred as I flashed them a grin.

"Liam, it's good seeing you again. This is my sister, Waylynn. She lives here in New York."

Waylynn reached her hand out, and I was surprised by the firmness of her shake. "Liam, it's a pleasure meeting you."

"Pleasure is all mine."

Her brow quirked, and she leaned in closer. "You harm one hair on her head and I'll shoot your ass. We clear?"

I swallowed hard and my eyes darted to Amelia. She shrugged, then winked. "Just agree and you'll be fine."

"Ah," I mumbled as I looked back at Waylynn. "Not a single hair on her head will be harmed."

Waylynn grinned, reached for her shot of whiskey and downed it. "Good, my five brothers will be happy to hear that."

"*Five*? You have five? Brothers?"

Waylynn looked me over. "Do you often stumble on your words, pretty boy?"

"No, ma'am, but I don't often come across beautiful women who threaten to shoot me within the first two minutes of meeting them."

With a sinful smile, Waylynn replied, "It wasn't a threat, sweetheart. It was a promise."

Jesus, who is this woman? Annie Oakley?

Glancing back at her sister, she waved. "Have fun, Amelia. See you in the morning."

Amelia lifted her hands and wiggled her fingers at her retreating sister. I watched Waylynn walk out of the bar, her high heels clicking against the tile.

"Holy fuck. She's terrifying."

Amelia laughed. "Don't let her scare you off. Please sit, let me buy you a drink."

I slid onto the barstool and pointed at what Amelia was drinking. "Is that an old fashioned?" I asked.

"Yep."

"I'll have the same," I said. The bartender quickly went about making my drink as Amelia and I slipped into a comfortable conversation.

"What brought you to America?"

"Modeling."

She chuckled. "Of course."

"What's that supposed to mean?" I asked before taking a sip of the godawful drink in front of me.

"I figured you were either going to say actor or model. My sister swears she's seen you on the side of a bus."

I shook my head and laughed. "She might have. I did an ad campaign for a high-profile chain store. They fucking had my face everywhere. Even I got sick of seeing it."

She smiled, and my cock jumped. Oh, yes. I wanted in this girl's knickers.

"I'm not sure how anyone could tire of that face," she said.

I took another drink. "You'd be surprised."

The heat between us was undeniable, and I wondered if she felt it, too.

"So, you moved here to be a model. How did you end up voice acting?"

"My ex got me into it. She's an actress, or trying to be. She did a little voice work and always told me I had a sexy voice. I auditioned for a job she told me about, I got it, and the rest is history. Now I get paid to recite how much your characters love fucking in showers."

There went that sexy-as-fuck grin of hers. This time she raised the ante and ran her tongue along those plump lips.

Goddamn, I was attracted to this girl, but I couldn't very well ask her to head up to her room yet and fuck her every way I could imagine

"Do you want to grab something to eat?" I asked, finishing off the dreadful drink.

"What are you in the mood for?"

Your pussy.

"Ladies first," I replied with a wink.

She rested her chin on her hand and looked at me with sultry eyes. "Listen, Liam, I'm going to be up front and honest with you."

My heart raced. "Okay."

"What I really need is a beer and a damn good slice of pizza."

I stared at her for a few seconds to let what she said soak in, then laughed. "Beer and pizza. I think I can deliver that."

I threw some money on the bar and reached for her hand. As we stood to leave, she said, "You better be able to deliver more than that before this night is over."

Oh, yes. Amelia Parker was going to be a lot of fun.

CHAPTER 6

Amelia

My phone buzzed on the table and I glanced at it. Waylynn. Again.

Waylynn: *So? How's it going? Have you dusted the cobwebs?*

Me: *No. At dinner, still talking.*

Waylynn: *Hmm. Maybe he's not into you. Dry spell continues.*

Me: *Fuck you.*

Liam walked back to our table and set a beer in front of me. He pointed to the pizza and asked, "You want the last piece?"

I held up my hands. "No! Have at it. I'm good."

He did just that. Where the man kept it all was beyond me. From what I could tell, he had a rocking body.

"I love the pizza here," he said.

Laughing, I replied, "I see that. It was good, but my mother makes a better pizza."

His eyes lifted. "Were you born in Texas?" He wiped his mouth and tossed the napkin on the table.

"Yep. My parents own a ranch. Been in our family for years."

"Cows?" he asked with a snarled lip.

"Yes. Do you have something against cows?"

"I don't eat meat."

Oh, hell.

"Seriously? You just ate pepperoni!" I chuckled.

"Yeah, well, that doesn't count. Bacon doesn't either. Gave up the rest of it a few years back. Well, really I did it because Nancy ate that way."

I lifted a brow. "Nancy?"

"My ex."

"Huh. Sounds like Nancy had a lot of influence on you."

He leaned back in his chair, crossing his arms over his massive chest. "Not really. She ate that way, I tried it and felt better. So, I stuck to it."

"What happened between y'all?"

He leaned forward, looking uncomfortable. Well, too bad. He brought Nancy up. If he thought I wasn't going to ask, he was stupid.

"We were better friends than lovers."

"Oh please," I spat.

Liam raised his brows. "What?"

"Isn't that code for 'I'm cheating on you and don't have the guts to tell you'?"

This time he pinched his brows together and studied me. "Well, neither one of us was cheating. It was Nancy's idea to break up. In the end, it was best for our friendship. Doesn't faze me when she brings someone home and the same goes for her."

My mouth fell. "Wait. Y'all still *live* together?"

Liam smiled and my stomach pulled with desire. *Geesh*, this guy was even more handsome when he let that smile loose.

"Do you know how expensive it is to live in New York? Besides, Nancy has a killer place with views of Manhattan."

"I've heard it's pretty expensive," I admitted. If I was looking for more than a simple hook-up, I might have been bothered by the fact that he still lived with his ex. But I wasn't looking, so I wasn't bothered.

Leaning close, Liam placed his hand on my bare knee, and I was a bit bummed not to get those butterflies in my stomach. "Where to now?"

I moved toward him. "My hotel? I need to work off the beer and pizza."

Liam's mouth rose at both corners. "And I need to fuck you."

His dirty mouth made my libido shoot straight up and out the building. I gave him my sexiest smile and lifted my hand for the check. "A man who gets straight to the point. I like it."

"I need to make a call," Liam said as he stood. "Will you excuse me?" With a quick nod, I watched as he made his way out of the restaurant. I couldn't help but wonder who he was calling.

The ex?

A friend, to cancel plans for later?

My mind raced as I pulled out my phone and sent Waylynn a text.

Me: *Looks like the cobwebs will be wiped out this evening and I'm hoping the boy from down under has a big duster.*

Waylynn: *LOL! Glad we picked up the extra-large condoms! Have fun, baby sister, and be careful, okay? Are you going back to your place?*

I watched as Liam talked on the phone. He threw his head back and laughed, then looked into the restaurant. When our eyes met, he smiled.

Me: *Yes. I'll text when I get back there.*

Waylynn: *Okay. Love you.*

Me: *Love you back.*

Liam had left his card on the table, but when the waiter brought the check, I paid in cash. Grabbing Liam's card, I made my way outside, my curiosity getting the better of me.

When I stepped outside, I instantly got a chill. It was still cold in New York City and I had opted to not wear a heavier coat.

"Right, Mum. I know. I won't, I promise you."

My heart melted. He was talking to his mom. Oh, my God. Sexy as fuck.

"What am I doing? Um…about to workout."

I had to cover my mouth to hide my chuckle. When he turned and saw me, he shrugged, a slight blush moving across his cheeks.

"I will. Tell Dad I said hi. I'll call tomorrow night."

When he hit End, we stood there staring at each other. The sexual attraction between us was insane. If I thought I could get away with it, I would have stripped down and asked him to screw me up against the restaurant window.

Wait. Didn't I write that in a book once?

"I've got to tell you, Amelia, my cock is rock hard."

Slipping closer, I cupped him and lifted my brows. He wasn't lying. He was hard and huge.

It was worth repeating. Thank God for the extra-large condoms.

The ride up the elevator nearly killed me. An older couple was on the same floor as mine so Liam and I waited not-so-patiently behind them. His thumb brushed across the skin of my back, driving me insane. The older couple chatted nonstop about some charity event as Liam's hand moved down to my ass. I gasped when he pinched it. The old man glanced over his shoulder at us.

"Good evening, sir," Liam said in that damn Australian accent. The guy smiled, then turned straight ahead. When Liam's hand snaked around to my front, I stepped to the side. No way was I going to let him touch me with people standing there.

The doors opened and Liam dragged me out and past the couple. "Room number?"

I was dizzy with desire. "Um, twenty twenty-four."

At my hotel room door, Liam's hands desperately tried to find a way under my dress. I fumbled for my room key while trying not to pant like the sex-starved woman I'd become.

"Hurry, love," he said. "I'm aching to be inside of you."

The lock made a sound and we were soon pushing through the door and into the room. I'd never acted this way before, but there was something about Liam. Something that made me crave him. I could practically smell the sex in the air.

Our hands roamed everywhere, and we soon stood naked in front of each other.

"Fucking hell, you're sexier than I imagined," Liam said, his hand bringing my nipple up to his waiting mouth.

My head dropped back as I ran my fingers through his hair. "Yes! God, yes! I have condoms!"

He chuckled against my breast and pulled back to look at me. "No foreplay, Amelia?"

"Screw foreplay, Liam. I haven't had sex in a year. I want to be fucked six ways to Sunday."

With his hand cupping my pussy, I let out a moan. "You're not shy, my sweet Amelia Parker."

Not wanting to wait a second more, I reached for my purse. Pulling out a condom, I dropped to my knees. Cradling his balls in one hand, I slowly ran my other one over his hard length.

Oh, yes. He was huge. I was going to be sore. And this was going to be amazing.

I ripped open the condom and slowly sheathed Liam. His moans and hiss had me dripping wet with desire.

He reached down and grabbed my arms, pulling me back up.

"Turn around. I want to take you over this table."

Smiling, I did as he said. When my breasts hit the cool surface of the wood, I gasped. The feel of Liam's fingers slipping inside me caused me to let out a long, low groan.

"Yes!" I panted as he pushed my legs apart. From behind was probably going to hurt like a son-of-a-bitch, but I didn't care. I was acting like a crazed woman. I'd never wanted to be fucked so much and so roughly in my entire life.

"Fuck me now and stop making me wait, Liam."

He pushed in and I let out a loud whimper-groan, grabbing the sides of the table.

"You okay?" Liam asked, slowly pulling out and then going back in even slower. Pure, unadulterated, blissful torture.

"Yes, keep going!" I panted as I tried to relax around his girth.

"Give me ten seconds to adjust to you. You're so fucking tight I'm going to come before we even get started."

He gently ran his fingers over my ass as he worked his way in and out, causing goosebumps to race across my body.

"You feel so damn good, baby," he said.

I glanced over my shoulder and smiled. "No small talk, Liam. Fuck me. Hard and fast."

Liam did just that. After screaming out his name on the table, I called it out again while he fucked me against the wall, on the sofa, in the shower, then one last time in the massive, king-sized bed.

I was spent and my body ached. I'd never been fucked with such commitment and ferocity. We certainly hadn't made love, and I was perfectly fine with that.

"You're going to be sore, love," Liam whispered as he pulled my body flush against his.

"Hmm."

I waited for that pull in my chest at his use of a pet name, but it never came. Letting it go, I slowly let myself drift off to sleep.

CHAPTER 7

Amelia

My body ached in the most delicious way as I opened my eyes and stared at the ceiling.

"Jesus," I whispered as I slipped my hand between my legs. My vagina had been thoroughly fucked. When Liam woke me up earlier with his cock pushing into me, I murmured, "Yes, please." He pulled out another amazing orgasm, and I was sure the poor people on either side of us got no sleep last night. Not with all the screwing in this room.

The smell of bacon quickly had me sitting up. Liam must have ordered room service. I swung my feet over the bed and reached for my robe, heading to the living area of my suite.

"The last time I checked, you weren't my mother, Nancy," Liam muttered into his phone while he stood and looked out the window.

I frowned. Ugh. The ex.

"Yeah, well, I just spent an amazing evening fucking, and I wasn't about to stop what I was doing because you needed me."

Lifting my brows, I let his words sink in. So, they either had an open relationship, or they really were just roommates. Still, I didn't like him talking about our night like that. Maybe it was because I felt like a total whore for letting a man I hardly knew screw my brains out.

Or maybe it was because his words made me feel that way.

When he turned and saw me, I sensed regret in his eyes.

He mouthed *I'm sorry*, and I shrugged. Snagging a piece of bacon, I flopped onto the couch and reached for the remote along with my phone. Clicking on the TV, I searched for HGTV.

"I'll fix it when I get home," he said. "I've got to go."

Liam sat down next me and sighed.

"Do you always talk on the phone naked?"

He laughed. "No. Not always."

I knew he was probably waiting for me to ask him about Nancy, but I honestly didn't care. It wasn't like Liam and I were dating. We'd hooked up and had an amazing night. He didn't owe me anything.

"What are your plans for today?" I asked as I finished the bacon, still searching for a damn TV show I wanted to watch.

"I was kind of hoping we could spend the day together."

I stared at him. After a few seconds, I responded with, "Um, you want to hang out?"

Liam laughed. "Well, did you really think I was going to fuck you all night and leave in the morning?"

"Well, yeah. I mean, kind of. Isn't that what guys do?"

He lifted his hand and pushed my hair behind my ear. "Not all guys, love."

I smiled. This was kind of nice. Too bad he lived in New York and I lived in Texas. We might actually have a good time dating.

"Okay, well, I need to see what my sister is doing," I said.

"Let's all do something together." Liam suggested.

Grinning bigger, I jumped onto my knees. "That sounds amazing! Like what?"

"How about take a drive out of the city. I know this great little restaurant that a friend of mine opened about a year ago in Highland. Do you like Italian?"

"Like it? I freaking love it!"

Liam pulled me to him and pushed my robe open. Pressing against his warm dick instantly turned me on.

"I was going to suggest calling Waylynn right now, but I'm thinking that can wait."

With a sexier-than-hell smile, Liam cupped my breasts and chuckled. "I agree."

After a serious make-out session on the couch, we were in my bed and he was making love to me. It was so different from the night before, and a part of me wanted that crazed man who couldn't keep his hands off me. This felt too intimate, and I couldn't figure out why I wanted him to stop. Closing my eyes, I let Liam work in and out of me slowly until I couldn't take it anymore. Wrapping my legs around him, I dug my nails into his back.

"Fuck me, Liam. Hard and fast."

With a smirk, he did exactly what I asked for.

"Oh, my goodness. This is the cutest town. How have I never been here?" Waylynn asked as we walked along the shoreline to Liam's favorite restaurant.

Liam held my hand as we approached Marco's. My mouth was watering from the idea of food. After last night's sexcapade and this morning's sequel, I was starving.

Opening the door for us, Liam said, "Here we go. Best Italian restaurant on the east coast."

I loved his Australian accent. A few times he had dropped a word that I didn't recognize at all, but it didn't matter. He was fun to be around, and I could tell Waylynn thought so too.

Walking through the door, we were greeted by a warm voice. "Liam! When I got your text, I was over the moon!" an older gentleman said. Waylynn and I glanced at each other and grinned. I'd had it in my mind the owner was going to be young and Italian.

"Marco! Buongiorno!"

The older man kissed each of Liam's cheeks and rattled something off in Italian. Waylynn leaned in and said, "He just asked Liam how he ended up with two beautiful women on his arm."

My cheeks blushed. Waylynn had taken six years of Italian, but I decided to keep that information to myself.

"I'm a lucky bastard, that's how," Liam said.

"I see that," Marco said. "What brings you here, my friend?"

Liam grinned. "We needed a change from the city and I bragged about your food. Don't make me regret it."

Marco pretended to punch Liam in the stomach before turning to us. "Come, come. I've got the perfect table for you. You can see the water, very romantic." He wiggled his eyebrows before leading us to our seats.

"Marco is a bit of a character, but he's a good guy," Liam said as we followed a few steps behind. "He did business with my father a few years back."

"Really? What does your father do?" I asked.

Liam let out a snarky growl. "He makes money and likes to tell everyone how much."

Note to self: Liam's father is not a happy topic.

Ahead of us, Marco and Waylynn were speaking in Italian. Well, there went my secret.

"Your sister speaks Italian?" Liam asked.

I nodded. "Yeah, she took six years of it."

"Wow. What about you? Do you speak another language?"

Laughing, I shook my head. "I took two years of Spanish and not one word stuck with me."

Behind Liam, a couple caught my attention. I stopped walking and started staring.

Holy shit balls. My heartbeat doubled as panic set in.

Liam stopped. "Hey, is everything okay?"

I slowly shook my head and whispered, "No. This is far from okay."

Following my gaze, Liam stared at the couple who were now locked in a kiss. It wasn't hard for him to see what I was staring at. They were the only two people sitting in the corner.

"Do you know them?"

I pulled my eyes off the couple and looked at Liam. "The guy lip-locked with that woman is Jack...Waylynn's husband!"

Liam's head jerked. "Shit's fucked."

"What?" I asked.

"That's fucked up," he translated.

"Yeah, it is. Shit, this is bad." My eyes traveled to my sister. Marco and Waylynn figured out we had stopped, they stopped and turned to face us. Waylynn wore a huge smile, but it quickly dropped. She must have sensed something because her eyes swung from me to Jack and then to the young bleached-blonde who had stopped sucking his face long enough to feed Jack something off her plate.

"Oh, no. Waylynn sees him."

"Okay, well, should I go beat his ass or something?"

Waylynn had frozen with a stunned expression. Glancing at me, she forced a smile then walked straight over. "We need to leave."

Nodding, Liam and I followed her out of the restaurant.

"Is everything okay?" Marco asked. Liam told him what had happened in a rushed whisper.

Waylynn got in the car faster than I could even say goodbye to Marco. My heart ached for my sister. My first instinct was to call my parents, but this was Waylynn's problem, and I had to let her decide how to handle it.

"Liam, I'm so sorry to cut today short, but I think it's best if I head back to my sister's place."

"Of course, yes. I'm more than happy to drive you back there, love."

With a smile, I reached up on my toes and kissed him on the lips. "I had a lot of fun."

He frowned. "This is not you saying goodbye, is it, Amelia Parker? Because Texas or not, I plan on seeing you again."

I could feel the burn of heat on my cheeks. "I'd like that."

Liam's arm draped across my shoulders as he walked us to his car. I slipped into the backseat with Waylynn, expecting to see her crying.

But that's not what I found. My sister's head was high, a look of determination on her face.

A true Parker.

CHAPTER 8

Liam

The keys rattled as I dropped them on the side table. Walking into the apartment, I glanced around for Nancy. The moaning from her bedroom meant she was screwing some guy.

"Great," I huffed, making my way to the kitchen.

"Oh, John! Faster! Harder!"

The container of milk stopped at my lips. Her damn door was open. I sighed and took a long drink as she kept up her little show.

"Yes! That's it! *Don't. Stop.*"

After grabbing an apple, I headed down the hall. My stomach growled; I hadn't picked up lunch after the whole mess at Marco's.

"Nancy!" a deep voice cried out.

Stopping at her door, I took a bite of the apple, and Nancy's eyes met mine. She smiled and moaned again.

"Want to join us?" she asked as the guy on top of her went to town, not even bothering to see who was there.

"No, thanks. Sloppy seconds aren't my thing."

Before she could respond, I pulled the door shut and headed to my room. Two days ago, I might have said yes to that invitation—with the ground rule that cocks don't touch under any circumstances. But now, all I could think about was the beautiful, blue-eyed redhead who rocked my world last night and again this morning. Amelia was heading back to Texas and I already hated the thought of it.

I reached for my work calendar to see when I had a few days off. With a smile, I circled two weekends from today. One quick text to Amelia, and I would be making plans to fly there.

Me: *I need to see you again, love. Are you free in two weeks? I could fly in on that Friday and leave Sunday the second.*

Staring at my phone, waiting for a reply, I had to laugh at myself.

"Jesus. I'm waiting by the phone." I chucked my phone across my bed. Heading to the shower, I decided what I needed was a good jacking off to the image of Amelia in my head.

When my phone buzzed, I damn near leaped across my bed for it.

Amelia: *I'm free that weekend. Are you serious? You'd come to Texas?*

For that sweet pussy, I'd fucking go around the world twice.

Me: *Yes. To see your beautiful face, I'd travel the world.*

Okay, so maybe I didn't tell her what I was really thinking, but I meant what I texted.

Amelia: *I've got you down! I thought I might be able to see you again, but Waylynn has packed a bag and we're heading to my hotel to get my things. We're leaving tonight.*

My hand scrubbed down my face as Nancy made it clear they had both orgasmed. Hitting Amelia's number, she answered on the second ring. "What time does your flight leave?"

"We're taking Jack's private plane. Waylynn told him she had an emergency and had to get to Texas. He was more than willing to let her take it. Guess he's spending the weekend with the woman we saw him with at Marco's."

I shook my head. "Damn. I'm sorry about that."

"It was overdue. Her leaving, I mean. Jack never treated her right."

"Are you back at your hotel yet?"

"A few minutes away, but traffic is a bitch."

I quickly headed back out of my bedroom, dressed in the same clothes I had on last night. "Text me when you get there. I want to kiss you goodbye again."

"That sounds amazing."

Nancy walked out of the kitchen naked. She licked something off a spoon, and I tried my best to ignore her. Grabbing my keys, I replied to Amelia, "I'll make sure it's a hell of a lot better than amazing."

I couldn't get the image of Nancy and the guy fucking out of my head. Her moans replayed until I finally asked the taxi driver to turn up the radio. By the time we pulled up to the front of the Ritz, I was wound tighter than a damn yo-yo.

My phone buzzed.

Amelia: *I'm at the bar with Waylynn. She needed a drink.*

Thank fuck.

The moment I walked into the small bar, I saw her. She sat at the bar with that red hair piled on top of her head. My cock strained against my pants, and I needed to sink deep inside her.

Waylynn was deep in a conversation with a lady dressed in a business suit next to her. She didn't even see me walk up.

I stopped behind Amelia and leaned down, my lips inches from her ear. "I need to fuck you now. Get your ass in the ladies' toilet."

Turning, I walked away.

No one responded to a quick knock on the door to the toilet, so I walked in. Not ten seconds later, Amelia walked in.

"Liam," she said, heat and desire pooling in her eyes.

"Do you have a condom?" I asked.

With a nod, she reached into her purse and pulled it out. I grabbed it and pushed her against the bathroom door, locking it in the process.

"Wow. If this is how you say goodbye, what is hello going to be like in two weeks?"

I smiled and unzipped my pants, pulling my hard cock out. My hand stroked it lightly as I watched Amelia gaze down and lick her lips.

"Do you know how fucking hard it's going to be waiting two weeks?" I asked.

Ripping open the condom, I sheathed myself and reached under her short little dress. Her panties were soaked and that only made me want her even more.

I pushed them to the side and sank two fingers in. Amelia gasped and grabbed my arms. I knew she had to be sore from all the fucking. I started to slow my pace when the image of Nancy moaning and looking straight at me flashed through my mind.

"Fuck," I groaned and picked Amelia up. "Are you sore? Can you take a good fucking right now?"

Her eyes widened. "Y-yes. I can."

Lining my cock up to her pussy, I pushed in. "Good. Take all of me, love."

Amelia's face strained, so I backed off a little. "No! Keep going."

"Tell me to fuck you, Amelia. Tell me how you want it."

Her fingers dug into my shoulders. "We shouldn't be doing this, Liam. We're in a public restroom! But, my God…"

I drew back and looked into her blue eyes. "Do you want me to stop?"

If she said yes, I would. I'd fucking hate it, but I would.

Her head went from side to side. "Don't stop."

My mouth crashed to hers as I took her up against the door. Anyone walking by would know exactly what was happening and that made it all the more thrilling.

Amelia attempted to keep her voice low as she cried out. "Liam! Oh, my God, Liam!"

Coming, she pulsed against me, bringing me to my own orgasm. Burying my face in her neck, I cursed. As much as I tried to tell myself this behavior was brought on by my need to have her and give her a proper goodbye, I knew it wasn't the truth. Seeing Nancy being fucked by another man brought it out. I was using Amelia to rid myself of that vision. And that made me feel guilty as hell when those baby blue eyes drew back and looked into my green. Her chest rose and fell and a gorgeous smile grew across her face.

"That. Was. Fun!" she said with a giggle. Her cheeks were flushed, and I wasn't sure if it was from the good fucking I gave her or not. The innocence spilled out of her in that moment. I got the feeling Amelia Parker wasn't the type of woman to let guys fuck her in ladies' toilets, but for some reason, she let me. My chest pulled with a dull ache, and my guilt grew.

CHAPTER 9

Amelia

Jack's private plane was insane. There were six leather recliners and one leather love seat. All done in a cream color. The wood in the cabin looked nicer than my parents' formal dining room.

"Holy private plane!" I said, spinning around in a circle for good measure.

"Jack spares no expense." Waylynn's voice was sad, but there was also a bit of anger in there.

Placing my hand on hers, I knelt in front of the chair she was sitting in. "You don't need him, Waylynn. He took everything away from you and made you into something you're not happy with. You and I both know that."

She nodded, her eyes filled with tears. "I love him, I really do. It's just, I haven't been *in* love with him since he made me give up dancing. Why were his dreams more important than mine?"

"What?" I asked in a shocked voice. "Waylynn, he made you stop dancing a year after you got married. Why would you stay with him for so long?"

She wiped away tears with the back of her hand. "I don't know. At the time I thought it was what I wanted, even if I moved to New York to become a dancer. I let Jack Owens make me believe I'd never be good enough. That the only reason I got as far as I did was because I had a pretty face. He actually asked me if I slept with someone to try and secure a spot with the Rockettes."

"Mrs. Owens, you'll both need to be seated and buckled. We've been cleared for taxi and take-off," the pilot said over his shoulder from the cockpit.

I quickly sat in the seat opposite my sister. "Fuck him. You don't need him, Waylynn. And if you want to move out and get a place in New York to follow your dream, I'll support you."

She smiled. "You'd move to New York and share an apartment with me?"

Oh, shit. I wasn't expecting that. "Um, sure, I suppose I could hang out in New York for a bit. I know a guy who rocks my world in the sex department."

Waylynn snarled then rolled her eyes. "Ugh. Don't think I don't know what the two of you were doing in the bathroom. You came back oozing with that *just fucked* look. There seriously could have been a sign above your head that flashed *I had hot sex*."

I chuckled and looked out the window. "I have to admit I was taken aback when Liam showed up demanding sex like that. There's no denying the heat between us."

"No kidding. Besides the sex, do you like him?"

I waited for that feeling. The one where my stomach dropped, or my chest fluttered. But it didn't happen.

"I do like him. We had a nice time together, and he's coming to Texas in a few weeks. Maybe we'll be able to get to know each other a bit better."

Waylynn laughed. "You mean if y'all can keep your hands off each other."

I smiled, but an ache grew in my chest. Would I ever find a guy who swept me off my feet? A smile to melt me into a puddle of happiness and desire? The guy who made my stomach tumble with a simple touch? Whose hands caused mind-numbing orgasms...

Like the mythical unicorn, this creature didn't seem to exist. Or maybe worse, he didn't exist for me. I wrote about love, but had I ever truly felt it? No. Not the kind of love my parents had. Or the kind that Steed and Paxton shared. I thought I had it with Ryan, but quickly realized our high school first love hadn't grown and lasted like I thought it would.

Waylynn and I were both lost in our thoughts as the plane took off. I wasn't sure how long we sat there before my sister finally spoke.

"I thought love was going to be so different."

Turning my head, I stared at her. She had voiced the very same thing I'd been thinking. "Yeah. Me, too."

With a shake of her head, she glanced at her rings. "When I look at Mom and Dad, my heart soars. The way Daddy looks at Mom is how I want a man to look at me. I've never had that, and I can't believe it took me so damn long to realize it."

She looked out the window, then back at me. In that moment, the oddest thing happened to Waylynn...and I got to witness every moment. A wide smile grew across her face. "I feel like a bird who's been let out of her cage. I'm ready to find my wings and heal my heart. Start over. Start living."

Finding a smile, I asked, "Will you go back?"

"To New York?"

"Yeah."

Her brows pinched slightly as she thought. "No. I don't want anything from him. Everything I have is from him. Besides, I can borrow some of your clothes when I run out of what I brought, right?"

Laughing, I nodded. "Of course, anything for you."

Waylynn reached into her bag and pulled out one of my books.

"You're reading one of my books?" I asked, my cheeks instantly heated.

"Hell, yeah. I read them all. It's nice to know there really is love out there."

"Um, you do know they're fiction, right, sis?"

She rolled her eyes. "A girl can dream. Besides, it sounds like Liam is going to be the perfect inspiration for giving you some writing material."

I forced a smile. "For the sex scenes, maybe. The boy has a way of drawing out a darker side of me, that's for sure."

Waylynn's grin faded. "Gross. TMI, Amelia." Her body shivered as she shook her head. I was positive she was trying to rid herself of the mental image.

We spent the next hour in silence. I pulled out my laptop and started writing while she read. Well, if you could call staring at the computer screen "writing." I had no idea why I couldn't get into it. Nothing was motivating me. I needed to spend some time around Steed and Paxton, maybe. The way those two loved on each other was sure to be inspirational.

"Do you think it will last?"

My sister's voice caused me to peek at her over my screen. "What?"

"Your love affair with Liam."

Love affair. That sounded so old-fashioned.

I shrugged. "I'm not sure. The sex is amazing. He's already made an effort to come to Texas to see me in two weeks."

"Yeah, but will you fly back to New York to see him?"

Chewing my lip, I glanced at what I had written almost an hour ago.

My heart hammered as I anticipated his smile. His arms wrapped around my body while he pulled me in for a soft, gentle kiss. I longed for him to make love to me. To show me with the touch of his hands how much he wanted me.

Did I anticipate Liam's smile? His touch? Or was it the idea of his cock buried deep inside me that thrilled me?

Focusing back on my sister, I grinned. "I guess when I'm in the mood to be fucked seven ways to Sunday I'll fly back up."

A sadness swept across her face. "There is more to a relationship than fucking, Meli."

Yeah. No shit.

"Well, that's all I'm interested in. Besides, I might write about love, but I know for a damn fact that none of this shit is real."

Her head tilted as she stared at me. "Steed and Paxton have the real deal. So do Mom and Dad."

I couldn't argue with her point.

"Well, then, maybe it's not in the cards for this Parker."

Waylynn's shoulders slumped. "Or this Parker."

We sat in a welcome silence before an evil smile moved across my sister's face.

Waylynn stood and grabbed a bottle of wine. After she opened it and poured two glasses, she raised hers. "Looks like we're gonna have to raise some hell now that both Parker sisters will be back in Oak Springs."

I shut my laptop, not even caring that I didn't save my work. It was one damn paragraph anyway.

Toasting back, I added, "Hell, yeah. Trouble's back in town, gentlemen. Watch out."

CHAPTER 10

Amelia

"Wait! I haven't checked on April!" I shouted as we headed to my rental car. Since we were back earlier than expected, I went ahead and rented a car instead of calling one of the guys to pick us up.

"Flipping hell, Meli. Why are you obsessed with that giraffe?"

"*That* giraffe? April is not just any giraffe. She is teaching the world about conservation."

Waylynn rolled her eyes. "Keep telling yourself that, sis. Whatever keeps the crazy out of your head."

After putting my luggage and Waylynn's in the trunk, I sent Liam a quick text.

Me: *Landed in San Antonio. Thanks again for the fun times! I'm looking forward to seeing you in a couple of weeks.*

Liam didn't respond right away. I figured he wouldn't if he was working or with friends. As I slipped into the car, I remembered him saying he still lived with his ex.

"Hey, let me ask you a question," I said as we got in the car.

Waylynn pulled the sun visor down and applied lipstick. "Go for it."

"Should it be a warning sign that Liam still lives with his ex?"

She stopped and faced me. "He lives with his ex?"

"Yeah, he said apartments are expensive, and I guess they had decided they made better friends than a couple. He said that living together made financial sense."

Leaning back in the seat, Waylynn gave it some thought. "Who broke up with whom?"

I shrugged. "No clue. Wait, I think he said she broke it off."

"It's probably okay. I mean, it would bother me a little, but if he was honest about it then you have nothing to worry about."

Traffic was light as I pulled out onto the highway. "I mean, it's not like we're dating."

Waylynn chuckled. "Right. You're only fucking."

"You're so crude."

"What! It's true, and you said so yourself."

The heaviness in my chest returned. "Well, whatever. If we become something more than sex buddies, I just wondered if that was something that should alarm me."

"Does it now? After you've had lots of orgasm-inducing sex?" she asked.

"Not at all." And it didn't. Maybe that should have been alarming.

I could feel Waylynn's eyes. "Huh. Well, then, you have your answer."

"Yeah. I guess I do."

"Whoa, is this a welcome home party?" Waylynn asked.

Laughing, I pulled around all the cars and parked next to Steed's truck. Paxton and Steed were back from their honeymoon, and I couldn't wait to talk to Paxton about it.

"Aunt Vi is in town," I said. "Mom mentioned me missing her birthday party. I'm guessing that is what we're fixin' to crash."

Waylynn let out a roar of laughter. "Oh, hell. Aunt Vi will love that!"

The moment I stepped out of the car I heard music. "Did they hire a DJ?" Waylynn asked.

Trying to hold back my laughter, I said, "I think so. Or maybe it's a band." Waylynn had begged for my parents to hire a band for her twenty-first birthday and they refused. Said it was a waste of money.

"Hell's bells, why can Aunt Vi have a live band and I couldn't?"

Wrapping my arm around my sister, we made our way around the house. A large, white tent was set up and I could see my parents standing next to Aunt Vi. She was my father's sister and she split her time between San Francisco and Paris. When she came home to Texas, Daddy always made a huge deal out of it.

"Look who I brought back with me," I said as we stepped into the tent. Our parents turned to see Waylynn and my mother let out a scream.

"Waylynn! Amelia! Girls, what are you doing here?"

Before I could respond, Waylynn spoke. "Amelia wanted to surprise Aunt Vi and come back for her birthday. I tagged along."

I smiled. Waylynn wasn't about to steal the show from our aunt. If she mentioned what had happened with jackass Jack, the fun times would be over.

After fifteen minutes of hugging and walking around to say hi to everyone, Waylynn and I found ourselves in front of the bar.

"I'll take a shot of whiskey," Waylynn said with a wink.

"Whiskey?" I asked with a chuckle.

"I need something strong to get me through this shit of pretending all is well."

"Diet Coke, please," I said with a smile.

The DJ was spinning tunes, and I wasn't surprised to hear Frank Sinatra singing. He was one of Aunt Vi's favorites.

"Well, hey there, sisters," Trevor said, giving me a hug and a kiss on the cheek. "I see you came back early and brought a surprise with you, Amelia."

Trevor kissed Waylynn on the cheek, then froze. "What did the fucker do?" he asked under his breath.

We both looked at him and spoke at the same time. "What?"

Trevor took a drink of his beer. "I see it on your face, Waylynn. He did something. If he hurt you, I'll fucking kill him."

We both stood there staring at Trevor, and Waylynn finally laughed. "If I promise to tell you later, will you drop it for right now? I want Mom, Dad, and Aunt Vi to enjoy the party."

Trevor's eyes searched both of us. "Fine. I'm letting it go…for now."

Waylynn hugged him, then stole his beer and scanned the dance floor.

"Helllllooo, holy hotness. Who in the hell is dancing with our niece and clearly stealing her heart?" Waylynn asked.

Searching for Chloe, my eyes landed on the most handsome man I'd ever seen.

"*Wow*," I breathed.

"Isn't She Lovely" by Sinatra was playing and this guy was spinning Chloe around. My heart melted. "He's singing to her! Who is that?"

Trevor laughed. "That would be Wade Adams, the friend I picked up the day I dropped you off at the airport. He works for us now," he said, nudging Waylynn.

"Hello, Wade hotter-than-hell Adams," Waylynn said.

The way Chloe was smiling made me smile. "He sure knows how to swoon a six-year-old."

Trevor laughed. "He can swoon more than a six-year-old."

I laughed. "Not these two Parker women."

Waylynn lifted her drink and agreed. "Girl power all the way."

Trevor narrowed his gaze and said, "Watch this."

He headed over to the band. The players were setting back up after their break. He talked to them and then shook what looked like the lead singer's hand. Turning to the mic, Trevor tapped it and got everyone's attention.

"So, as most of you know, we have a new guy on the ranch. He's our new agricultural engineer. Fancy name for a fancy cowboy."

Cheers rang out, and I couldn't help but glance over to Wade. He smiled and tipped his cowboy hat to the crowd.

"But what you don't know is that Wade here is also a musician."

Wade's smile faded. He shook his head and mouthed *Don't*.

Trevor smiled from ear to ear. "Dude, come on. Entertain the ladies, please. I've got a challenge going on. For a friend?"

When Wade laughed, something in the air changed. I swallowed hard and tried to ignore the way it made my stomach drop slightly.

He had a nice laugh. That was all, right? And he was good looking. And he was dancing to Frank Sinatra with my niece.

Ah, hell.

Wade glanced around the room and our eyes met for the briefest moment before he looked away.

Every nerve in my body felt like it caught on fire.

What. The. Heck?

CHAPTER 11

Amelia

My sister's voice broke my trance. "If he wasn't so young I would probably find out what other talents he possessed."

With a giggle, I hit Waylynn on the shoulder. "You're still married, remember!"

I glanced back to Wade, who was arguing with Trevor. "Nah, no one wants to hear me play."

One of the band members handed Trevor something. He held up a harmonica and said, "I think you're wrong. Come on, dude. Let's get in a state of mind."

I couldn't help the grin that moved over my face. Clint Black. Trevor wanted him to sing that song. Every single time he played that song he would say we needed to get into the right state of mind. Wade tossed his head back and laughed as Trevor worked the crowd into chanting *Wade*.

I needed a distraction. "There's Steed and Paxton!" I grabbed Waylynn's arm and pulled her over to their table.

Paxton smiled, jumping up to hug us. Steed stood and kissed me, then Waylynn. "What are you doing here?" Steed shouted over all the noise.

"Long story. Tell ya later."

We sat, and I focused back on Wade, who had walked up to the stage. Trevor hit him on the back and handed him a guitar and the harmonica.

Turning to Steed, I asked, "Is he going to sing?"

He shrugged.

"Alright, y'all. Seems like Trevor ain't gonna stop till I give you a little song."

Waylynn turned to me and wiggled her eyebrows. "Yummy."

I laughed and turned to the stage. Wade was talking to the band, his back to us.

Then he spoke into the mic. "Clint Black was always one of my favorite country singers growing up. I made the mistake of playing the beginning of this song once for Trevor and a few guys in college. Now they think I need to sing it whenever a band is around."

Everyone laughed, including Trevor who was making his way over to us. He sat down behind me and laughed at something Steed said. For some reason, I couldn't pull my eyes away from Wade. His smile was beautiful. Big and bright, like he lit up the area around him. He instantly melted into the band like he had been a part of it from the very beginning, but there was also a sadness to him. I saw it in his eyes.

Wade started counting down, and I was acutely aware of the crowd going silent with anticipation.

"Three, two, one."

The sound of the harmonica filled the air over the rhythm of the drums.

"Holy shit!" I said with a laugh as I watched him fill the air with amazing music.

Cheers and hollers rang across the tent as Wade really got into it. I'd never heard anyone play the harmonica like that. Okay, besides Clint Black. It wasn't lost on me he went a little longer with the intro.

"Get after it, cowboy!!" Waylynn shouted as Wade held the last note.

"Hell, yeah!" Trevor shouted as the whole band started to play. Wade strummed a guitar the moment he started to sing, and I thought I was hearing Clint Black.

Glancing back to Trevor, I smiled. "Wow!"

"I know, right?" he shouted back to me. "He turned down a record deal!"

My brows lifted before I focused back on Wade. He owned the stage, and I loved how he looked at everyone as he sang.

A strange sensation came over me as I watched him reach down and help Chloe up beside him. She danced around the stage as Wade kept playing and singing, not missing a beat.

Waylynn stood and was singing along before turning back to yell to us. "Holy shit, that man is going to make some lucky woman very happy one day."

Paxton laughed and shouted, "I know! Chloe adores him!"

I smiled and watched the scene play out. Wade smiled at everyone, and I kept my eyes on him. Watching his every move. Every now and then he would spin Chloe. My gaze felt locked until the last note sounded. Everyone stood and clapped as Trevor headed back up and shook Wade's hand, revealing a tattoo along his right arm.

To quote Waylynn, *Yummy*.

Trevor grabbed the mic. "That's Wade Adams, y'all!"

Wade laughed as he handed the guitar back to one of the band members. He lifted his hand and nodded before reaching down and picking up Chloe and jumping off the stage.

Jesus. My stomach dropped at the sweet gesture, and I stared as they made their way over to our table.

Waylynn was the first to speak. "You killed it!"

Wade let out a soft chuckle. "Thank you. You are?"

"Oh, sorry, dude," Trevor said. "This is my older sister, Waylynn." Turning to me, he added, "And my baby sister, Amelia. They just got in from New York."

Wade shook Waylynn's hand then turned to me. His gray eyes captured mine, and his knock-me-to-my-knees smile grew wider.

Wow. What is this guy doing to me?

"It's a pleasure meeting you, Amelia. You're a very talented writer."

I pulled my head back in shock. "You've read my work?"

He grinned, showing off matching dimples. "Yes, ma'am." He turned back to Waylynn. "I got to see your first recital, as well!"

Waylynn laughed. "What? How!"

"Mom busted everything out for Wade when he got here," Trevor said with an eye roll. "Showed him Waylynn's dance tapes and gave him one of Amelia's books, bragged about Steed's ability to beat me at ropin', and Lord knows what else."

My eyes scanned the room and landed on my mother. She was laughing at something my father had said. The way she looked up at him with such love made my chest squeeze.

"Wade! Dance with me again!" Chloe said, tugging on his arm.

Steed let out a laugh. "Chloe, honey, let's let Mr. Wade have a break, okay? He may want to ask another girl to dance."

Eyeing Steed as he spoke to Chloe, I couldn't help but cover my mouth to hide my smile. Poor little Chloe looked devastated.

The band started up with a cover of "Banjo" by Rascal Flatts. Wade turned to me. "Want to dance with us?"

"Us?" I asked.

"Me and my girl, Chloe."

"Yes! Aunt Meli, dance with us!"

I glanced at Steed and he nodded. I knew he had just told Chloe no more dancing so I wanted to make sure he was okay with it.

"I'd love to dance with y'all." My phone started ringing, and I glanced at it. "Darn it. It's Liam," I said to no one in particular.

"Her new guy from New York!" Waylynn added.

"New guy, huh?" Steed and Trevor said in unison.

I shot them both a dirty look as I swiped my finger across the phone and gave Wade a quick glance. "Sorry, I need to take this."

He winked at me…and my stomach dropped.

What the fuck?

"Waylynn?" Wade asked as he held his hand out. My breath caught as I paused. I'd never been jealous of my sister until this very moment.

"Hello, Liam? Can you hear me?" I shouted into the phone as I watched Waylynn, Wade, and Chloe take off for the makeshift dance floor.

"Yeah. Where are you?"

"Give me a second!" I headed out of the tent and into the house. "Sorry! My parents are throwing a party for my Aunt Vi. There's a live band playing."

"Sounds like fun. I got your text. I'm glad you made it home. How's Waylynn?"

I watched as my sister danced with Wade and Chloe. My smile grew bigger as I watched Chloe having an absolute blast.

"She's okay for right now. I think she is in pretend mode. She doesn't want to spoil the party so she's telling everyone we came back to surprise my aunt."

"Makes sense." His voice dropped. "By the way, my cock is hard from just hearing your voice."

Turning away from the window, I leaned against the counter. "Someone feeling a little lonely, huh?"

"Rough day. The girl I like jumped on a plane and left me too soon."

Grinning, I shook my head. "What a bitch."

"I know. She should make herself come over the phone so I can feel better."

My cheeks heated. "Is that right?" The fact that I was even entertaining the idea surprised me.

"Are you alone right now, Amelia?"

Swallowing hard, I whispered, "Yes."

"My hand is stroking my hard cock."

I closed my eyes and pictured what he was doing. "Mmm, Liam."

"Are you wet? Touch yourself."

Slipping my hand into my panties, I answered. "I'm so wet, Liam."

"Fuck. Make yourself come for me. Let me hear you moaning my name as you finger fuck yourself."

My eyes snapped open. I was standing in my parents' kitchen with my hand down my panties. What in the hell was I doing?

One quick glance over my shoulder outside proved that everyone was still out there.

"I don't know, Liam. I'm standing in the kitchen. Anyone could come inside any moment."

"That makes it even hotter. Oh, fuck. Amelia, I'm so close. Put it on speaker and touch yourself."

Turning away from the window, I put the phone on speaker and set it on the counter. I slipped my hand back into my pants and spread my legs open. "I'm touching myself."

"Yes. Go fast."

Christ Almighty. I'd written scenes like this before, but never in my life had I been part of them.

My breathing picked up as I pushed two fingers inside and played with my clit.

"Liam," I whispered, eyes closed as I finger fucked myself. My other hand ran over my nipple, causing me to moan.

"Tell me when you're about to come."

"I…ohhhhh…oh, my God, Liam, I'm almost there…" I panted through my almost-orgasm, knowing how close I was to ecstasy.

Then it dawned on me. This felt like a scene from one of my books because it *was* a scene from one of my books. The one that Liam was narrating for audio. The hero called the heroine when she was out of town and talked her into phone sex. A part of me was bothered that Liam was playing out a scene I'd written. My libido quickly took a nose dive.

"I'm so close, Amelia. Tell me how you feel, baby."

My hand stopped moving, and I swear I felt him before he even said anything. Opening my eyes, I turned to see Wade standing there.

"So sorry!" he whispered and turned to leave.

"No! Wait!" I cried, not really thinking about what I was saying as I pulled my hand out.

"Wait? Baby, I can't wait," Liam said.

"No, Liam. I have to go."

"What?"

I spun around and quickly washed my hands while Wade stood there awkwardly since I had shouted for him to wait.

Shit. Shit. Shit.

"You've got to be fucking kidding me," Liam said in an angry voice.

Fumbling with my wet, soapy hands, I took it off speaker and said, "I have company. Someone from the party."

"Oh. Well, that made my dick go down. Cock block, party of one."

I forced a laugh. "I'll call you later."

Hitting End before Liam could respond, I turned to Wade. He held up his hands.

"You don't have to say a word. I'm sorry I didn't know you were in here…um…doing…yeah. Your mother sent me in for a bottle of wine."

I was positive my face was as red as the apple in his hand. Why was he holding an apple?

"No, it's fine. I mean. That's not something I normally do. I, ah, got caught up in the moment."

He smiled. "Hey, judgment-free zone. I'm sure it was hot as hell for y'all. Lucky bastard."

Wade started to walk off in his search for the wine.

My mouth opened, but nothing came out. "It's not what you think," I finally said.

He laughed. "Really? I'm not sure what else that could be but phone sex, plain and simple."

"I'm really embarrassed now. Not the first impression I wanted you to have of me."

Wade found the bottle and picked it up. Turning to me, his eyes swept over my body, causing my lower stomach to pull. I wished it had been Wade asking me to make myself come.

Wait, what?

"What would you want my first impression to be of you?"

I let out a gruff laugh. "Well, not some whore standing in her kitchen getting off with a guy on the other end of the phone."

He frowned. "I don't think you're a whore, Amelia. I don't even know you. I walked in on a private moment, and I'm sorry I embarrassed you."

Okay. Where did this guy come from? First he danced with little girls to Frank Sinatra, then he sang, and to top it all off, he was being such a gentleman in this crazy, weird situation.

"Um, can we pretend this never happened?" I asked.

A strange look moved across his face before he cleared his throat. "Forgotten."

I grinned, and he returned the gesture. "I better get this out to your mother."

Swaying back and forth nervously, I replied, "Yes. It's her favorite wine."

When he walked out of the kitchen I buried my face in my hands and moaned.

"That did not just happen!" I said as I sank down on a chair.

CHAPTER 12

Wade

My heart pounded hard as I smiled at Amelia. "I better get this out to your mother."

She nodded. "Yes. It's her favorite wine."

With a polite nod, I headed out of the house and toward the party as fast as I could. When I had first walked into the kitchen and saw one hand in her panties, the other hand touching her tits, I had to look twice. I thought my eyes were playing tricks on me. When she let out a whimper, my cock instantly went hard.

Then I realized she was on the phone with, I guess, her boyfriend from New York. The sound of him talking and moaning was ice water across my libido.

I dragged in a deep breath and headed back out to Melanie and John. I couldn't get the look on Amelia's face as she made herself feel good out of my mind. The moment I laid eyes on her across the dance floor, I had been instantly taken with her. Then to find out she was Trevor's little sister…

Damn. This day was starting to suck.

"Here ya go, Mrs. Parker," I said as I handed the bottle of wine over.

"Wade, if you're going to be working here, you need to stop calling us *Mr. and Mrs. Parker*. You're family now. It's Melanie and John."

"That's right, son, first-name basis around here," John said.

I forced a smile. He wouldn't be so friendly if he knew how racy my thoughts had been about his youngest daughter a few moments ago.

"Thank you, sir."

"Wade! Wade! Dance with me!" Chloe begged as she pulled on my hand.

"Chloe Lynn Parker. You leave this poor boy alone. He has spent enough time dancing," John said as he picked up his granddaughter.

"Granddaddy, will you dance with me?" Chloe asked, eyes full with hope. Damn, she was a cute little thing. She'd captured my heart the first moment she looked up with those big blue eyes.

"It would be my honor, Chloe."

We watched as John walked out on the dance floor and started to swing her around.

"We're so happy to have Steed and Chloe here," Mrs. Parker said. "And with Paxton expecting a baby this summer. My cup runneth over!"

Turning to her, I smiled. "You're very blessed Mrs....I mean, Melanie."

She nodded. "What about you, Wade. Where is your family?"

My chest ached at the mention of my family. It was something I'd never get used to. I thought for sure Trevor would have told his parents.

"My parents and two younger sisters died in a car accident a few years back. Both sets of my grandparents are gone. I do have an aunt and uncle in San Antonio."

The empathy in her eyes was clear. "Oh, Wade, I'm so sorry. I had no idea or I would not have asked."

With a forced grin, I kissed her on the cheek. "It's okay. Thank you, though, for your kindness. When Trevor offered me the job, I have to admit I was excited to meet y'all. With how he talked about his family in college, I knew I would be happy here. Family business and all. My Daddy had a cattle ranch in Colorado. His dream was for me to run it."

"Do you still have it?"

I kicked at a rock at the edge of my boot. "No, ma'am. I sold it. After what happened to them, the memories were more than I could take. Trevor knew I was in a bit of limbo and I think that's why he offered me the job. I'll be honest, it came at the perfect time. I was a bit...lost...you could say."

Melanie pulled me in for a hug. "Wade Adams, you are a part of this family, and I promise you that you will never be lost again."

Tears threatened to build as I wrapped my arms around this amazing woman. Everything Trevor had ever said about his mamma was true. "That means more to me than you know, ma'am."

We both drew back at the same time. She gave me a wink. "Why don't you go find you a pretty little thing to dance with? I'm sure you've noticed your fan club already beginning to build." She motioned with her head to a group of young ladies who were all looking my way.

"I believe I'm going to call it a day, if you don't mind. I've got a bit of work to catch up on. I've sent out a sample of y'all's dirt from the east pasture. I received the report back earlier."

Melanie shook her head. "I like your work ethic, son, but don't be running off to hide. You stay for a bit longer and enjoy yourself. Why don't you ask Amelia or Waylynn to dance? They both love to two-step."

I swallowed hard as the memory of Amelia rushed back into my mind. "Yes, ma'am."

Turning, I headed over to Trevor. He was surrounded by his siblings. All the Parker brothers, and the two sisters. As I approached, I couldn't help but feel the heat of Amelia's eyes on me. She was probably worried I'd say something about what I caught her doing.

As I approached the table, a young woman stopped me. "Wade? Hi, I'm Amanda Poteet. It's a pleasure meetin' you."

I tipped my hat and replied, "The pleasure is mine."

"Um, do you want to dance?"

My eyes swung over to Trevor. He smiled big, and I knew that was his way of telling me this girl was safe to dance with. The first night I got to town I got a stage three clinger. Took me three hours of trying to shake her before Trevor finally told her a lie...that I was gay.

"Sure, I'd love to dance with you, Amanda Poteet."

She giggled and I forced myself not to roll my eyes. She couldn't have been older than twenty. Taking her in my arms, we started to dance. The poor thing couldn't really keep up, and we spent more time tripping over each other than anything. When I felt a tap on my shoulder, I turned to see Amelia. Her smile nearly blew me out of my boots.

"Mind if I cut in, Amanda?"

Amanda frowned. "Sure. I guess, if Wade wants to dance with ya."

Great. She left it in my corner. "Sure, I don't mind."

The disappointment in Amanda's eyes was evident. She forced a smile before spinning on her boot heel and walking off. Amelia held her arms out, and we started across the floor to "No Can Left Behind" by Cole Swindell.

"Listen, I'm sorry I walked in on you in the kitchen."

Her cheeks blushed. "No, I shouldn't have been doing that in the first place."

I lifted a brow.

"Not that I didn't want to do it. I did. I think." Her brows narrowed.

"You think you wanted to have phone sex? Forgive me, Amelia, but you either know if you do or don't."

She sighed. "Can we please forget that ever happened?"

I looked at her with a raised brow.

"Please?"

"Consider it forgotten."

"Thank you, Wade."

Yeah, there was no way in hell I was going to forget that. But, since I knew she was embarrassed, I changed the subject. "Your mother was right, you can dance."

Amelia laughed. "So can you, cowboy."

"This ain't nothin', darlin'."

She drew back and lifted a brow. "That right? Why don't you show me your moves, then?"

"Is that a challenge?"

"Hell, yes, it is."

"Country swing?"

"Bring it," Amelia purred.

Smiling, I pulled her tight, and we took off two-steppin'. The girl *could* dance. After a few trips around the floor we got after it. A few twists and turns led to some dips and even a few lifts. It was like we had been dancing together our whole lives.

I could hear Trevor and Cord yelling out for an aerial spin.

Amelia laughed as she spun like a pro. Pulling her to me, she straddled my leg, and I dipped her back. Jesus, this girl was amazing.

Hoots and hollers tugged me from the dirty thoughts running through my head. I noticed, with a jolt, that only the two of us were dancing. When the song came to an end I slowly dipped her back. The smile on her face was something I wouldn't soon forget.

I lifted her up and she threw her arms around my neck with a laugh. When she pulled back, her eyes caught mine. "That was the most fun I've had in a long time."

I wanted to make a sarcastic comment about being in the kitchen with her New York City man *not* being fun, but I let it go.

"Same here. Where did you learn how to dance?"

She blushed. "My older sister is a dancer. I was dragged to all her practices and recitals. Guess I picked up a few things here and there."

Giving her a *yeah, right* look, I spun her around one last time before walking her over to her family's table. Cord stood and reached his hand out to shake mine.

"Dude, I'm going to need you to hang out at my place. Sing a little, dance a little. The women are going to go nuts over you."

I let out a chuckle. "I don't know about that, but I'd love to sing sometime."

Trevor hit my back and pulled a chair out for me. He pointed over to his two sisters and yelled, "I told y'all he had the moves."

"Well, I can tell you one thing, Wade. My daughter is smitten with you," Steed said with a smile. "And I'm not so sure how I feel about that."

The whole table let out a round of laughs. "No dancing with my wife!" Steed added.

Paxton rubbed her stomach. "I'm afraid I couldn't dance like that even if I tried."

"Your daughter is a joy," I said. "She brightens my day when I see her walking into the barn with her goat, talking to Patches like they are long-lost friends."

Steed groaned. "That damn goat. Dad and his great ideas."

Glancing around, I asked, "Where did Tripp and Mitchell go?"

Trevor handed me a beer. "Tripp took off to pick up Corina from the airport, and Mitchell said something about having an early shift."

"Corina?" I asked.

The family shared a look as if it was a subject no one wanted to talk about.

"Corina's my best friend," Paxton said. "She's also a teacher at the elementary school. She and Tripp are sort of dating."

Trevor laughed gruffly. "Mitchell has the hots for Corina. Tripp knows it and that's probably the only reason he keeps dating her."

"Oh, well, hell. I'm not touching that with a ten-foot pole," I said.

"Yeah, don't," Steed added.

Waylynn stood. "Well, as much as I love y'all and as fun as Aunt Vi's party is, I'm in serious need of a hot bubble bath."

"When you gonna tell us what's wrong?" Cord asked with a raised brow.

Waylynn snarled. "Do you boys all have some radar that alerts you when something's wrong?"

"Yes!" Amelia said with a chuckle. "They do."

"I see it in your eyes, big sis," Cord said.

She gave him a sweet smile. "I promise I'll tell y'all tomorrow. Right now I need to be alone and do some thinking."

They all nodded, and I felt like I was invading a private family moment.

"Night, y'all," Waylynn said. "Wade, it was nice meeting you."

I stood and tipped my hat. "The pleasure was all mine."

Waylynn headed over to her parents while I reached across the table for Steed's hand. "Thank you so much for letting me dance with your beautiful daughter."

Steed shook my hand firmly. "Thanks for being so patient with Chloe. She adores you."

"You got yourself a future heartbreaker."

Both Steed and Paxton groaned as I chuckled.

I turned to Cord and extended my hand. "Let's plan something at your place soon."

"Yeah, I'll give you a call this week. I'm serious."

"Me, too!" I said with a grin.

Trevor slapped me on the back. "Thanks for helping me prove something to my sisters, but I'm afraid I might have started the Wade Adams fan club."

I shook my head. "Payback's a bitch, my friend." I swung my eyes to Amelia. She was staring at me with a look I couldn't read.

She smiled. "Where are you staying, Wade? In the foreman's cabin?"

"Well, that was the plan, until your father found out there were bees in the walls."

Her eyes widened in shock. "What?"

"Yeah, Dad's having it fumigated so Wade's staying at the main house in Steed's old room."

I glanced over to Steed. "By the way, I found your stash of *Playboys* in the closet."

"Damn, I was looking for those."

Paxton hit him on the chest. "Steed Parker, you do not have *Playboy* magazines!"

Laughing, he shook his head. "Dude, those are Mitchell's. I stole them from him years ago. He was pissed. I forgot all about them. Well, now I know what I'm giving him for Christmas this year."

"I'll be sure to have them delivered over to your place. Wrapped to keep them from prying eyes, of course," I said as I peeked over at Chloe who had crashed asleep on a table.

"May I walk with you to the house?" Amelia asked.

"Sure."

Lifting my hand, I glanced around the table. "Evening, y'all."

"Bye, Wade. You calling it a night, as well, Meli?" Paxton asked as Steed swept up his sleeping daughter.

"Yeah. Night, y'all."

Amelia and I headed to the house. The large oak trees that lead to the house cast a shadow from the rising moon. When I looked up, I was in awe at the endless amount of stars I could see. There was something about a Texas sky. No matter if it was day or night, it seemed to go on forever.

"You don't want to say goodnight to your folks?" I asked.

She shook her head. "Nah. They're talking to friends. I'll see them in the morning."

We walked in silence until we got to the back door. Opening it for her, I motioned for her to go in first.

"So, will you be joining us for breakfast?" Amelia asked as we made our way to the back stairs.

I couldn't help but like the way she was looking at me. I wondered if she looked at her city slicker the same way.

"No," I said, holding my hat in my hand. "I'll be up and out of the house early, checking on a few things."

She tilted her head and stared at me. "Wade, you do know you're welcome to join us for breakfast."

My chest tightened. "I know. I don't want to intrude on your family."

"You are family already, and I know how much you mean to Trevor, so please don't think that way." There went that brilliant smile again. "I wanted to say thank you for being a gentleman about earlier. I appreciate you keeping what you saw to yourself."

Laughing, I pushed my fingers through my hair. "Well, if your brothers found out what I walked in on in that kitchen, I'm afraid they'd all kick my ass. I'll take it to the grave, darlin'."

Her cheeks flushed as we walked farther into the house and stopped at the bottom of the stairs. We both stood for a few seconds, staring.

"Good night, Wade. It was nice meeting you and thanks for the dance." Her teeth dug into her lip as she grinned. "I really had fun."

I returned her smile. "Night, Amelia, and the honor was mine."

She headed up the stairs. I waited for about ten seconds before I followed.

First thing on the agenda for this evening?

A *very* cold shower.

CHAPTER 13

Amelia

By the time I got downstairs, everyone was gathered in the kitchen. Everyone but Waylynn. The moment I stepped in, all eyes were on me.

"Why did you come back early and what happened with Waylynn? And why is some boy named Liam sending you flowers?" my mother asked.

"Momma, I need a cup of coffee before you start with your barrage of questions."

Sliding past my father, I reached for a mug. "Morning, Daddy. Morning, Aunt Vi."

"You look like hell, sweetheart. Did you sleep at all last night?"

Rolling my eyes, I replied, "Thanks, Aunt Vi. I worked up until around two."

"Writing?" my mother asked.

After I poured my coffee, I leaned against the counter. I took a sip and the hot liquid rolled down my throat.

"Yes. It's weird. I've been in somewhat of a writing funk, but last night I wrote more than I have in weeks."

Daddy kissed me on the forehead. "I'm glad you're home. I'll find out who this Liam is later. I've got a meeting in town. Enjoy the morning, ladies."

I watched as my father drew my mother to him and kissed her. I took it all in, smiling. So did Aunt Vi.

Daddy turned to Aunt Vi and kissed her cheek. "Later, my lovely sister. Behave, will ya?"

Vi let out an evil laugh. "I always behave." Glancing over to me, she winked.

I sat, reached for a banana, and started to peel it open.

My mother scooted next to me the second my father left. "Okay, spill it, young lady. Liam?"

I sighed. "He's a guy I met in New York."

"That much I figured out," she said.

"He's recording my last book."

Vi drew her eyebrows together. "Recording your book. What does that mean?"

"It's for the audiobook version. You know, if you don't like to read the books, you can listen to them. He's voicing the male character."

Her eyes lit up. "Holy shit. I didn't know there was a such a thing. Do they get into the sex scenes?"

I chuckled. "Boy, howdy, do they."

"That's it. How do I sign up for them?"

"Vi! Really?" my mother said as she tried to contain her smile.

"What? I may be an old woman, but my vibrator still works the same as hers." She pointed to me and my face heated.

Trevor walked into the kitchen and right back out. All three of us busted out laughing. Tears were streaming down my face. I hadn't laughed that hard in a long time.

When we finally got things under control, I told Aunt Vi and my mother the facts about Liam: he was a hot Australian actor I had met and basically hooked up with.

"He's, um, he's actually coming to visit in a few weeks."

My mother's jaw nearly dropped to the floor.

"Ah, hell. That must have been some good sex you gave him, sweetheart," Aunt Vi said.

Jerking her head to Vi, my mother said, "Vi! Don't you ever think about what you say before you say it?"

She shook her head. "I speak the truth. Look at the girl. You can tell by the look on her face she's been thoroughly fu—"

"Jack's cheating on Waylynn!" I nearly yelled.

"What?" they said as one.

I dropped my face into my hands and groaned. I sold my sister out just to get my aunt to stop talking about Liam "thoroughly fucking" me. I'm an awful sister.

My hands dropped to my lap. "Mom, please, don't tell her I told you. It slipped," I said as I glared at Vi. She took a sip of her coffee and shrugged.

"Oh, my poor baby. Don't worry, sweetheart. I won't say a word." I knew I could count on my mom to not confront Waylynn…who was now standing in the doorway.

"Don't worry, y'all," Waylynn said. "I heard Amelia practically scream it as I walked down the steps."

I made eye contact with my sister. "Waylynn, I'm so sorry."

She waved me off and headed to the coffee pot. "It's okay. I also heard Aunt Vi about to tell the world that Liam fucked you in the bathroom at the Ritz before we left New York City."

I choked on my banana as Aunt Vi gave me a nod of approval. My mother, on the other hand, looked like she was about to be sick.

She stood and turned to face the window. Her hands resting on the sink, she bent over almost in prayer. "Oh, Jesus. I did not hear that. I'm going to my happy place."

Waylynn leaned down and kissed Aunt Vi on the cheek before turning to me. "Payback is a bitch."

I slowly shook my head. "Oh, just wait. You're fixin' to find out just how bad."

She leaned toward me. "Bring it."

"Oh, I will!"

"I'm not afraid."

"You should be!"

My mother spun around and shouted, "Stop it! Both of you are acting like children."

Waylynn leaned back in her chair, but not before sticking her tongue out at me.

"Oh, really? You're thirty-two and you're still sticking your tongue out?" I asked.

"Amelia! I'll deal with you in a minute," my mother said before facing Waylynn. "Sweetheart, I'm so sorry."

Waylynn shrugged. "I'm not, Mom. I had a chance to think about things last night. I gave up everything for Jack. My career, my family. Now I know why he kept putting off having a baby. He didn't really want to be with me. I was the thing he conquered. The young girl he was able to sweep off her feet with promises of a happily ever after. He never wanted that with me. He wanted a Barbie doll on his arm. Well, I'm glad I found out before it was too late."

"Too late?" my mother asked.

"I'm thirty-two years old, Mom. I want to have babies. I want to dance. I want to have the life I always dreamed of. Well, I guess some of my dreams will never come true, but I got to thinking. The last time I was here, at Christmas, Paxton mentioned something about how the old studio where I used to take lessons closed down. I'm going to buy the building and open a dance studio."

My mother's eyes widened. "What?"

"Waylynn!" I gasped. "That's an amazing idea."

She grinned widely.

"You're...you won't go back to New York?" my mother asked. It was obvious she was trying to hide her tears.

"That is a dream I need to let go of. Jack took that one from me, but that's okay. I was able to live it for a little while."

"It's a great idea. If you need an investor, I'm in." Aunt Vi said as she reached for Waylynn's hand.

"I appreciate that, Aunt Vi. But I'm pretty sure Jack will be more than happy to give me the amount we settled on in the pre-nup, plus a little extra to go away quietly."

"That fucking dirty, rotten bastard."

"Momma!" I gasped. "Look at you pulling out all the dirty words you know."

"Waylynn, sweetheart, are you sure you're okay?" my mother asked.

"I really am, Momma. For a few hours last night I cried, but only for the things I gave up for that man. I knew it was coming. It's best it happened now rather than in fifteen years."

Aunt Vi piped in, "I agree. Best to start over while you're young and your boobs aren't touching your vagina."

We looked at Aunt Vi with stunned expressions. She stared back.

"What? It's true. Do you know how hard it is for me to pick up a man these days? Especially the younger ones. There's a reason I have a personal trainer, ladies. That man keeps me in shape. I've got to be able to do a reverse cowgirl with these boys."

Waylynn and I stood, barely containing ourselves. "I'm in the mood to go shopping," I said as I quickly headed to the sink, rinsed out my cup, and put it in the dishwasher.

"Same here." Waylynn was right behind me.

As we walked around the corner Waylynn stopped and grabbed me by the arms. "I'm never going to be able to get that visual out of my head. Never!"

A week after Waylynn and I came back from New York, I met her at the old dance studio early in the morning to walk through it together. Jack had already agreed to a quick divorce, and Waylynn had been right. He was giving her double what the pre-nup stated. He never even bothered to deny the affair. My heart broke for Waylynn, even though she seemed to be the happiest I'd ever seen her.

"Cord has a friend who owns his own construction business. I called him yesterday and he's going to meet us here to give me some rough figures on what it will take to get this place how I want it."

"When do you close?"

Waylynn turned to me and smiled. "Two weeks. When I told the owner I would be paying cash, she was ready to close that day!"

There was a knock on the door and Waylynn and I turned to see who it was. Jonathon Turner--Cord's best friend from high school, not to mention a guy I used to have the biggest crush on.

"Jonathon?" I said as I made my way to the door.

"Hey, Amelia, how are you doing?" Jonathon said as he leaned in and gave me a hug.

"Little Jonathon Turner? You're Jon Turner?" Waylynn asked as she reached out and gave him a hug. "I didn't make the connection when Cord mentioned his friend owned a construction business. Wow, you've changed a lot."

Jonathon flashed a smile. "I'm all grown up. Call me Jon."

One look at Waylynn and I was pretty sure she was calling him a lot more than Jon in her mind. By the way her eyes traveled over his body and that wicked smile on her face, I could tell she was enjoying quite a few naughty thoughts about Jon Turner.

We stood there in a weird silence for a few seconds before Waylynn popped out of whatever dirty fantasy she had going on in her mind. "So! How about we take a tour and I give you my ideas?"

Jon nodded. "Sounds like a solid plan. What's your timeline on the project?"

"I'm not in a rush, but I don't want it to take a year, either."

"I got ya."

As they walked ahead, Waylynn turned around and fanned herself, mouthing '*Holy shit, he's hot*'. Attempting to hide my chuckle, I nodded in agreement.

"Don't you have an appointment you need to be at, Amelia?"

My jaw dropped. When she looked at me I mouthed, '*Whore*'.

"Takes one to know one," she whispered.

"Yep. I guess I should be going. It was great seeing you again, Jon."

He was taking out a tape measure and glanced my way. "Yeah, you too, Amelia."

Pointing to Waylynn, I whispered, "Behave!"

She winked and I couldn't help but laugh.

Trouble was indeed back in town.

Sitting in the cabin, I stared at the computer screen. With a deep sigh, I shut the laptop and stood. This place was my safety net. Where I could relax and totally get lost in writing. The only thing I was getting lost in was an endless array of useless thoughts—and then the sound of whistling caught my attention. I jumped up and made my way over to the window.

Wade.

My heart started to beat a little faster as I watched him on his horse rounding up a lost calf.

I swallowed hard. *Jesus Christ, that guy is good looking.* He finally got the calf and was guiding her back out into the open field. *Damn, that cowboy is one hot son-of-a-bitch.*

A slow smile pulled at my lips as I was hit with inspiration. I sat down and opened my computer. Pulling up my manuscript, I started to write. I was on a roll, the words flowed from my fingers. I squirmed a bit in my seat as I wrote the scene. An evil smile spread over my face as I took my characters on an erotic ride. Before I knew it, I was writing them both coming at the same time. My heart raced and I took a deep breath. I slowly blew it out as I pushed back my chair.

"Holy shit. That was hot."

I chewed on my lip, but couldn't help the chuckle that rose up. I walked over to the window to where I'd seen Wade earlier.

I was finally getting my mojo back, and I knew exactly whom I could thank for that.

CHAPTER 14

Amelia

Wade was the first person I saw when I walked into Lilly's Café. Our eyes met and I couldn't ignore the small twinge of excitement.

"Hey, how are you?" I asked as I approached his table.

He nodded, then sighed. "I'm good. Waiting on a lunch date, but it looks like she isn't showing."

I pulled my brows together. What idiot in her right mind would stand up Wade Adams?

"What's her name?" I asked.

"Kendall Young."

Fighting to hold back my smile, I pulled out the chair and sat down. I raised my hand and got the attention of Lucy, Lilly's daughter. "I'll take my regular."

When I turned back to Wade, he was smiling. "Please feel free to join me, won't you, Amelia?"

I chuckled. "Yes, thank you. Let me tell you why I felt confident enough to have a seat and share my lunch with you."

Wade leaned back in his chair and folded his arms across his massive chest.

Shit, this boy has a body. No. Not boy. Man. Wade Adams is all man.

Lucy set down a Diet Coke in front of me, not bothering to hide a grin.

I took a drink. Long and slow, building up the anticipation of my big reveal.

"Please, take your time while I sit here with bated breath, awaiting your explanation."

Gosh, he was cute when he was frustrated. "Okay. I'll be frank. Kendall Young won't be joining you for lunch."

His left brow lifted along with the left side of his mouth. "Really? And you know this how?"

"'Cause she's married."

Wade's smile dropped, along with his arms. "Are you shitting me right now?"

I had to force myself not to laugh. "Nope. Dead serious. Let me guess. You met her at Cord's, she flirted, probably kissed you, promised to meet you for lunch here?"

He snarled. "Yeah. Pretty much."

I shrugged. "Kendall got pregnant right out of high school and her parents forced her and Leo to get married. About once a month she gets a wild hair and goes to Cord's Place with the intention of having an affair. She always backs out."

"Motherfucker."

"Oh, you won't be fucking her anytime soon. She's actually very much in love with Leo. Just a little bitter she missed out on that part of life."

Wade shook his head. "No, I didn't say I wanted to fuck her, I said *motherfucker*."

With a wink, I replied, "I know."

Dropping back in the chair, Wade let out a frustrated groan. "Are all the women in this town crazy?"

Lucy set my hamburger down. I lifted my gaze from my burger to Wade. "You want the truth or want me to lie?" Looking at the empty spot in front of him, I said, "You gonna eat?"

He shook his head. "I'll just have a salad, please."

"A salad? What kind of pussy cowboy orders a salad?" I asked before taking a bite of my hamburger.

"The kind who just got stood up by a married woman. The idea of hooking up with someone's wife makes me feel sick. I'm not that kind of guy."

His words were so sweet I almost *awwww*ed out loud.

Setting my hamburger down, I stared at him. "You're not like normal guys, Wade."

Now it was his turn to laugh. "What do you mean?"

I half-shrugged. "I don't know. You're...different. It's obvious you care about people. The way you are with Chloe is adorable. Do you have a younger sister?"

His face dropped, and he moved around in his seat. "I, um...had two younger sisters. They died in a car accident along with my parents a year ago."

Now I felt sick. "I'm so sorry, Wade. I didn't know."

He forced a grin. "It's okay. I probably need to start talking about them more. At least that was what my counselor back in Colorado told me."

"I'd love to hear about them. And your parents. If you feel like talking."

His body relaxed, and the way he was looking at me warmed me through. I'd never had a guy look at me that way before. I wasn't sure if he was thankful for my offer or if it was something else.

When Lucy brought over his salad, Wade said, "I think I'll take a burger and fries, if you don't mind."

I smiled, as did Lucy. "Not at all. How do you want it cooked?"

"Medium well. Thanks."

After Lucy turned to leave, he continued to speak. "I grew up right outside of Colorado Springs. My father owned a cattle ranch. My great-grandfather actually started the ranch, and it was passed down to his son and so on. The plan was for me to go to school, get my degree, and take over. My father wanted to spend more time with my mother and sisters. It gutted him when I decided to go to college in Texas."

"Why did you?" I asked.

"Texas A&M had the best program for my field. He got over it quickly. I went home as much as I could, so it wasn't all that bad."

I smiled. "How old were your sisters?"

He played with his fork as he answered. "Grace was eleven and Anna was fifteen. I was ten when my parents told me they were having another baby. Then again at fourteen I got the news our family was growing. Man, I prayed so hard for a baby brother." Wade let out a soft laugh. "But when I held Grace in my arms for the first time I knew I was meant to be her big brother. It was my job to protect them."

His voice cracked, and he closed his eyes. I reached across the table and took his hand.

It took a few moments for him to continue. "I'd been home for a couple years. Running the ranch and all. Anna had begged my folks to go to Denver for the weekend. My father didn't want to go, said he had too much to do. I talked him into going. Said I'd stay behind and make sure everything got done. Anna was so angry with me. She wanted us all to go as a family."

He closed his eyes and shook her head. "She accused me of staying behind so I could be with Caroline, the girl I had been dating since high school." When he opened his eyes, he looked straight at me. "She told me I picked a girl who didn't deserve me over my own family. It wasn't true. Caroline wasn't even in town that weekend.

The only way I could get my father to go was if I stayed behind. I told her that."

"Did she finally believe you?" I asked, while silently saying a prayer she had.

"Yeah." He laughed. "She sent Caroline a text asking if she wanted to go to Denver."

I grinned. "Smart girl."

"She really was. Caroline told her she was in San Francisco with her grandparents that weekend, but I could still see the hurt in Anna's eyes. She wanted me to go and couldn't understand why I didn't go with them. They were on their way back, not very far from the house. A young kid was texting and crossed the center line. Hit them head on. My mother and Grace held on for a few days. My father and Anna died instantly."

Tears rolled down his cheeks, and I had the urge to reach over and wipe them away.

"I rotated between their rooms. Praying to God not to take them. They died a day apart. My mother's heart gave out, and Grace... They couldn't stop the internal bleeding. It felt like my life was over."

I squeezed his hand, and he looked at me. "I tried to hang onto the ranch, but I couldn't do it. Everywhere I turned there were reminders. I sold it six months after my folks passed away."

My heart dropped. "Oh, Wade. I'm so sorry."

"I didn't know what else to do. I wasn't about to let it go, not after all the hard work my dad had put into it. His best friend and another local rancher bought it. Promised me if I ever changed my mind he'd sell it back to me."

I smiled. "That was nice of him."

Wade grinned slightly. "Yeah. He's good people."

"What happened with Caroline? Was she upset when you moved to Texas?"

"Yeah, no. She broke up with me shortly after the accident. She thought that I was giving up and said she couldn't emotionally deal with helping me through it all."

I gasped. "What?"

"Yep. Those were her exact words. I spent the next four months drinking myself to death. Felt like I didn't have anything to live for. Then I got a phone call from Trevor. He'd flown up for the funerals and had kept in close contact with me since the accident. Called me damn near every day."

I now remembered Trevor going to Colorado to help out a college friend. He never did tell me the story though. My chest filled with pride as I thought about how caring my brother had been.

"He offered me a new start. I spent about a month getting my shit together and settling up everything in Colorado, then headed to Texas."

I smiled. "I'm glad Trevor called you."

For the first time since I had met Wade, I saw a light in his eyes. "I am, too. Your brother saved me, and I'll forever be in debt to him for that."

It wasn't lost on me that I was still holding his hand. I didn't let go, and he didn't pull away. His thumb brushed over mine, and I couldn't ignore the way my chest fluttered. Our eyes locked. Awkward, yet mesmerizing at the same time. He withdrew his hand as Lucy set his food down.

I watched while he took a bite and moaned in appreciation. "Damn. That's a good burger."

"It is!" I said with a smile.

We sat and ate for a few minutes. Pushing my plate back, I placed my elbows on the table and stared at him.

"I know your loss is still very new. And I'm not saying I want my family to replace yours, but I know you're staying in the main house for another few weeks. I want you to start eating with us."

Wade stared at me like I'd lost my mind. "What?"

"I've seen you sneak out at the crack of dawn, and I know it's so you can avoid breakfast. I want you to join us. You ain't got nowhere to be that early in the morning that can't wait. Trevor eats with us, so can you."

"Amelia, I appreciate you trying to make me feel welcome."

"I'm not making you feel welcome, Wade Adams. You *are* welcome. You're part of our family whether you like it or not. That means eating with us. At least breakfast. Will you do that for me?"

A wide smile built over his face. "Yes. I'll do that for you, Amelia."

His words touched me more than I thought they would, and I had to push away my growing feelings.

We stared at each other until my phone started ringing. Glancing down, I read the caller ID.

"It's, um, it's Liam."

Wade nodded. "No dirty sex talk at the table, please."

I swiped across my phone. "Hey, Liam. What's up?"

"I'm not going to be able to make it this weekend."

Disappointment should have rushed through my body; it didn't. "Why not?"

"Nancy got me an audition for a Broadway play. I can't turn it down."

"Of course not," I said. "When is the audition?"

"Saturday afternoon."

"Really? What play?" I asked.

"It's for a dramatic adaptation of a 19th century literary piece."

I grinned. "Walter Theatre Productions?"

"Yeah. How did you know?"

"One of the girls I went to college with works for the production company."

"Really? Small world. Think she can help me get the part?"

I was stunned for a moment by his request for her to help him with the part. "I doubt it."

Wade laughed and shook his head.

"Who's that?" Liam asked.

"I'm having lunch with Wade."

"What the fuck? Why?"

"Why not?" I asked, not the least bit pleased with his outburst.

"The guy clearly wants in your pants, and you're having lunch with him?"

I stood and covered the phone. "Excuse me. I'll be right back."

Wade nodded and continued to eat his hamburger. The second I left the café, I ripped into Liam. "How dare you! You don't even know Wade. He works for my father and brother and happens to be a friend of mine and part of our family. You don't hear me complaining that you're living with your ex. And the last time I checked, Liam, I don't remember us being exclusive."

"Is that what you want? To see other people?"

"Liam! We've barely gone out on two dates."

"We've fucked plenty of times."

"Oh, so that makes us boyfriend and girlfriend?"

"Maybe!" he shouted over the phone.

"Have you gone out with anyone since I've left?"

"No."

I sighed. "Neither have I, but Liam, I also wasn't out to be in a serious relationship."

"Then I want to be exclusive."

Rolling my eyes, I asked, "Why?"

"Because I don't want you having lunch with this Wade guy."

Anger pulsed through my body. "You're being a complete dick. I'll have lunch with whomever I damn well please. You don't see me telling you to move out of the apartment you share with your ex, and I know for a fact she walks around naked! You told me."

"That's different."

I groaned. "I'm not doing this. The only time you ever call is when you want phone sex. If you need sex that bad, fuck your ex."

Hitting End, I stared at my phone. I was about to go back in when it rang.

Liam.

I debated sending him to voicemail, but answered. "What?" I snapped.

"I'm sorry. I got jealous, and it's only because I want to be the one having lunch with you."

"Wade is just a friend. Liam, maybe what we shared in New York was just meant to be fun. You and I both know this isn't going to work. Not with you being in New York and me in Texas."

"I'm not ready to just give up like that, Amelia. Are you?"

I wanted to be honest with Liam. I was forcing myself to feel things for him that just weren't there. I didn't want to tell him over the phone though. It was better to do it in person. "I'm not sure what I want at this point, Liam. Why don't you go to the audition, and we'll talk about visits after?"

Liam let out a sigh. "Okay, I might not be able to make it to Texas if I get the part."

"We'll talk Saturday night, okay?" I asked.

"I want to see you, Amelia. How long are we going to have to wait?"

My chest felt like someone was sitting on it. "Let's talk about it after your audition, and we have a better idea of things."

The silence on the line proved that Liam was not happy about having to wait.

"I'll call tonight, if I can."

"Okay. Talk soon."

"Bye, Amelia."

"Bye, Liam."

The line went dead, and I walked back into the café. At the mere glimpse of Wade my stomach dropped. I stood frozen in place as I stared at him. He was talking to Lucy and wore a huge smile. There was something about him that held me captive, and I knew that I couldn't go on with Liam. It wasn't fair to him or me. When Wade looked at me my breath would catch, and I got excited at the chance of glimpsing him. I wanted to explore these feelings. Especially since I'd never really felt them before.

I knew then what I had to do.

I will end things with Liam this weekend.

CHAPTER 15

Liam

I dragged in a deep breath as I walked into the apartment. Nancy sat at the table surrounded by a few of our mutual friends.

"Liam!" they all called out. "We need another player."

Forcing a smile, I made my way over to them. "For what?"

"Strip poker, and don't say it."

I lifted a brow. "Don't say what?"

"If you say one of the five forbidden words, you have to take a shot."

Nancy was looking up at me with a smirk. She must have had ten layers of clothing on.

"Afraid you'll lose, Nance?"

She laughed. "You know how bad I am at poker. How was the audition?"

I was still pissed about not being able to make it to Texas. Amelia seemed to have something on her mind, and I had a feeling I knew what it was. Things weren't going to work out between us. I think we were both lonely when we hooked up in New York. I wasn't going to lie to myself and say I didn't crave her. I did. But not in a healthy way. I was using her to fill up an empty space. I just didn't know why it was empty.

"I got the part."

Everyone cheered, and Nancy wore a smug expression. I had nothing to do with landing that role. Nancy did with the strings she pulled with whomever it was she knew. It was her way of keeping me in New York and away from Amelia.

"Then we need to celebrate. Come on. Join us for some fun, won't you?" Linda said. She was one of Nancy's best friends.

I had sent Amelia a text and still hadn't heard from her. I had a sneaky feeling she was with that asshole Wade.

Damn it. Why am I so jealous of this guy?

"I'll play. Why not?"

It didn't take long before I was halfway drunk, and a part of me was saying the forbidden words so I could have an excuse to get wasted. I was glad I'd gotten the part, but pissed I wasn't in Texas with Amelia. Nancy kept flirting with some guy named Rich. I had no fucking clue who he was. All I knew was she was doing her best to make me jealous and for some reason, it was working.

I placed my winning hand on the table and looked straight at Nancy. "Strip."

Standing, she pulled her shirt off to reveal she hadn't been wearing a bra. Her tits bounced, and Rich reached up to cup them. "Are they real?" he asked as everyone around the table laughed.

Reaching for the bottle of whiskey, I poured myself another shot. This was going to be a long night.

My eyes snapped open when I heard Amelia's voice. It came from out in the apartment, where people were still partying.

"Is Liam around?"

"Yeah, he's in his room."

I sat up and looked to my right. Nancy was sprawled out in my bed, naked.

"What in the fuck?" I muttered.

My head was pounding. I couldn't remember a damn thing from last night. The last thing I remembered was losing a hand at poker and having to take off my strides.

Shit. Fuck. I slept with Nancy.

The door to my bedroom opened, and I glanced over to see Amelia standing there. She looked between Nancy and me and slowly nodded her head.

"Wait, Amelia, it's not what you think!"

"It's pretty clear, Liam. Why don't you get dressed? I'll meet you at the coffee shop across the street."

She shut the door, and Nancy rolled over. "Well, talk about busted."

"What in the fuck did you do?" I asked as I jumped out of the bed and searched for something to put on.

"Me? I didn't do a damn thing, Liam. You're the one who told me you needed to fuck me. And fuck me, did you ever."

I groaned. "Jesus Christ. Nancy, you knew I was seeing Amelia."

"Was that an exclusive thing? You barely just met her."

"If you fucked up this job for me…"

Nancy frowned. "Job? Liam, did you just hear yourself?"

I stopped moving. I had talked about my job rather than hurting Amelia. Christ. What was wrong with me?

"I've got to go. Amelia is waiting."

Slipping on a pair of shoes, I quickly made my way to the coffee shop. I hadn't brushed my teeth or even splashed water on my face. I was regretting that more than anything.

The door chimed when I walked in, and Amelia faced me. She didn't look angry. In fact, she looked almost relieved.

"Amelia, let me explain."

Holding up a hand, she replied, "Don't. Liam, this wasn't ever going to work. It's pretty clear you still have feelings for Nancy. I should have seen it from the beginning. We had fun, it was an adventure being with you here in New York. You got me to do things I probably never would have done, but I think we both know this is over. Even before you slept with Nancy, it was over. I planned on telling you when you came to Texas, and when you canceled, I knew I had to fly up here and end things."

The girl behind the counter called out two black coffees. Amelia took them both and handed me one. "Here, you look like hell."

I laughed. "I feel like it. I don't remember anything about last night. I didn't mean to sleep with Nancy. I didn't want to hurt you. I guess this explains why you were so calm when you walked into my room."

Amelia gave me a sweet smile. "Liam, I think we both know what we had going on was nothing serious. You can't build a relationship on great sex."

"Great sex, huh?" I said, wiggling my brows.

"Yes. I'm not going to lie. That was some of the best sex of my life, and it was also a rush to do something I'd never really done before. Sure, I've slept with guys, but I've always known them beforehand. With you, it was different. Almost like a dare to myself. A few forbidden moments to go wild and crazy."

"You liked the toilet sex, I take it."

We both laughed. "It was a rush, like I said. But that's all it was. I only want to be honest with you. I don't have feelings for you. At least, not the kind that make me think we have a future together."

I nodded. "Friends still?"

"Of course. Plus, you've still got three more books in my series to record! You're the perfect James."

"Thank you, Amelia. Listen, I'm sorry I acted like a jealous ass with this Wade character."

She shrugged. "No worries. So, what's really going on with you and Nancy?" she asked while sipping her coffee.

My hand pushed through my hair. "Hell if I know. She's driving me crazy. I do love her. A part of me will always love her." I took a deep breath and slowly blew it out. "But she's manipulative. I don't think that is a relationship I can honestly go back to."

Amelia leaned back in her chair. "What are you going to do?"

"I think I'm going to go home for a few weeks."

Her eyes widened. "Really? What about the new role you landed?"

I shrugged. "My eyes have been opened this morning. Maybe this isn't the life I wanted after all."

Amelia reached for my hand. "Follow your heart, Liam. Sometimes our dreams have been staring us right in the face, and we've chosen to ignore them for whatever reason. Your heart will never lead you the wrong way."

"Spoken like someone who has found her path."

Amelia's smile faded some. "No. But hopefully someday I'll stumble upon it. I've come to realize that it's easier to write words about happiness than it is to make your own."

I reached for her other hand, and we sat there smiling at one another. "You're an amazing woman, Amelia Parker. You're worth more than some asshole begging you for phone sex. Someday you're going to meet a man who will treat you the way you deserve. Don't settle for anything less. Promise me that."

She blushed. "Thank you, Liam. And I promise I won't. I'm not so sure love is in the cards for me, but I won't give up."

"He's out there, and he's not one of your fictional characters. Follow your own advice, sweetheart. He's probably right in front of you, and you just haven't opened your heart to him."

Her eyes filled with tears, and she cleared her throat. "I'm stealing that and putting it in a book!"

Kissing both her hands, I replied, "Do it. But please remember it, okay?"

Nodding, she added, "You do the same. You're a great guy, Liam. Any girl would be lucky to capture your heart." Amelia stood. "I guess I should probably head out to the airport."

I followed her lead, guiding her out of the coffee shop with a hand on her lower back. "See ya around?"

Reaching up on her toes, she kissed me gently on the lips. "See ya around."

With a wave, I got a taxi to pull over for her. "I'm sorry you came all this way."

She slid into the back seat and looked up at me. Those big, bright blue eyes sparkled. "I'm not."

"Bye, Amelia Parker."

Sinking her teeth into that lower lip, she smiled big. "Bye, Liam Jones."

As the taxi drove off, I lifted my hand again. I would never forget Amelia Parker. Those blue eyes and red hair would forever be ingrained in my memory. She was the woman who showed me it was *okay* to want more out of love and life.

CHAPTER 16

Wade

I brought my horse to a stop and gazed over the hill country. Storm clouds slowly covered the sky. Thunder rumbled closer as I waited for heaven to rain down on me.

"You do know a storm is coming, right?"

The sound of her voice did something to me. I hadn't really put my finger on it yet, because I refused to go there. First off, she had a boyfriend. Second, she was Trevor's baby sister.

"I do."

"You always leave yourself open for lightning to strike you?"

I glanced to my right and smiled at Amelia. She was on her precious horse, Stanley. "I could say the same thing about you. Why are you out here?"

She took in a deep breath and slowly let it out. "Something about a storm clears my head. Besides, it's still miles away."

"Lightning can strike up to ten miles, ya know."

Amelia turned in her saddle to look at me. "I'd say that storm was at least thirty, forty miles away."

I lifted my brow. "You think?"

"Yep. I'm an expert when it comes to storm clouds."

A hint of sadness was evident in her voice. I looked away. "Yeah, me too. I'd say it's closer to thirty."

"Just enough time for us to get back."

Drawing Rio back by the reins, I turned around. "What are you doing here? I thought you went to New York to visit your boyfriend."

Amelia let out a curt laugh. "Liam wasn't my boyfriend. We had a bit of fun together, but that was all it was ever going to be."

I kept my expression tight. There was no way I would let myself celebrate the fact that she let that asshole go. I'd save it for later when she wasn't around.

"I'm sorry to hear that."

"Don't be. I'm not. I never felt anything for Liam but attraction. He's a great guy, but he wasn't *the* guy."

Thank fuck. Amelia deserved better than some schmuck who was only interested in sex.

"I guess it's good you figured that out before it was too late."

She laughed. "Yeah. So how are things going? Are you settling in with everything?"

"I am." We rode next to one another as the storm moved in closer. "Your parents are amazing. First, your dad had the foreman's cabin fumigated and now he is insisting on updating everything. He really doesn't have to go through all the trouble."

"He wants to. Besides, it needed some new paint. It was remodeled a few years back, but Daddy never replaced the old crap furniture."

Letting out a chuckle, I replied, "Well, I would have been fine with it."

"Have you been to Cord's to sing yet?"

"Nah. We're all going out tonight, though."

"Who's *we all*?"

"Your brothers. I guess it's the first time in a while they've all had the same night off."

Amelia whistled. "Ah hell, look out. All five Parker boys out at the same time...and with you. The girls will be swarming tonight."

"Very funny."

"Wade, have you not been out yet with all my brothers?"

I shrugged. "Trevor and I have gone out."

"Take that and multiply it by five...no, six. Six hot guys, most of them on the prowl, and the women come out of the woodwork."

"You think I'm hot?"

She was looking straight ahead, and then her head snapped over to look at me. She faked a shock expression. "Did I say that?"

Tipping my cowboy hat at her, I replied, "Yes, ma'am, you did."

With a half-hearted shrug, she added, "I mean, you're decent lookin', I guess."

"I'll take it. What about you and Waylynn? Would y'all like to join us?"

"That might be just what the doctor ordered for both of us."

"Now, don't feel obligated. I don't want to cramp your style. Two beautiful women in the company of five hot guys and one half-decent looking one."

Amelia fought to hold her smile back. "You think I'm beautiful, Wade?"

Our eyes locked. "Yes, I do, darlin'."

Her smile faded.

Shit, that came out too soon. I don't want to scare her away.

Pressing her lips together, she asked, "Can I show you something?"

I grinned. "Of course, you can."

She kicked her horse lightly and started off in a trot. "It's right up here."

We were soon going down a path and an old cabin appeared.

"Wow."

She glanced over her shoulder. "I know. It's beautiful, isn't it?"

I slid off of Rio and draped his reins over his neck.

The smile Amelia wore was contagious. She grabbed my hand and hauled me up the porch. She unlocked the door and walked us in.

"This is beautiful," I said.

"The cabin," she whispered. "I have written a lot of books here. I love it. My thinking is clearer here. Well, when my damn brothers aren't bringing women here to fuck."

I swallowed hard. The sound of that word coming from her lips instantly made my dick hard.

"I can see why you'd love to write here. It's very inspiring."

The way she looked at me made my chest tighten. Her eyes turned dark, and I could have sworn she had naughty thoughts running through that pretty little head of hers.

"It's very inspiring." Her teeth dug into her lip. If we stayed in this cabin much longer I was afraid I might do or say something I couldn't take back.

Finally, she broke eye contact. "Anyway, you're more than welcome to come here if you want."

My brows pulled together. I wanted to ask what made her think I'd need to come to the cabin.

"I'm just saying it's a nice escape. You know if you wanted to disappear for a bit, this is the place to go. The key is under the mat if you ever...want...something. Um, if you want to...get um..."

It was cute as fucking hell how she was stumbling over her words. I wouldn't have thought Amelia Parker was one to stumble over anything.

"Get lost?" I asked.

She pointed and jumped. "Yes! Get lost."

I nodded.

"You want to race back to the house?" she asked, changing the subject before the sexual tension in the room grew.

I let a crooked grin spread over my face. "You don't think you could beat me, do you?"

Her hands went to her hips. "Think? Oh, Mr. Adams, I know I can."

We were soon back on our horses, making our way into the pasture. I kicked Rio and took off as Amelia yelled out, "Cheater!"

"Dude, why do you keep staring at the door? You waiting for someone?" Trevor asked.

"No. I'm not waiting for anyone."

Trevor grinned. "Good. Look around, brother. Endless pussy at your disposal. You walk up to any of them, and I promise you'll get some. Even if it's only a hand job."

I laughed and took a long drink of my beer. "You haven't changed a damn bit, Parker."

"Learned it from the best."

Trevor pointed to the dance floor and his brother, Cord. He was currently sucking the face off of a blonde. His hands roamed all over her ass as they danced.

"And if you need more proof." He pointed to Mitchell who was talking to a girl who looked like she was ready to drop to her knees for him.

I glanced around our table to find Steed and Tripp talking. Steed wasn't about to step out on Paxton, and Tripp was in a relationship with Corina. Or at least I thought he was. I still wasn't sure on that whole thing.

"Why aren't you out there?" I asked Trevor.

"I'm waiting."

"Waiting?"

Trevor nodded and placed his beer to his mouth.

"For?" I asked.

"The girl I know will be a sure hook-up. I haven't had a decent fuck in a few weeks. I need to release some steam."

I shook my head. "You don't ever get tired of one-night stands, Trev?"

He looked at me like I'd lost my damn mind. "Hell, no. And bite your tongue. If you had any sense, you'd be looking, as well."

After taking a look around the bar, I knew there were plenty of attractive women to pick from. I was positive I could easily get laid tonight, but I wasn't interested in a mindless hook-up. I wasn't interested in anything, to be honest.

Maybe there was something wrong with me.

"Look at the chick down at the end of the bar. She hasn't stopped eye fucking you since you walked in. Go dance with her."

"I'm not interested in a hook-up, Trev. Besides, what would I do? Bring her back to your parents' place?"

"Have you ever heard of the back seat of your truck?"

I stared at Trevor. "Are you serious? You're still screwing women in the back seat of your truck?"

"Hey, if they're up for it, so am I."

"Evening, boys."

Trevor, Steed, Tripp, and I looked over to Waylynn.

Steed stood and kissed his sister on the cheek. "Hey, sis. You look nice."

Waylynn blushed. She did look nice. She had on a long skirt and a blouse that hinted at how nice her body was underneath it all.

"Hey, glad you made it. Where's Meli?" Tripp asked. Waylynn pointed to the bar.

My mouth dropped when I saw her.

"What in the fuck is she wearing?" Trevor said as he stood.

"Oh, settle down. She just has on jean shorts and a shirt."

"I can see her ass!" Tripp said. "She needs to change."

Waylynn laughed. "Okay, which one of you is going to tell her that?"

"I will," Steed said. "She doesn't need to be dressing like that. Look how nice you look and you're covered up...kind of."

Waylynn raised a brow. "The girl is twenty-two years old. I'm thirty-two. That's why I'm in the long skirt, and she's pulling off the daisy duke shorts."

Trevor punched me in the chest.

"Ouch. What in the fuck, dude?"

"Stop staring at my sister like that, you asshole."

"What? I wasn't staring at her."

"Dude, you were staring." Tripp said. "*Hard.*"

"Well, hell. What do you expect? She's a beautiful girl. I'm not the only one staring."

Steed, Tripp, and Trevor scanned around them and Trevor growled, "I'll kick the ass of any fucker who touches her tonight."

"Then I guess y'all better make sure her dance card is full. I see someone on the approach."

Trevor grabbed me by the arm and pulled me up. "Go ask her to dance."

I stared at him, confused as hell. "You just punched me for looking at her, and now you want me to dance with her?"

"You, I trust. These others, I don't."

Swallowing hard, I looked over to Waylynn. She was wearing a shit-eating grin. If I hadn't known any better, I'd swear she set it all up.

"Go. Now."

He pushed me, and I stumbled forward. I could see the guy coming up on Amelia's right. I picked up my pace, and when I reached her I placed my hand on her lower back. The feel of her soft skin instantly made my body come to attention. Amelia jumped. "Hey, Wade."

"Dance with me, darlin'?"

A wide smile moved over her face. "I'd love to."

I looked over her shoulder at the guy who had been about to hit on her as he came to a halt. I shot him a smirk and led Amelia to the dance floor. She dropped two beers at the table and then took my hand.

The second we hit the dance floor a slow song started. I pulled her body against mine and we started to two-step. The feel of her in my arms was nice. It was something I could let myself get used to, but I wouldn't. I slowly took in the way she smelled. Like honey-dew. Soft, yet sweet.

"Your brother nearly kicked my ass earlier," I said.

Amelia drew back and looked up at me. "What do you mean?"

"I guess I was looking a little too long at you standing by the bar. Fair warning, your brothers all think you need to change your outfit."

She giggled and shook her head. "The joys of having five older brothers."

"They love you and worry about you. That's all."

"So, did they force you to dance with me?"

"Oh, darlin', I don't need to be forced to have you in my arms."

Amelia dug her teeth into the corner of her mouth before she replied. "Why, Wade Adams, did you just flirt with me?"

Grinning, I pulled her closer. "Yes, ma'am, I did."

Her fingers came up and pushed slightly against the back of my neck. "Don't stop. I liked it."

Fuck if I didn't like it, as well...but...

"And risk getting my ass whooped by five cowboys? No way. One flirt a day. That's all you're getting from me."

She let out a roar of laughter. "One a day? Damn. I guess I'll take it."

The song changed to "Night's On Fire" and Amelia let out a little yelp. "Let's show them how to dance!"

And show them we did.

CHAPTER 17

Amelia

I was out of breath by the time Wade and I left the dance floor. Four songs in a row, and we tore up each one. As we walked to the table I couldn't help but notice Waylynn dancing as well. I did a double take when I saw that she was dancing with Jon.

"Damn, y'all," Tripp said as we reached the bar. "I think you should enter a competition with the way you two dance."

"Yeah, I'm not too sure how I feel about where your hands were on my sister, dude," Trevor said.

I glared at him. "Seriously? We were dancing. Give it a rest, Trevor."

When Trevor did the whole *I'm watching you* thing with his fingers toward Wade, I had to laugh.

"Ignore this jackass, Wade. He actually beat up my prom date because he thought he took my virginity."

Wade's eyes widened as he looked from me to Trevor. "Dude, you didn't."

"I sure as fuck did. Little prick went around town bragging he took her flower."

"See! I'm not the only one who calls it that, Meli!" Steed cried out.

Rolling my eyes, I grabbed Wade. "Come on, I'm ready to dance again."

"Wade! Hold up!" Cord called out. "The band does tons of Clint Black covers. I told them you sound just like him. They want you to sing."

My heart dropped. If Wade got up on that stage, all the girls in the place would be after him all night and the idea pissed me the hell off. Which shocked me. I wasn't the jealous type, and this new feeling had my stomach twisting.

Wade gave me a questioning look. "Do you mind?"

I already knew how much he liked to sing. Who was I to keep him all to myself?

A selfish bitch. That's who. What is going on with me?

"No, I don't mind at all."

Lies! I speak nothing but lies!

As I made my way back to the table, Cord got everyone's attention.

Waylynn was back at the table sitting next to Trevor. She smiled and motioned for me to sit by her.

"So, we have a little special treat for y'all tonight. You're familiar with The Country Boys, our local band that plays here, but you haven't heard this guy sing yet. I'd like to welcome Wade Adams to Cord's Place. Give him a big round of applause, y'all."

The place went wild, women screaming. I had to force myself not to make a gagging sound.

When the spotlight hit Wade, I smiled. He really did look at ease up on the stage.

"Thanks, y'all. I appreciate the warm welcome. So, the boys here told Cord they like to cover a lot of Clint Black songs. He was

my idol growing up. I drove my mama crazy asking her to take me
to his concerts. Never did get to go, so singing his songs has been the
next best thing. I hope y'all enjoy it."

He turned and said something to the band. I held my breath and
waited for him to start on that harmonica. When the steel guitar
sounded instead, I was thrown off.

Wade sang Clint Black's "Nothing's News." He sounded so
much like Clint it was eerie.

Waylynn leaned close. "He has such a sadness to his voice."

I nodded as I watched him sing. He looked around at the audi-
ence, and when he smiled it didn't touch his eyes.

"Damn, that boy can sing," Cord said as he sat down at the table.

"I'm telling ya, he turned down that record deal in college. His
number one goal was running his dad's ranch."

The song ended and the crowd went wild.

"Thanks, y'all. I'll do one more song, then let these guys take
over."

When the piano started and I recognized the song, I had to fight
back tears.

"Oh, God," I whispered as Waylynn grabbed my hand.

Wade started singing Rascal Flatt's "I'm Movin' On" and no
one made a sound.

As I listened to the words I was taken back to the day in the café
when he told me about his family. The song seemed to be have been
written for Wade. My heart broke as I watched him sing. His eyes
were closed mostly, only looking over the crowd every now and
then.

I glanced to Trevor, and my breath caught when I saw the tears
in his eyes. It was clear that he thought of Wade as a brother. In that
moment, I could believe that what Wade had said in Lilly's was true.
Trevor had saved him.

A single tear rolled down my cheek as I focused back on Wade. He had such a pained expression. I had the urge to run to him and take him in my arms.

When he opened his eyes, they met mine and my heart stopped as he sang the title words. When the last note played I couldn't believe how everyone clapped. My brothers all stood, as did Waylynn. She yelled out Wade's name. Our eyes were still locked. It wasn't a stare. It was a connection that I couldn't deny, and I was positive he felt it as well.

Wade finally looked away, and I placed my hand over my chest. My racing heart confused me. What was happening between us? I stood and clapped while Wade handed one of the band members his guitar back.

He lifted his hand and jumped off the stage, and I lost sight of him in the crowd.

"Damn, that took everything out of me not to cry," Steed said.

"I hate that he lost his family," Tripp said.

Trevor cleared his throat. "Yeah. He's good people. I'm glad he took my job offer."

Waylynn took my hand. "Are you okay, Amelia?"

All eyes were now on me. "I guess I was overcome. That's a pretty powerful song."

My sister stared into my eyes. She knew it was more than that, but even I wasn't exactly sure what had happened.

The band started playing, and everyone began dancing again.

"Well, I'll give him one thing. He recovers well," Steed said as he pointed to the dance floor.

What?

Wade had a girl in his arms, and they were dancing. Cord walked up to me, blocking my view of Wade. "Dance with your brother?"

With a forced smile, I nodded. "Of course. It's about damn time one of y'all asked me."

Trevor and Waylynn headed out to the dance floor with Cord and me behind them.

I tried my best not to look for Wade. What in the hell was wrong with me? Why did I care that he was dancing with another woman? I had no right to care.

"Who are you looking for, Amelia?" Cord asked against my ear.

"What?" I shouted. "No one."

He gave me a doubting look. "Seems to me you're searching. Wade, maybe?"

I laughed. "Please! He's a friend. I'm not interested in anything more than that."

"Good. Then you won't be bothered by the fact that he's walking out with some girl."

My smile dropped, and I spun around to see Wade doing just that. I had no idea who the girl was. A blonde. Of course. Why did guys like blondes? And why were there so many blondes in Oak Springs, damn it?

Putting my attention back on Cord, I shrugged and faked a grin. "Let's hope he uses protection."

Cord tossed his head and laughed. "You and your condoms, baby sister."

"Extra-large is all I'm interested in, if you catch my drift." We continued dancing, which kept my mind off Wade.

After dancing with Tripp, Steed, and Trevor, I called it a night. Waylynn was still having fun, so Steed offered to take me home. The moment we got into his truck, I put my head back and pretended to fall asleep. The last thing I wanted to do was talk. Not when all I could see was Wade walking out with some girl to do God-knows-what.

At some point on the drive back, I actually fell asleep. My brother's strong arms carried me up the stairs to my bedroom. When he gently set me down on the bed, he brushed my hair back from my face.

"Thank you, Steed," I mumbled, too tired to look at him.

The bed moved slightly, warm breath at the side of my ear. "Goodnight, darlin'. Sleep good."

Wade's voice caused warmth to rush through my body. When his lips touched my cheek, my breath caught in my throat, I didn't move. Not one inch. I listened to him slowly retreat and walk out of my room, gently shutting my door. The second it shut, I sat up in bed and placed my hand over my cheek. It still tingled from his lips.

It was Wade who had carried me upstairs. Not Steed. What in the hell? Where was Steed?

I jumped out of bed and rushed to the window that faced the front of the house. Steed's truck was driving off toward the house he shared with Paxton.

Facing my bedroom door, I wrapped my arms around my body. Wade must have offered to carry me up to my room. My heart was beating so hard I thought for sure it would pound right out of my chest. I wasn't sure how long I stood there and stared at the door. Once I heard Wade's bedroom door shut, I slowly sat on my bed.

A million things ran through my mind. When did Wade get to the house? What about the girl he'd left the bar with? Maybe they had sex and that was it. Maybe he just left her. Would Wade do something like that?

Wade Adams had managed to do what no other man had ever done: gave me a sleepless night filled with one question after another.

CHAPTER 18

Amelia

I walked into the kitchen and stopped when I saw Wade sitting next to Trevor. He glanced up and smiled. The way my stomach dipped surprised me.

"Good morning," I said with a grin.

"Morning, sis," Trevor said.

I could feel Wade's eyes as I made my way over to the coffee maker.

"How did you sleep?" Wade asked.

I glanced at him over my shoulder. Did he know I'd stayed up half the night?

"I slept like a baby," I replied with a fake smile.

Trevor pointed toward the stove with his fork. "Mom made some potatoes and eggs. Grab 'em while they're still hot."

After making up a plate, I sat back down, the weight of Wade's stare still heavy. "You sounded amazing last night," I said as I sipped my coffee.

"Thanks. I didn't realize how much I missed singing."

"You could be making millions, especially if you had let me be your manager like I said." Trevor huffed.

Wade chuckled. "Manage a country singer and a ranch. How would you make that happen?"

Trevor shrugged. "I'd manage. Can you imagine the endless puss—"He stopped talking and looked at me. "Sorry, sis."

Instead of responding to Trevor, I turned my attention on Wade. "You had a bit of a little fan club last night."

Wade nodded, but his eyes grew intense. Like he was trying to read me.

"Speaking of fans, who was the little blonde you left with?" Trevor asked, causing my fork to freeze mid-air.

"I didn't leave with her."

"You walked out of Cord's Place with her," I added. Trevor looked over at me with a surprised look on his face.

I wanted to crawl under the table. The way it came off made me sound like a jealous girlfriend. I didn't want to draw Trevor's attention to even the slightest feelings I might have for Wade.

Which I didn't. At least, I didn't think I did.

Wade leaned back in his chair and tossed his napkin on the table. "Lacy was her name."

I found myself holding my breath. At least he remembered her name.

"I met her a few days ago. She works at Ace Hardware."

I couldn't help myself. I lifted my brow and said, "Seems like you'll fit in good with my brothers."

Wade's forehead pinched. "What do you mean?"

I'd lost my appetite. "Nothing," I mumbled as I cleared my plate in the trash and rinsed it.

Trevor laughed. "She's calling you a manwhore, dude."

"If the shoe fits," I said with a wink. I was trying not to let it bother me that Wade had had a one-night stand—then carried me up to my bed like a gentleman. Ugh. To think I stayed up practically all night trying to talk myself out of having feelings for him.

"Well, maybe you should have let me finish my story. Lacy's husband texted her and said their truck battery was dead. I happened to be standing there and offered to help. We used my truck to jumpstart theirs. After we got it running, I took off and came back here."

The defensive tone in his voice had me wishing I could take back the last few minutes and start over.

I swallowed hard. "That was nice of you."

Trevor stood and grabbed his plate and Wade's. "That's Wade for ya. Always helping people out."

I smiled and my eyes caught Wade's. "I'm sorry. I didn't mean to offend you."

He stood, grabbed his cowboy hat and nodded. "No worries. Trevor, I'm going to take that soil sample on in and have it tested."

Trevor gave Wade a nod. "Sure. Hey, when you come back, you mind helping me vaccinate those goats?"

"Nah, I don't mind. I'll be back in a few hours."

"Where are you going?" I asked.

"San Antonio." Wade didn't even bother to look over as he answered and that bothered the hell out of me.

I had no idea what came over me, but I asked, "Mind if I tag along?"

Trevor turned and stared.

Wade didn't bother to even look my way. "If you want. I'm only dropping off a soil sample."

"If you don't want the company, I totally understand. I just figured if you're heading that way, I might be able to stop at a print shop that has an order of swag for me."

"Swag?" Wade asked.

Trevor laughed. "Yeah, like pens with her book covers on it. Shit like that."

"It's not shit, Trevor."

"I don't mind you tagging along," Wade said. "I have to make another stop if you're not in a huge rush to get back."

With a smile, I shook my head. "Nope, not in a hurry at all."

Wade looked at Trevor. Almost like he was asking him for his okay. When Trevor nodded, my mouth fell slightly open.

What in the hell?

"You ready to go now?" Wade asked, causing me to pull my death stare off Trevor.

"Ummm…" I glanced at my clothes before looking at Trevor. "Can I have five minutes?"

"Plan on that being twenty," Trevor said while slapping Wade on the back.

I shot Trevor the finger.

Wade laughed. "I'll meet you out at my truck in ten."

I dashed out of the kitchen and ran up to my room, the anxiety kicking in.

What do I wear?

I threw open my closet door and stared.

My teeth! I need to brush my teeth.

I rushed into my bathroom. Toothbrush in hand, I made my way back to my closet and stood there, brushing and staring.

I reached for a dress, then shook my head and tossed it onto my bed. Next came a shirt.

"Nope," I mumbled and threw it. Another vetoed dress followed, landing in the growing pile of clothes.

"Do you need help picking something out?"

I screamed and toothpaste went everywhere, including on Waylynn's face.

"Gross!" she cried out and wiped it off with her shirt. "What in the hell, Meli?"

Dashing back to my bathroom, I rinsed out my mouth and threw my hair into a ponytail.

"I have zero clothes."

Waylynn pulled out a romper I bought in New York. "You have a ton of clothes. This will be perfect."

Narrowing my eyes, I replied, "You don't even know where I'm going."

"I can put two and two together. This has to do with Wade going into San Antonio and you going along."

My mouth dropped. "How did you know?"

She laughed. "I just saw him. He told me."

I reached for the jumper and held it up to myself. It was cute, I couldn't deny it.

"You like him, don't you?"

My eyes found Waylynn's in the mirror. "Don't be crazy."

With a look that said she didn't believe me, she shrugged. "Well, if you did like him and wanted to keep it on the down low for a bit, but still be flirty, go with the romper. If you're only interested in friendship, I'd wear the jeans and maybe that blue shirt. The one that hangs off your shoulder a little bit."

I lifted my chin and nodded. "Thanks for your help."

Waylynn folded her arms across her chest and waited for me to make my pick. It was clear she wasn't leaving until I made my choice.

"Ugh! Fine! I'll wear the romper!"

She jumped and clapped her hands. "I knew it! I knew you were crushing on him. He's hot as hell and could sing the panties off any woman."

Rolling my eyes, I grabbed the romper. "I have to hurry. He's waiting on me."

"Put a little bit of mascara on…but that's it!" she called out to me.

I slipped the romper on and reached for my makeup bag. After putting on mascara, I added a bit of blush and a light shade of pink to my lips. I'd fix my hair in his truck. For now, the sloppy pony would have to work.

As I made my way out of the bathroom, Waylynn held up a pair of Jimmy Choo flats. "Here, wear these. The bow on the flats will look adorable with the romper."

"You'd let me wear your expensive shoes?" I asked as I slipped them on and tied them both.

"Why not? Someone has to wear them."

I glanced at my watch and saw I had gone past the ten-minute mark. "Shit! I've got to go."

I reached for my work bag and tossed it over my shoulder.

"Amelia Parker, you better not have your laptop in that bag!" Waylynn shouted as I ran down the steps.

"Thanks, Waylynn!" I rushed out the door, not expecting Wade to be standing on the front porch. I slammed right into him. Knocking us both down.

"Ohmygawd!" I cried out as I landed right on top of him. Immediately, naughty things ran through my mind and I jumped up. "I'm so sorry!"

"My goodness, Amelia, why in the world did you come rushing out like that?" my Aunt Vi asked. A look of pure wickedness gleamed in her eyes. Oh, she knew damn well why I came rushing out.

"Wade was waiting on me," I panted.

Why am I out of breath?

"I couldn't find anything to wear."

Vi raised a brow. "Really? Is this a date?"

"What?" I asked with an awkward laugh. Wade was brushing off his jeans, and I couldn't help but notice his ass. Well, hell, it was right there. How could I *not* notice it? When I pulled my eyes away, I caught Vi grinning from ear to ear.

"Nice view?" she asked.

"What? I wasn't staring at his ass!"

I covered my mouth with my hand. Wade turned and looked at me. "What?"

Vi lifted one brow in that oh-so-perfect way that said she was calling bullshit. "She said she wasn't staring at your ass when I clearly caught her staring at your ass."

With pleading eyes, I looked at my aunt. Then I laughed. Again. Awkwardly.

Turning to Wade, I said, "I wasn't, Wade. I'm not interested in your ass. Well, I mean, not that you have a bad ass because you don't. You have a great ass."

His smile grew, and I closed my eyes.

Oh. My. Gosh. Jesus, take the wheel.

"Um, you ready to go?" Wade asked, and his gray eyes seemed to sparkle. It was clear he had been attempting not to laugh.

Holding my head up, I nodded. "If you are."

Aunt Vi chuckled as we made our way down the porch steps. Turning back, I shot her the finger. She might have been my aunt, but she was the first person to teach me how to flip someone the bird.

"That's my girl!" she called out.

Wade walked to the passenger side of his truck and opened the door. Holding his hand out for mine, he winked and said, "She's a different character, isn't she?"

With a sigh, I replied, "You have no idea. The things she taught me with my Ken and Barbie...I'm convinced she is the reason I write romance."

His laugh rumbled through my body, making my chest squeeze. When he grabbed my seat belt and pulled it out for me, I had to force myself not to lean in and smell him.

I took the belt. "Why, thank you, cowboy."

He smiled, those dimples on full display.

Lord. Help me right now.

The urge to wrap my arms around his neck was insane.

Wade lingered a little longer than he probably should have before he stepped back and shut the door to his truck. I watched him walk around the front, and I swore it looked like he was talking to himself.

Taking in a deep, calming breath, I pulled my laptop out from my bag and opened it. Wade climbed into his truck and started it up.

"You don't mind if I work, do you? I'm writing a book and I can't seem to shut the voices off in my head."

"I don't mind at all."

"How about music? Would you mind if we listened to my playlist?"

Wade smiled and reached over to his stereo. "Let's Bluetooth so I can hear what inspires you."

"Okay!" I said with probably a little bit more excitement than the situation warranted.

Once my phone was synced to Wade's truck, he started down the driveway. I closed my eyes and let myself enter the world of Mike and Amy.

"Damn it!" Wade said. He pulled over and grabbed his phone.

"What's wrong?" I asked.

"I need to check on something."

Peeking over to his phone, I watched him pull up what he was looking for.

Oh. My. Gawd.

I slowly lifted my eyes and stared at him. He smiled, and my heart melted. Like in a puddle. Right there on the floor of the truck.

"You watch April?" I asked, my voice slightly shaky.

Wade peeked over at me. "I know, it's stupid, but I'm invested. I feel like if I don't stick with it until the end, I've somehow failed April."

Swallowing hard, I placed my hand over my stomach to calm the butterflies. "You've been watching from the beginning?"

He looked my way. "Well, kind of."

The way his cheeks were flushed was the cutest damn thing I've ever seen.

"I've been watching her, too!"

His eyes lit up. "No shit?"

"Yes! I'm actually obsessed. I usually have it pulled up on my phone, truth be told."

"Me, too! Just don't say anything to your brothers or I'll have my man card revoked."

We started laughing.

"Well, she's not in labor yet. I thought for sure she'd have the baby on April first," Wade said. He placed his phone down and started driving again.

With a tilt of my head, I asked, "So, you pulled over just now to check on her?"

He gave a half shrug. "Yeah. Figured I had better check before taking off."

I nodded. "I'll pull it up in another window on my laptop. I have a hotspot on my phone."

"A girl after my own heart."

His words shouldn't have made my chest feel so tight, but they did. Boy, did they ever. In the few weeks I'd known Wade, he had affected me in more ways than I could count.

CHAPTER 19

Wade

I could barely hear Amelia's tapping fingers on her keyboard over the sound of her playlist. The girl had good taste, although I couldn't figure out for the life of me how she typed in a moving vehicle.

I pulled into the parking lot and put my truck in park. "I'm gonna run this sample in. It'll be less than ten minutes."

Amelia shot me a smirk and then giggled. "Make sure no one checks out that ass of yours."

I turned back and winked. "I'll be quick."

I walked into Ralph Minor, Inc. and glanced around. Ralph's son, Tyler, went to Texas A&M with me and Trevor. A younger lady glanced up from her computer and flashed me a welcoming smile.

"Hello, may I help you?"

"Morning, ma'am. Tyler in?" I asked with a tip of my hat.

Her teeth sank into her lip, and she didn't try to hide the fact that she was eyeing me from top to bottom.

"He is. May I tell him your name?"

"Wade Adams."

She picked up her phone and hit a few numbers. "Mr. Minor, there is a Mr. Wade Adams here to see you. Yes, sir."

She hung up the phone and stood. "If you'll follow me, Mr. Adams. I'll show you to his office."

I did as she asked. I couldn't help but notice how she threw her hips out while she walked. She stopped and stepped to the side, inviting me to enter Tyler's office.

Tyler stood and rounded his desk while he reached his hand out to shake. "Damn. It's good seeing you, Adams."

"Good seeing you, too."

"You want coffee, water?" Tyler asked while motioning to the receptionist. "Laney can get it for you."

I held up my hands. "No, I can't stay, Amelia's waiting in the truck for me."

Tyler drew his head back in question. "Amelia...as in Trevor's *little sister*, Amelia?"

"Yeah. She needed to pick something up in town so she drove along with me."

"Uh-huh. Did Trevor buy that excuse?"

Hitting him on the shoulder, I rolled my eyes. "Knock it off. It's not like that."

"Is she hot?"

"I'm not answering you, Tyler. Now, do you want this sample or not?"

He reached for it and sighed. "I can't believe you won't even throw me a bone."

I sighed, knowing that if I didn't give him something, he would keep at it. "She's a very attractive young woman."

Tyler packaged the sample and handed it to Laney, who was still waiting. "Here you go, Laney. Will you get that going for me?"

She nodded then excused herself, but not before giving me another once-over.

Tyler went on. "In other words, you think she's fucking hot, but won't admit it because she's Parker's baby sister."

Laughing, I replied, "Something like that."

"I always figured she was hot. Hell, look at Parker. Never in my life saw a guy get as much pussy as him."

I pushed my hands into my pockets. "Trevor wanted me to invite you out, two weeks from this Friday. He's having a party."

Tyler's brows lifted. "Oh, yeah? What kind of a party?"

"Welcome home party for his sister, Waylynn. She moved back to Texas from New York a few weeks back."

"Count me in. Have him text me the details. Would he mind if I brought a date?"

"A date?" I asked with a surprised look on my face. "You still with Lee?"

He grinned. "Planning on asking her to marry me soon. Just haven't found the right ring."

I nodded. "Good for you. Y'all were always good together. Okay, well, I best get going. Amelia is sitting in the truck."

Tyler motioned for me to head out of his office. I knew he was planning to walk me out just so he could get a look at Amelia.

"What about you, Adams? You dating anyone?"

"Nah, I'm not looking right now. Not after what happened with Caroline."

He slapped my back and pushed the door open. "I get it, man. I do."

Letting out a whistle, Tyler looked at me then back to Amelia. She glanced up and smiled.

Damn. She is *beautiful.*

Her light red hair was pulled up into a sloppy bun on top of her head. A pencil was pushed behind her ear, giving her a look of innocence.

"Holy shit. She *is* fucking hot."

As we got closer to the truck, Amelia rolled the window down.

"Amelia, this is Tyler Minor. Trevor and I went to school with him at A&M."

She stuck her hand out the window and flashed him an adorable smile. "Pleasure to meet you, Tyler."

"Pleasure's all mine. Heard a lot about you."

Amelia rolled her eyes. "Lord knows what Trevor has said."

"I believe he said you were joining a convent."

Laughing at the memory, I shook my head. Trevor had told us everything to keep us uninterested in his sister—even said she was a lesbian.

"Trust me, a convent has never crossed my mind," Amelia said.

Her eyes swung over to me before she brought her attention back to Tyler. I hoped he didn't read anything into that. Even though I definitely had.

"A woman as beautiful as you? I'm sure your brother would say anything to turn away his horny, college friends."

She laughed, and I was startled by how it made my body warm. I cleared my throat and said, "Well, we better get going. Still have a few stops to make."

Tyler shook my hand. "I'll get those results back to you right away."

"Appreciate that, Ty. I'll see you in a few weeks, then?"

He gave my shoulder a good squeeze. "Hell, yeah. I'm in."

After shaking hands once more, I walked around the truck and got in.

"So, is that the Tyler who ran around A&M naked?"

I started the truck and faced her. "Um, no. That was me."

Her mouth fell open. "What? I thought Trevor said it was his friend Tyler."

"Oh, Tyler did it too…after I bet him he wouldn't. He just happened to be the one who got caught."

The corners of her mouth rose. "You surprise me, Wade Adams."

"I do?" I asked in an innocent voice.

"Just when I think I've got you figured out, you tell me something unexpected."

I shrugged. "Stick around, and I'm sure I'll do something else to surprise you."

Her eyes turned dark as she pulled her lower lip between her teeth. "I hope so."

We both turned away at the same time. *Fuck. Does she have any idea how damn sexy that is? Of course she does. She writes romance.*

The air in the truck seemed to crack with a strange tension.

Ten minutes later I pulled up to a gated house.

"Where are we?" Amelia asked.

"A children's home that my grandparents founded. They adopted my mother when she was fourteen. It killed them to see the older kids being tossed around from house to house. They set up the Wrangler Home for kids who had been in the system for years with no luck at being adopted."

Amelia stared back at the house. "A home for kids. How sad."

"Yeah. There aren't very many kids here like when my mother was young," I said as I typed in the gate code. "My aunt and uncle live here and are pretty much these kids' parents. I've lost count of how many kids they've raised and sent on to bigger and better lives. Each of them went to college, paid for by my grandparents' foundation. A few of them are now married with kids of their own, and they give back to the foundation if they can."

Amelia sat in silence as she took in the grounds. "Your grandparents must have been wealthy to be able to operate something like a childrens' home."

"Oil," I responded.

"This place is amazing."

To my right, my aunt was giving two girls riding lessons.

"It is pretty amazing. These kids are lucky, at least they have a stable home and people who love and care for them. Mick and Wanda are their family."

"Is that your aunt and uncle?"

I nodded as I pulled up to the front of the circular drive. Mick walked out, wearing a giant cowboy hat, his smile as wide as a Texas sky.

Jumping out, I walked toward him. "Mick, it's good seeing you."

He pulled me into his arms and held me longer than normal. It was the first time I'd seen him since the funeral.

"How in the hell are you, boy? Damn it, I'm glad you're back in Texas, son."

"Me, too, Mick. Me, too."

Mick's eyes wandered over my shoulder, and he smiled big.

"Don't be gettin' any ideas. She's a friend and that's it," I said in a hushed voice.

"She's one hell of a pretty *friend.*"

I couldn't help but chuckle. He was right about that.

Before I knew it, Amelia was wrapped in my uncle's arms, and he was leading her up the stairs.

"Wait until the boys see you. They're gonna think they've died and gone to heaven," Mick said with a loud, deep laugh.

Anxiety prickled as I followed him, and I was hit by a wave of nerves. Maybe I shouldn't have let Amelia come along. This was personal. Something I didn't share with many people. S*o, why did I think I could share it with her?*

I got my answer the moment I stepped into the house. Four of the kids surrounded her and little Annie, who was ten, tugged Amelia toward the playroom. With a huge smile, Amelia took it all in.

"What are we going to do?" she asked with anticipation in her voice.

"Dress up!" Annie said as the older kids groaned.

As they walked into the other room, my cheeks ached from my smile. Mick stood next to me and bumped my shoulder. "Boy, that look on your face isn't screaming that's my *friend*. It's screaming she's the *one*."

I was so fucked.

CHAPTER 20

Amelia

Two hours had passed since we arrived at Mick and Annie's place. I'd met all twelve kids, each with their own shining personalities. Little Annie was the youngest and seemed to crave all of my attention. I gave it to her the first forty minutes and then suggested we head outside for a game of volleyball. The older kids loved the idea, and even Annie was in on it.

Wade played on the opposite team, and I couldn't believe how much fun I was having. After the game was over, we headed back in, and I got to know Mick and Wanda a little better. They were amazing people. Mick was Wade's mother's brother. They had been super close growing up. He had been adopted, as well, a few years after Wade's mom.

"It seems like this is very rewarding, yet hard work," I said to Wanda as I helped her load the dishwasher with the bowls we had used for ice cream.

"It's a lot of work, but we love them all. Annie is our biological daughter. James, the oldest, is, as well. He's heading off to Texas Tech next fall. Makes me so sad."

I leaned against the counter and looked into the living room. James was sitting next to Wade and a boy named Thomas, playing a video game.

"My parents had seven kids, so I love the chaos."

Wanda chuckled. "Chaos, indeed. We wouldn't change a thing."

I couldn't pull my eyes off of Wade. He had amazingly spent equal amounts of time with each kiddo. I would have never known seven of the kids were not his own blood. He treated them all like kin.

"Wade sure is good with the kids," I said, my internal thoughts slipping out.

"He is. Always has been. Lord, that boy was good with his little sisters, too. There wasn't anything he wouldn't do for them. Broke his leg once climbing up a tree to save Grace's cat who was stuck. A branch he was standing on snapped, sending him to the ground. Do you know he got up and climbed back up and got the cat?"

Grinning, I replied, "That sounds like something he would do. He's such a gentleman."

"Indeed, he is. How do you know Wade?"

Her question pulled me from my trance. "He's my brother's friend from college. When Trevor found out what had happened to Wade's family, he offered him a job on my father's ranch."

She lifted a brow. "What does he ranch?"

"Cattle, mostly. Goats, grain for feed. They want to go organic, and Trevor said Wade was the guy to do it."

Wanda grinned. "Well, it's good seeing him smile. The last time we saw him he was a bit of a mess. I think coming to Texas was the right thing for him to do."

I nodded, not really sure how to respond.

"Go on in there. If you don't pull him from the game now, y'all might be spending the night."

With a chuckle, I made my way into the living room. Wade glanced up and smiled. My stomach dropped and I prayed like hell my cheeks hadn't turned red. The naughty things that had been running through my mind about Wade were starting to get out of control.

Zeroing in on his lips, I let my wayward thoughts run wild again.

What would those soft, plump lips feel like on my skin?

Was Wade into rough and fast sex? Or slow and romantic? The latter I'd never experienced before. I only wrote about it.

The idea of his hand slipping into my panties and making me come was almost too much to take.

Jesus. What is wrong with me?

I sat down on the sofa, keeping a good distance between us.

"Can you play, Amelia?" James asked.

Laughing, I said, "The only thing I can play is Frogger. I'd kick your butt, though."

Wade looked at me. "Want to make a bet?"

My smile grew. Boy, oh boy, could I think of some things for us to bet on.

"What should we bet?" I asked.

Wade pointed to James. "You pick."

Damn it. My bubble popped.

"How about loser has to cook dinner for the winner."

Okay, that was safe. Although not what I had in mind. By the look on Wade's face, I was going to guess he had some different ideas, as well.

"Sounds perfect!" I said.

After changing out the games, I was handed a controller and Wade and I started to play.

Ten games later, I was up nine to one. "I'm pretty sure I've won," I said while attempting to hide my victory smirk.

Wade rolled his eyes. "Whatever. I let you win."

"You did not!" I gasped while pushing his shoulder.

He looked at me in that moment and we burst out laughing. He'd been schooled in Frogger…by a girl. And he knew it.

Wade dropped the controller on the coffee table. "We need to run, y'all. Let's plan something soon."

The next thing I knew, Wade was grabbing my hand and leading me out of the house. I'd never in my life felt my heart pounding like it was in that moment. The feel of my hand in his was the most amazing thing ever.

What. In. The. Hell.

He was guiding me out of the house, not kissing me! Yet, by the way my heart raced, you'd think we were making out in the truck. When he dropped my fingers, I instantly missed the connection. I shook my hand to get the tingles out of it.

Oh, dear Lord.

I'm falling for Wade.

This is not good. Not good at all.

Or is it?

Wade walked out of the print shop carrying two boxes filled with pens, magnets, and notepads. He only teased me once about the cover of my last book while I was looking over the swag. The model on it had his shirt hanging open, abs on full display. It was a steamy cover, if I did say so myself.

"So, what got you into writing romance?" Wade asked.

With a shrug, I responded. "Jane Austen. I fell hard for Mr. Darcy, and the rest is history."

He gave me a blank expression.

"Please, tell me you've read *Pride and Prejudice* by Jane Austen."

Nothing. His gray eyes seemed to be lost. "Nope."

I clutched my chest while he put the boxes in the back seat of his truck. "Wade, tell me you're kidding. You had to have read it in high school."

"I remember *The Scarlet Letter,* but no *Prejudice and Pride.*"

My knees wobbled. He couldn't even get the title right.

"There has been an injustice in your life. This is something we have to fix. Right away. Immediately." My fingers went to my temples. "I'm not sure we can be friends right now."

Wade laughed. "Why don't you read it to me on the way back?"

I nearly pulled a muscle in my neck as I looked back at him. "You want me to read *Pride and Prejudice* to you?"

He shrugged. "Why not? Unless you don't have the book on your phone or you need to work."

The way my head was spinning was not good. Wade Adams was inching his way into my heart. The heart that I had on lockdown. No man was ever going to break it again.

Before I could stop myself, I was agreeing. "I'm actually ahead on my word count goal. What makes you think I have it on my phone?"

He flashed the smile that made me want to rip my panties off and tell him to take me right in the cab of his truck. "My mother loved to read. She had a Kindle app on every device she owned. Phone, laptop, iPad. She could access any book at any given moment. When one device's battery died, she just powered up the second or third. I figured you were the same. I mean, you have to have a love of reading to be a writer, right?"

I want this man. Like...right...this...second.

"You're killing me."

He frowned. "Huh?"

Shit. I hadn't meant to say that out loud. With a wave of my hand, I brushed off my outburst. "Nothing. You're right. I have it on my phone. I'll read it off my Kindle, though, since it's also on there."

Reaching into my bag, I pulled out my Kindle Fire, causing Wade to chuckle.

"Hey, laugh now, but I promise you, you will be in love with Mr. Darcy," I shook my head and giggled. "I mean, you'll be in love with Elizabeth Bennet within the first few chapters."

"Bring it on."

I pulled up the book and cleared my throat. My heart was racing, and I couldn't help the heat on my cheeks. I had no idea why I was so nervous. Maybe because I was sharing something with Wade—something I loved.

Before I started, I glanced over. With a smile, I focused on my Kindle and started to read aloud. We were soon lost in the world of Mr. Darcy, Charles Bingley, Elizabeth, Jane, and Mrs. Bennet.

Before I knew it, Wade was parked in the driveway and I was still reading.

Hitting the top of my Kindle, I bookmarked the page and turned it off, stowing it in my bag.

"What are you doing?" Wade asked.

I tried to hold back my smile. "We're home."

"So? What happens next?"

I stared at him. "Are you for real? I mean, you check on April. You adore kids, you like classical literature. You're like a dream man."

He smiled. "Your dream man?"

My heart plummeted. I had the urge to say *yes*. Instead, I winked. "You wish."

Before he could say anything else, I grabbed my bag and got out of the truck, my pulse racing. I had never walked so quickly up the steps of my parents' house in my entire life.

"Hey!" Wade called out. "What do you want to do with your swag?"

I stopped and spun around. "I'll put it in my office."

"You have an office?" Wade asked.

I stood there like an idiot. No, I didn't have an office. I shared one with my mother. I had taken up half of it storing boxes of books and swag items.

I started to have an anxiety attack. *What if things do go to the next level with Wade? Or any guy? I have no house! I still live at home, for fuck's sake!*

The feel of Wade's hands on my arms caused me to jump.

"You okay, Amelia?"

Wade's eyes were filled with concern. Tears filled mine, and I had no idea why. "I still live at home. I'm almost twenty-three years old, and I still live at home and share an office with my mother. How sad is that?"

He leaned down, eyes level with mine. "I don't think it's sad. You're lucky to be able to get along with them well enough to live with them. Besides. Your parents' house is damn huge. I don't think I've even seen them in passing one time."

With a half-hearted smile, I shook my head. "I need to grow up and move out. It's not like I can't afford to live on my own."

With pinched brows, Wade asked, "Amelia, what in the world brought this on?"

I shrugged. "I don't know. I'm feeling emotional. I'm sorry. If you could please put the boxes in my mother's office, I'd really appreciate it."

Stepping back and out of his grasp, I turned on my heels and headed straight to my room. By the time I hit the top step, tears were streaming down my face, and I had no fucking clue why.

CHAPTER 21

Wade

Mitchell handed me a beer and sat down next to me. He was staring out at the dance floor with a scowl on his face.

"You look like you want to beat someone's ass," I said.

He let out a gruff laugh. "I do. My brother Tripp."

I followed Mitchell's gaze to the dance floor, where Tripp was spinning Corina around.

"You like her?" I asked.

He pressed his beer to his lips and took a long drink while shrugging. "I don't think he's that into her. He's only dating her because he knows I was attracted to her."

"Why did you let him ask her out?"

"He said he liked her first. Brother code, and all that shit."

Two women walked by, batting their eyelashes and laughing.

Mitchell and I tipped our heads to them and said hi. I was glad when they kept walking, and I got the feeling Mitchell was, as well.

"They're not exclusive though, are they? I saw Tripp all over another girl the other night."

Mitchell turned to me. "No shit?"

I nodded.

Leaning in close, Mitchell demanded, "Define *all over*."

"Kissing, hands on her ass, grinding into her while dancing. That type of shit."

Now Mitchell looked pissed. "I can't imagine Tripp would ever cheat."

Focusing back out on the dance floor, I said, "Why don't you ask him?"

"That's a great idea," he said. "Go cut in and start fishing Corina for answers."

My head snapped over to him. "What? I said for *you* to go ask. Not me!"

Mitchell was still watching them dance. "If Tripp thinks I'm the least bit interested, he'll play games with me."

"Really?" I asked with surprise. "He's your brother. Why would he screw around with you like that?"

Mitchell grinned. "That's what I would do."

I shook my head. "Seriously? Why would you mess around with Corina's emotions?"

"Corina's, I wouldn't. If it was a random hook-up, I would."

"And you think Tripp would do that to Corina?"

Mitchell looked back at them. "No, they've been dating for a few months now."

Right about then, Tripp and Corina stepped apart. She headed to the bathroom while Tripp made his way to us. The girl from last night stepped in front of him. He smiled and shook his head. I couldn't help but notice how Mitchell sat forward and took it all in.

Tripp leaned down to her ear and said something, then laughed. They parted ways and he walked straight to us.

"What's up, boys?"

Now *I* was pissed. I didn't like picturing any of the Parker brothers as cheaters.

I wasn't giving Mitchell the chance to think about this any longer. It was time to nip the shit in the bud. "Dude, I saw you with that girl last night. You're not stepping out on Corina, are you?"

Tripp stared at me like I was insane. "What? No. Corina and I broke up a couple months ago."

"What?" Mitchell and I said at the same time.

"Why are y'all still going out?"

Tripp looked at Mitchell. "I ran into her. She's here with Paxton. Girls' night."

Mitchell dropped back in his seat.

Taking a seat next to Mitchell, Tripp slapped his back. "I know you like her. I liked her, too, but we never connected. I'll admit I was being a dick by hanging on longer than I should. Corina told me a few months back she didn't have strong feelings for me, which is probably why we never slept together."

Now Mitchell was sitting straight up. "What? Y'all never slept together?"

Tripp took a drink of beer. "Nah. I'm going to take a guess that she was probably still hung up from that one-night stand y'all had."

My eyes widened. "You slept with Corina?" I asked, staring at Mitchell.

Mitchell closed his eyes. "Dude, I was going to tell you, but Steed told me to let it go."

Laughing, Tripp shook his head at his brother. "That's why a part of me wouldn't let her go. I was pissed. It's water under the bridge. If you like her, Mitch, go for it."

"Go for what?" Cord asked as he placed three beers on the table in front of us. "Girls at the end of the bar bought them for y'all."

I leaned around Tripp and tipped my hat. They all waved and giggled.

With a sigh, I sat back. "Don't y'all ever get tired of this game?"

"Endless pussy? Fuck no," Cord said before heading back to the bar. I glanced over my shoulder to see Trevor behind the bar. He was busy, but not too busy to stop and flirt with a girl standing there.

"Trevor and Cord, I get." Looking back at Tripp and Mitchell, I narrowed my eyes. "But you two, I don't. You're not interested in settling down? Having a family?"

I could see it in both of their eyes. They were tired of the rotating door of women.

Tripp shrugged. "I guess if the right girl comes along. Mine came and went a long time ago. Haven't been able to find anyone like her since."

My curiosity got the best of me. "Who was it?"

He grabbed the beer and took a long drink. "The one who got away." He stood and let out a sigh. "I'm calling it a night, y'all." He reached his hand out for mine. "Make him ask her to dance, will ya?"

With a grin, I nodded. "I will. Goodnight."

"Later, Tripp," Mitchell said.

Mitchell and I watched as Tripp made his way to the bar to say goodbye to Cord and Trevor. I swore he looked like someone had just delivered him bad news.

"Her name was Harley," Mitchell said. "High school sweetheart. Tripp was planning on asking her to marry him before they left for college."

"What happened?" I asked.

Mitchell slowly shook his head. "She didn't want the same things Tripp wanted. He wanted to come back to Oak Springs. Start a law practice."

"Let me guess? She was tired of the small-town living?"

"Pretty much. She loved horses. Went to vet school and never came back. Walked away from Tripp like it was no big deal. He never got over it."

I looked down at the table. "Damn. That sucks."

Mitchell hit me on the back. "Sucks is right. Now, if you'll excuse me, Mr. Adams. I see a beautiful blonde who needs dancing with."

I watched Mitchell make his way toward Corina. She wore a huge smile as Mitchell led her out to the dance floor.

"About damn time," Trevor said, sitting down next to me. "Boy's been pining for months."

I sipped my beer and turned to Trevor. "What about you, Parker? No girl caught your eye yet?"

He tossed his head back and laughed. "Hell, no. I'm only twenty-four. Why would I want to settle down when I'm having so much fun?"

When his eyes met mine, his smile faded some. "What about you, Wade? Don't you think it's time you moved on?"

My chest squeezed, and for a moment it was hard to breathe.

"I'm not in a rush. If it happens, it happens."

He stared like he could see into my lying eyes.

I do have feelings for someone. Your sister.

"You're a good guy, Wade. Don't let fear stand in your way."

I let out a chuckle and shook my head. "Yeah. Maybe I just need to get laid."

He waved his hands in front of him. "Take your pick. I'm pretty sure you could find a girl in here who would love to spend a few minutes alone with you. If that's what you want."

I knew he was right. Hell, I could probably take one in the bathroom and have a quick fuck. That wasn't what I wanted, though.

"Not interested."

He nodded. "Didn't think so."

We sat there for a few minutes as we watched the crowd.

I finally broke the silence. "I'm not going to lie to you, Trevor. You're too good of a friend. There is a girl I'm...I guess, attracted to. Have feelings for. Hell, I don't know what the fuck it is. I like her."

As we faced each other, I felt my heart pound hard. The last thing I wanted to do was ruin my friendship with Trevor.

"Amelia?" he asked with a half grin.

My heart dropped. "How did you know?"

He huffed. "Dude, you don't think I notice the way you hold your breath when she walks into the room? Or the way you stare at her with those fucking puppy dog eyes? Same goes for her. When she doesn't think anyone is paying attention, she can't keep her eyes off of you."

I broke our eye contact. "I wasn't looking for anything, Trevor. And you know I would never do anything to hurt you or your family."

Reaching over, he squeezed my shoulder. "Wade, I trust you. You don't think it crossed my mind if you came to work for us that you and Amelia might have an attraction? I'm not fucking stupid."

I grinned. "She is beautiful."

"Fuck yeah, she is. She's also been hurt. I think she guards her heart pretty tightly. The only thing I'm going to ask is that you don't push her. If it happens…like you said earlier….it happens. Just don't rush her, dude."

My pulse raced as I stared at my best friend. How in the hell did I ever luck out with him?

"You do know you saved my life, Trevor, right? I would never do anything to ruin our friendship, and I sure as hell would never do anything to hurt Amelia."

He nodded. "That's all I needed to hear."

I swallowed hard. "I have your permission to ask her out?"

"Oh hell, dude. Let me school you on the Parker women. They don't need their brothers' permission to do shit, even though we like to pretend they do. They're stubborn. Fireballs that love to have as much fun as their brothers do. Outlaws who have both been known to cause trouble. I love my sisters, but I pray for the man who can wrangle in their hearts."

He laughed and shook his head like he was thinking. "Just ask my daddy. He fought like hell for my mama." His eyes lifted and met mine. "You ready for a fight, Wade?"

The corners of my mouth rose into a full-blown smile. "I've always been one for a challenge."

"Good," he said with a chuckle. "Challenge is what you're gonna have with Amelia Parker."

CHAPTER 22

Amelia

I stood at the kitchen sink and stared out the back window. Wade and Trevor were pressure washing the pool deck for the party the boys were throwing to welcome Waylynn home.

Waylynn walked up next to me. "You do realize you've been holding that same plate for five minutes."

I jumped. Glancing at the dish, I replied, "No, I haven't."

My sister laughed. "You like him. Why can't you just admit it?"

After a quick glance over my shoulder to our mother and Aunt Vi, I glared at Waylynn. "Hush your mouth. If Mama even thinks I'm interested, she'll be trying to push us together. I want to see how things go naturally."

Her brows lifted. "You *really* do like him?"

My cheeks heated. "I don't know. Maybe."

Grabbing the plate, Waylynn dropped it back into the soapy water and spoke loudly. "I just remembered I need your help with something, Meli. Now. It's a letter. I need your writing expertise."

She dragged me out of the kitchen while Aunt Vi called out, "We need to go shopping, girls!"

"Okay, Aunt Vi!" Waylynn called back. She pulled me into Steed's office and shut the door.

"Spill it."

I stared at her. "Spill what?"

Waylynn lifted her finger and waved it back and forth. "Oh, no, don't play innocent with me. You said you like him. Spill it."

I let out a nervous laugh. "There's nothing to spill. I'm attracted to him. Have you *not* seen him?"

Her brows lifted. "Oh, honey, I've seen him. I've seen the way he looks at you and you look at him. Ever since that day you spent with him, and you've been walking around in a damn bubble."

"I have not been in a bubble!" I said, my hands landing on my hips.

Waylynn looked at me with a *really* look on her face.

"Fine! He wanted me to read *Pride and Prejudice* to him! What guy wants that? And have you seen how he is with Chloe? Or how he helped Steed make the crib for Paxton as a surprise? What about his *voice*?"

My hands clutched at my chest as I sat in the loveseat in Steed's office. "Oh. My. Gawd. His voice when he sings."

I groaned and dropped my head back against the cushion.

"Why are you groaning?" Waylynn asked.

My eyes squeezed. "I can't let him into my heart for so many reasons."

"Name one."

Lifting my head, I turned to her. "Trevor being the main one. He's Wade's best friend."

Waylynn half shrugged. "So what? When did you ever let that stop you? You've dated plenty of guys who went to school with Trevor."

"This is different. Trevor and Wade are close. *Brother* close. They probably have a bro code, or some shit like that."

She rolled her eyes. "Okay, what other reason do you have for not going after that fine piece of cowboy?"

"He's got a broken heart! I mean he lost his family *and* his girlfriend up and left him. I don't think he's looking for a relationship."

"Have you asked him?"

I laughed half-heartedly. "Why in the hell would I ask him that?"

"Because you want him."

My head jerked back. "I don't want him."

"You don't?"

"No."

"You're not the least bit curious about how big his cock is or what it would feel like inside you?"

"*What* in the hell did I walk in on?" Steed asked, standing at the door, his face white as a ghost.

I jumped up. "Nothing."

Waylynn, of course, wasn't about to let it go. "Amelia likes a guy."

Steed smiled as he headed into the room. "Oh, yeah? Wade?"

I had been walking toward the door to leave when I stopped. "What?"

"Is it Wade?"

My eyes shot to Waylynn. She made a face like she didn't have anything to do with Steed's knowledge.

"Why would you think it's Wade?" I asked.

Steed walked to his desk and before he had a chance to say anything, Chloe came rushing in.

"Daddy! I need a giraffe!"

Stopping what he was doing, Steed stared down at Chloe. "What?"

I turned to Waylynn and said, "That's another thing. He watches April!"

She smirked and rolled her eyes. "A match made in damn heaven."

"Chloe, why in the world do you think you need a giraffe?"

"Wade loves them, Daddy. He's watching one now, waiting for her to have a baby. We watched her eat her breakfast this morning and he told me all about them and how we need to protect them. Cause they are going *to stink* if we don't take care of them!"

"Oh, Jesus. I think my ovaries just exploded," Waylynn whispered as I covered my mouth to hide my chuckle at Chloe's faux pas.

"Extinct, pumpkin. Not stink."

Chloe stared at Steed, and my heart grew bigger for her, if that was even possible.

"Okay, well, can I get one?"

Steed chuckled. "No, pumpkin. You've got your goat you need to watch over."

I almost died when I saw her hands go to her hips.

"Oh, larwd," Waylynn giggled. "Here comes the Parker in her."

"Then I'm going to go talk to granddaddy about a giraffe. He'll get me one."

The look on Steed's face was priceless. "Have at it. Good luck with that."

Spinning on her heels, Chloe marched out of Steed's office.

Waylynn leaned on his desk. "You, my dear brother, are in a shitload of trouble."

He rolled his eyes and groaned. "Tell me about it. Thank God the next one is a boy."

I walked into the living room and came to a stop. My eyes landed on the coffee table. It was loaded with popcorn, licorice, Mike and Ikes, and fresh-cut fruit. Glancing at the TV, I smiled when I saw the screen.

Pride and Prejudice.

"Hey."

I turned to see Wade with a small cooler.

"Hey, back at you. What's going on?"

He set the cooler on the floor, opened it and pulled out a bottle of Bud Light.

"Did you get my invite?"

My stomach fluttered exactly like it had ten minutes ago when a note was slipped under my bedroom door.

Movie night in the family room.
Love, Wade

"What are you up to, cowboy?"

He smiled, and my knees wobbled. "I figured if I can't get you to read me the rest of the book, we need to watch it. I remember you said it had to be the one with Keira Knightley. So, I bought it off of Amazon."

I wanted to look around for cameras. Men like this didn't exist. How could his girlfriend have left him? He was amazing, caring, and so damn thoughtful.

"This is perfect!" I said as I made my way to the oversized leather sofa.

Wade sat down, leaving a buffer between us. "I wasn't sure what type of snacks you liked."

My eyes scanned the table again. A strange emotion rushed through my body, and I fought not to look at him. If I did, I was positive I would throw my arms around him.

"I've never had anyone go to this much trouble to watch a movie with me," I said, struggling to keep my voice even.

Wade took my hand and squeezed it. "This was fun, Amelia. Not trouble. I think one of my favorite things is to see your smile. It makes me happy. So, the more I make you smile, the better it is for me."

My entire body trembled. I wanted to tell him I loved his smile. His laugh. His kind heart. Instead, I looked away.

I wanted to let Wade in, but I was positive my heart wouldn't survive if he broke it.

"Popcorn and M&M's. That's usually what I like."

He dropped my hand and laughed. "Chocolate and salt. I'll remember for next time."

When he reached for the remote, I peeked at him. He didn't seem the least bit phased I hadn't responded to what he said.

I chewed on my lower lip for the first ten minutes of the movie. It was killing me to think I might have hurt his feelings by not responding. Or he only wanted to be friends, and I was reading into everything…

After another ten minutes, I pulled my legs up and tried to relax. Wade asked a question every now and then, and before I knew it, I was leaning against him, my head on his shoulder and my hand resting on his chest. I fought like hell to keep my eyes open.

Slowly drifting to sleep, I smiled slightly. I'd never felt so at peace as I did in that moment.

When Wade's arm wrapped around me, pulling me close, I let sleep take over.

CHAPTER 23

Amelia

"How do I look?" Waylynn asked.

I pulled my gaze from the window. My sister was wearing a blue dress that fell just below her knees.

"You look beautiful in *my* boots."

Waylynn grinned at my favorite pair of Ropers on her feet. "They're so comfy, Meli. *Please.*"

How could anyone say no to those pleading eyes? Sighing like it was a big deal, I waved my hand. "Fine. Just don't scuff them."

With a small jump and clap, Waylynn headed into her bathroom. "Are you gonna get ready?" she called out.

Looking down at the dress I had on, I frowned. "What's wrong with what I'm wearing?"

Her head popped out from around the corner. "It looks like a sack on you."

I snarled. "Gosh, thanks."

"It's my welcome back party, Meli. You know our brothers invited everyone. Do you really want to wear something that doesn't show off your killer body?"

Turning my gaze back to the window, I looked down at my brothers and Wade setting things up for the party. A few months ago, I would have been dressing sexier and sticking a few condoms in my purse just in case. Now I wasn't sure how to read my emotions. Maybe it was this book I was writing. Or the perfect evening I had spent with Wade watching movies.

I closed my eyes and took in a deep breath. I needed to have fun. To let loose and stop worrying about every little thing Wade Adams did or said.

"Did you hear? The foreman's house is finished," Waylynn called out from her bedroom.

My eyes snapped open. "Really? Wade will be happy to have his own space."

Waylynn walked past me to her closet. "Yep. I overheard him telling Trevor he felt like he was wearing out his welcome by staying in the main house."

Guilt washed over me as I thought about the last two days. When I woke up the other night, wrapped up in Wade's arms on the sofa, I freaked. We had both fallen asleep and I had never slept so well in my life. I had rushed away from Wade and avoided him ever since.

I stood and followed her into the closet. "He shouldn't feel that way."

Waylynn looked at me. "I also him heard him telling Trevor he thought it was time to maybe start dating."

A weight landed on my chest, and I gasped for a breath.

Handing over a green dress, Waylynn looked in my eyes. "Looks like he took the hint of you ignoring him the last two days."

My mouth fell open, but nothing came out.

"Wear this. It will make your eyes and hair stand out."

And like that, she walked away, leaving me in her closet with a feeling of dread so overwhelming I felt sick to my stomach.

A few pieces of curly hair fell from my bun. Waylynn was right. The green dress brought out the red in my hair and my blue eyes made for a bright contrast.

As I walked down the stairs, I saw my parents carrying two bags. Chloe walked a few steps behind them.

"Where are y'all going?" I asked.

My father turned and said, "We are taking Ms. Chloe to the Marriott resort for a couple of days."

I laughed. "You don't want to stay for Trevor's welcome home party for Waylynn?"

"No, sweetheart, I think we'll be skipping this one."

I kissed my father on the cheek. "Probably a good thing."

He rolled his eyes as my mother touched the side of my cheek.

"Oh, Amelia. You look stunning."

"You look like a princess!" Chloe said.

Leaning over, I kissed her on the forehead. "I'll miss you, Chloe. Maybe we can spend a couple days together when you get back? There's a carnival coming to town!"

Chloe jumped and cried out, "Yes! I love carnivals, Aunt Meli!"

Laughing, I ruffled her hair and looked back at my parents. "I promise things won't get rowdy."

My father stared like I was on drugs. "You do know this is Trevor throwing a party. And now that you're all old enough to drink… Please make sure no one drives afterward."

"I promise, we'll keep everyone safe, Daddy. Paxton and I will be on watch."

He smiled and kissed me on the cheek. "I love you, Amelia. Have fun."

"Have fun, darling," my mother added.

With a wave, I watched the three of them leave. I headed to the kitchen, listening to the music the DJ was spinning. The party had started an hour ago, and I was kind of surprised my parents lasted that long.

The second I stepped out the back door, I was transported to Trevor's parties back in the day, the ones that I would sneak into. Things changed after we all came back from college. Sure, we had fun at Cord's Place, but none of my brothers had thrown an infamous Parker party since I'd turned twenty-one.

"I'm the One" came on and I watched as mostly everyone danced on the makeshift floor. I searched for each of my brothers. Trevor was dancing with a girl I recognized from high school. She had been two years ahead of me but I couldn't, for the life of me, remember her name.

When I spotted Cord, I rolled my eyes. He was dancing with two girls at once. Steed and Paxton were sitting off in the corner, lost in each other and totally ignoring everyone else. Tripp was standing with a few guys from his class in high school, probably talking politics.

I couldn't see Mitchell anywhere. I was positive he had taken today off from work.

As I made my way through the crowd, I smiled and said hello to everyone. Up at the bar Cord had set up, I grinned at one of Cord's bartenders.

"Hey, Neil!" I shouted over the music.

"Hey there, Amelia! Want a drink?"

I shook my head. "Just a Diet Coke, if you've got it."

He grinned. "I've got it. You should be the one getting toasted, you know? The youngest and all. Not the *responsible* one."

Laughing, I took the can and shrugged. "I promised my parents I would keep everything in check."

He lifted his chin. "Ahh, the parental promise. No wonder Trevor was avoiding his father."

This time I laughed harder. "Probably!"

"Have fun!" Neil said.

"I will, but hey, Neil, try not to let people get too toasted."

He gave me a thumbs up. "We have a three-drink rule. Cord put it in place."

I grinned. "That makes me feel loads better."

Neil winked. "Your brother is smart enough to know the risks. They've even hired someone to make sure that no alcohol is being brought in."

"Wow. Sure is different from the parties they used to throw in the south pasture!"

This time we both chuckled, and I headed over to the two love birds, Steed and Paxton. I stopped short when I saw Wade talking with Debi Hamilton. Ugh. I couldn't stand her. She and I graduated the same year. She did everything in high school. Played every sport, slept with all the guys in our class except for my ex, Ryan. Of course, for all I knew, they could have slept together.

I made my way past them, trying not to listen. Or maybe trying *to* listen.

"You have a beautiful voice, Wade," Debi purred.

"Well, singing is fun. My true passion is the land. Ranching and farming."

"But you could make millions with a voice like that."

I snarled and drank my soda.

"One thing I've learned in life is money doesn't make you happy. Filling your heart with the things that bring out a smile creates true happiness." His words from the other night hit me square in the chest. I couldn't help but notice how somber he sounded.

"I think one of my favorite things is to see your smile. It makes me happy."

I stared at Wade and Debi as Miranda Lambert's song, "Well-Rested,"' played.

Something came over me, almost like an out-of-body experience, and I walked up to Wade.

"Will you dance with me?" I asked, hope in my eyes.

His grin nearly knocked me off my feet. "Of course, I will. Excuse me, Debi."

Wade wrapped his arm around my waist and led me to the dance floor. My chest fluttered at how his voice had changed when he spoke to me. He was happier. His eyes lit up when they moved up my body and focused on my gaze. Setting the Diet Coke on a table, I melted into his body. His arms brought me close, as if he knew the struggle my heart and mind were having with one another.

Neither one of us said a word as we danced. We didn't two-step—we barely even moved our feet.

His hand moved up my back and pulled me even closer. Each breath I took felt like it was a forced labor, like I was struggling for oxygen, the only thing that could come between our swaying bodies.

"Please talk to me, Amelia."

My eyes closed at the softness of his voice. I fought to hold back the tears. I had no idea why I was so emotional. Wade Adams brought out feelings in me I'd never experienced in my life.

Lifting my eyes to his, I said, "I'm scared of you, Wade."

He furrowed his brows and a sadness swept across his face. I didn't want him to misunderstand, so I continued.

"I'm scared of the feelings I have. I've never felt this way about anyone. Not even the man I thought I was going to marry."

The way his face relaxed made me grin slightly.

"Amelia, I feel the same way. Exactly the same way, darlin'."

My chin trembled and I fought for the strength to tell him exactly how I felt. "I'm realizing that you hold the power to destroy my heart and that scares the daylights out of me."

His eyes glassed over.

I took a deep breath and let my honest thoughts continue. "I'm struggling between admiring you from afar and falling into your arms and begging you to kiss me."

Wade cupped my face with his hands, his thumbs sliding across my cheeks, leaving a trail of heat over my skin. My chest rose and fell as a rush of tingles raced through my body.

"What fun would it be if we admired each other from afar? Look but don't touch? I don't think I'm that strong around you."

I gave a small laugh. "But what about Trevor?" I asked, my eyes searching his face.

"I've already told him I have feelings for you."

My eyes widened in surprise. "You did?"

Leaning in closer, his lips barely brushed against mine. "Yes, I did, darlin'. Now stop talking so I can finally kiss you."

I gripped his arms as he softly pressed his lips to mine. For as long as I live I will never forget the feel of that first time. Couples danced around us, but they seemed to fade into the distance. Leaving only the two of us. To say it was magical wouldn't be close to the way my body felt.

The kiss started off gently. Wade prompted me to open for him, but not too quickly. The moment I did, my legs felt weak. He dropped one of his hands and wrapped it around my waist, drawing my hips close. Our tongues danced in unison as well as our feet did. He wasn't hungry… He was exploring, learning our every move.

I never in my life imagined I could be kissed the way Wade Adams was kissing me. And his body heat against mine caused me to let out a soft moan. I was rewarded with him pulling me closer still, his desire apparent as he pressed into me. A low moan slipped from his mouth, as well.

When he drew back, I was breathless. My head was spinning, and my body yearned for more. I slowly opened my eyes. Our gazes met, and I knew he felt the exact same way I did.

"I've been waiting to do that since I first laid eyes on you, Amelia."

CHAPTER 24

Wade

My heart was pounding so hard I was sure Amelia could feel it as she pressed against me.

I drew back and fought to find air.

That kiss.

I was breathless, and that had never happened before.

That kiss.

It was everything I dreamed it would be and more.

Our eyes met, and I couldn't help the smile that spread over my face. "I've been waiting to do that since I first laid eyes on you, darlin'."

"You take my breath away, Wade Adams."

Tracing the back of my hand down her cheek, I replied, "You have no idea, darlin'. I wish we were alone."

Her teeth sank down on that sweet, soft lip, and my pants quickly grew tighter.

Slow. I needed to take things slow.

"So, are y'all going to stand here or dance?" Trevor asked as he spun a girl and took off into the crowd again. I was never more grateful for Trevor's interruption. I needed a distraction before I dragged her caveman-style to a hall closet or something.

Amelia lifted her brow. "Should we show him how it's done?"

"Hell yeah, we should."

It didn't take long for Amelia and me to glide over the make-shift wooden dance floor. It was like she was made for me with how she fit in my arms. For the first time in far too long, I felt like I was where I belonged.

Song after song, we danced. The sexual tension between us grew each time I pulled her close to me. Fuck, all I wanted to do was touch her. Feel her moan when I slipped my hand down her panties. Every time she laughed and winked at me, my dick grew painfully harder.

After six fast songs in a row, a slow song started, and I cursed under my breath. There was no way in hell I could hold her against me. Not with my dick about to bust out of my jeans. Thankfully, Amelia checked out. "I'm exhausted and thirsty!"

Thank God.

Laughing, I placed my hand on her lower back and guided her to where Steed and Paxton were sitting. It was hard not to notice the two of them looking at us with goofy grins.

I pulled out Amelia's chair. The second she sat down, Paxton dove in with the comments.

"Wow! That was some kiss!"

My face heated, and the most beautiful rose color moved over Amelia's cheeks.

"Yes, it was," she replied with a wink.

Steed glanced my way. His smile faded, and he looked straight into my eyes. "You hurt my sister, I'll break every bone in your body. No questions asked."

I had been midway to sitting down when I froze—but it wasn't from what Steed had said. It was the sight of Chloe's goat, Patches, running toward the dance floor.

"Oh shit," I mumbled.

"Ignore him, Wade. He's always been overprotective."

Standing up quickly, I said, "Patches."

"Goat," Steed replied, laughing. "Are we playing word games, dude?"

I shook my head and pointed. "No. Patches is running this way, and he has a look of determination on his face."

Steed jumped up. "Oh shit."

"Goat!" Amelia called out. "Goat on the loose!"

I wasn't sure what everyone thought they heard Amelia call out, but people started running everywhere.

"Grab him!" Trevor cried as he, Cord, and Tripp took off after Patches.

"Should we help?" I asked as Steed stood next to me, laughing his ass every time Trevor dove for Patches and missed him.

"Are you kidding me? This is the best entertainment I've seen in a long time."

I shook my head at Steed, and focused back in on the other Parker brothers, who were all attempting to get the goat.

Paxton was laughing so hard she had to take deep breaths. Amelia stood with her hand covering her mouth. "He's destroying everything!" she said, trying not to lose it laughing.

"Oh no! The food!" Waylynn called out as they chased Patches.

"I feel like we should help," I said with a chuckle. "I mean, it *is* your daughter's goat."

Steed was still cracking up, clearly enjoying this too much. Amelia pushed me and said, "Go help before Trevor pulls something."

"There's Leroy!" Steed cried out in a laughing fit. He was bent over holding his stomach and pointing to Chloe's other pet goat who came in unnoticed because of all the commotion and made a beeline for the food.

I made my way over to the long food table. Waylynn attempted to grab Patches by the collar. When she crawled up on the table I stopped and stared. She was crawling through the food, calling out for Leroy. Patches joined in and I swore he sounded like Chloe yelling.

"He's eating me! Get the beast off of me!" Waylynn said as Trevor rushed over, slipping on food and sliding right past the table. Tripp and Cord threw up their hands and tossed in the towel. I don't think I'd ever seen anything so damn funny as Trevor sliding under the table on his ass as Patches jumped on it, watching from above, like a king looking out over his dominion.

I whistled and Leroy and Patches stopped. That was something I had started doing right before Chloe and I fed the goats each morning. I'd been trying to teach Chloe to whistle, and it turned into a signal for the damn goats that it was breakfast time.

Leroy looked at me, a piece of fabric from Waylynn's dress hanging from his mouth as he chewed. They jumped off the table and followed me. Every now and then I'd whistle so they'd stay on track.

As I walked by Tripp and Cord, they glared. "And you didn't think to do that when they first ran in?"

With a shrug and a smug smile, I replied, "I was distracted by y'all chasing them. I wish I had recorded it."

"Fuck you, Adams!" Cord said as he turned and headed straight to the bar.

After getting Leroy and Patches back in the barn, I poured them some food and turned to leave. Amelia stood at the entrance of the barn looking sexy as hell.

"You saved the day. Although, had you done that earlier, people wouldn't be leaving, and Waylynn would have her dress in one piece."

With a smile, I sauntered to her. "What fun would that have been?"

Her eyes sparkled as a beautiful grin graced her face. "That's true."

I stopped short in front of her. "I can't stop thinking about kissing you."

Her eyes fell and her cheeks turned slightly pink.

"Same here."

Taking my finger, I lifted her chin, but she looked away nervously. "Do you have any idea how beautiful you are, Amelia? You take my breath away."

She rocked back, and I couldn't help but chuckle at how adorable she was.

When she met my gaze, she inhaled sharply and my chest squeezed. She closed her eyes briefly, and it felt as though time stood still.

I pushed a piece of hair behind her ear. "I would give anything to know what you dream of when you close your eyes."

Her gaze searched my face. I reached for her hand and laced our fingers together.

"I'm thinking you aren't real. You're a dream. Something I write about in books but never truly believed in."

With a half-smile, I leaned in and whispered against her ear. "If I were to pick my nose or fart under the covers and hold you down underneath them…Would that make me more real?"

Amelia pushed me back with her free hand and laughed. "I guess that means we have to get to know each other. Want to go out on a date with me, cowboy?"

The way she chewed her lip drove me insane. I leaned in and kissed her, pulling that lip into my mouth. My hands gently took her hips, and I pulled her body against mine. The low moan coming from her mouth moved through my body at light speed. After only two of her kisses, I was already addicted. My dick grew harder by the minute. I had to slow this train down before we ended up in one of the stalls with Patches watching.

We drew back from one another. Our chests rose and feel with each rapid breath.

"I'll take that as a yes," Amelia whispered.

Resting my forehead against hers, I replied, "That is very much a yes."

CHAPTER 25

Amelia

With a deep breath, I stared at my reflection in the mirror. My mind drifted back to the night before, when I was out riding. The sun had barely begun to set, and I found myself up by the foreman's house where Wade was now living. Placing my hand on my stomach, I closed my eyes and smiled, remembering…

Pulling Stanley to a stop, I stared at the foreman's house. How in the hell I ended up here was beyond me. My breath caught as I watched a naked Wade walk through the house, drying his hair with a towel. The urge to walk in and demand that he make love to me was overwhelming. He dropped the towel to his side, giving me a full-frontal view. My stomach pooled with a delicious ache.

Wade sat down and wrapped his hand around his dick and slowly started working his shaft. His eyes closed while his head dropped against the back of the sofa.

"Holy. Shit," I said as I backed Stanley up and tried to hide him *somewhat behind a tree. Jumping down, I peeked around the tree and continued to watch Wade. His hand sped up and I let out a soft low groan. His mouth parted open as he jacked off faster. I couldn't pull my eyes off of him. It had to have been one of the hottest things I'd ever seen.*

Stanley pushed against my back and voiced his unhappiness.

"Shh! Stanley, give a girl a break, will you? Look at him! Look at how...beautiful he is. How incredibly hot it is watching him. Who do you think he's thinking about?"

Jesus, why am I asking my horse this?

Stanley snickered and pushed me again. Clearly he was ready to move on. I wasn't. My heart was pounding as my breathing increased as I continued to watch. Wade was getting close, I could see it on his face.

"Christ almighty," I whispered as I took a step closer. *The urge to slip my hand into my pants was increasing by the second. Wade's hips jerked and he lifted his head to watch himself come. It looked like he said something as he hit that heavenly moment of his orgasm. His other hand catching his cum as he closed his eyes and dropped his head back. He slowly stopped pumping his dick and sat there for a few moments. I closed my eyes and tried to focus on calming my erratic breathing. My eyes snapped open when I realized I was standing out in the open. Quickly rushing back behind the tree, I waited to see what Wade would do next. Stanley had wondered off and was eating grass safely out of Wade's sight.*

Wade stood and walked back toward the bedroom. I turned and leaned against the tree. My hand covered my mouth and let out a giggle.

"Holy shit! That is so going into a book!" Closing my eyes, I let the image fill my head again. Wade had an amazing body, but add him naked and jacking off. A girl could only take so much! My body was on fire. I needed to get back and to a vibrator stat.

I peeked back around the tree and waited. Wade returned dressed in a pair of sweats. He grabbed something and the next thing I knew he was on his front porch, playing his guitar and humming a tune.

I stepped back before he saw me. My lower stomach pooled with desire. I made my way over to Stanley and hopped on. The mental image of Wade Adams' perfect, naked body on his sofa making himself come was seared in my memory, a mental image I put to use when my hand slipped between my legs that night.

The light knock on my door had me glancing over my shoulder.

"Hey. May I come in?"

I motioned for Waylynn to come in. She walked up behind me, put her hands on my arms and rested her chin on my shoulder. It had been a few days since the Patches incident and Waylynn had finally stopped threatening to slaughter the poor little goats.

"You look beautiful," she said. "Where are you going?"

My stomach rolled with nerves. "A date. With Wade."

A huge smile covered her face. "Really? How exciting. Where are y'all going?"

I shrugged. "I don't know. He wouldn't tell me."

Waylynn took a few steps back and chuckled. "Oh, man. He's playing that card, huh? Where do you think he'll take you?"

Pulling my hair up, I pinned it to the top of my head.

"I have no clue. With Wade, it could be dancing at Cord's, going for a horseback ride, or going out to dinner. The ball is totally in his court."

Waylynn sat crisscross on my bed. Her blonde hair was in two pigtails, and she looked like she was twenty instead of thirty-two. "Amelia, take a deep breath. You said you both agreed you wanted to go slow and get to know each other. Which, by the way, I'm sure our brothers will appreciate."

I rolled my eyes. "Steed's already threatened to beat his ass if he hurts me. I can't imagine what the other four have said to him or what they're going to do."

We let out matching chuckles. "Trevor's probably already laid it out in fine detail," Waylynn said.

My chest felt heavy with uncertainty. "Am I making a mistake by doing this?"

Her brows furrowed. "By doing what? Going out on a date?"

"Going out on a date with Trevor's best friend. A guy who works for our father. What if things go south?"

She grinned. "What if things go great?"

I sighed and sank down on the bed next to Waylynn. "I'm so afraid he's going to break my heart. After only two kisses, I crave him, Waylynn. And not even in a sexual way."

Her expression made me giggle. "No...I mean, yeah, I can't wait to be with him when we're ready. I crave him in a *different* way. One I've never experienced before. When I wake up, the first thing I think about is him. What is he doing? Where is he? When will I get to catch a glimpse of him? He smiles at me, and I swear to God it feels like my knees are going to buckle. His touch sends butterflies all over my stomach. This is stuff I write about... It's not real."

"But it is real, Meli. Look at Mom and Dad, or Steed and Paxton. You just needed to find the right guy. And the right guy might be Wade."

I chewed on my lip, grasping the enormity of what she'd just said. "Did you feel those things for Jack?"

Her eyes turned sad. "Yes, but I was too naïve to realize that he didn't feel them in return."

"How do I know if Wade feels them, then?"

Waylynn reached for my hands and squeezed them. "He will show you, Amelia. Look at how Steed takes Paxton out once a week and they do something together. He makes sure she knows how special she is to him. It might be a walk at sunset or a beautiful, expensive dinner in a fancy restaurant. It's the things he says to her, as well."

I smiled. "Paxton is so happy. They're both so happy and that makes me happy."

My sister nodded. "Me, too, but they had their fair share of heartache. Sometimes I think we have to walk down the darkest path before we can see the light through the trees. With Jack, I thought I found my light, but he wasn't it. He promised me a family if I gave up dancing and then hit me with every excuse under the sun as to why it wasn't the right time. I didn't listen to my heart, Meli. I listened to the idea that I couldn't have a failed marriage. My heart knew early on Jack wasn't the one."

"You'll find your *one.*"

Waylynn let out a sigh. "I know. Just look at our other brothers. Jesus. I'm beginning to worry about Tripp and Mitchell. Cord and Trevor, not so much."

"Yeah. What do you think will happen with Mitchell and Corina?" I asked.

Standing, she shook her head. "Girl, that is a conversation over drinks. Come on, let me braid your hair instead of wearing it up. You know, just in case Wade finds himself behind you he'll need something to grab onto."

My mouth dropped as I pushed her back. "Oh, my gawd! You're terrible."

She laughed. "No. I've been hanging around Trevor and Cord too much."

All talking stopped when I walked into the kitchen. Steed, Paxton, and Chloe were sitting at the kitchen island with my parents making tacos on the other side.

"What's up, y'all?" I leaned down and kissed Chloe on the head, then Paxton on the cheek. Steed stood and kissed me on the cheek. "How are you feeling, Paxton?"

My sister-in-law wore a bright, beautiful smile. "I feel amazing!"

"I do, too!" Chloe stated.

I giggled. "I'm so glad! Chloe, do you like to feel your baby brother moving around?"

She nodded and placed her hands on Paxton's stomach. "I'll tell you when he wakes up and you can feel him, too."

My heart melted. "Okay, pumpkin."

Steed and Paxton grinned from ear to ear. Turning, I faced my mother.

"Hey, Meli. You look nice. Will you be joining us for dinner?" she asked, her brow lifted in a way that said she clearly knew my answer was going to be no.

"Thanks, but I have a date."

Grabbing a water from the refrigerator, I held my breath. I had just put it out there for everyone.

What in the world is the matter with me?

When I turned around, all eyes were still on me.

"What?" I asked, my hand shaking while I took a sip of water.

"With whom?" Paxton asked, an evil little grin on her face.

"Yeah, Aunt Meli! Who you gonna kiss?" Out of the mouths of babes.

I laughed nervously. "I have a date with Wade."

Chloe's eyes widened. "What! My Wade?"

My head jerked to Steed and Paxton. "Um, I…Um…"

Shit. Shit. Shit.

Paxton came to the rescue. "Chloe cat, we talked about this. Wade is not yours."

Chloe faced Paxton, then me. "But he's my best friend. If he falls in love with Aunt Meli, he won't be my best friend anymore."

My heart was slowly breaking. Chloe actually had tears in her eyes. Here I was worried about Trevor, when the person I really needed to be worried about was Chloe.

"Oh, no, Chloe," I said as I rushed to her. "Wade will always be your best friend. I know there is nothing he enjoys more than your morning feed time."

Chloe's little lip trembled. "Did he tell you that?"

I nodded. "Yes."

"But…what if he forgets about me? And you forget about me, and we don't have our dates together?"

Cupping her face in my hands, I said, "Chloe, that could never happen. You're such a special little girl, and you always will be. And Wade is an amazing friend. He will always make time for you."

"Hey, y'all," Trevor said as he cleared his throat. Chloe and I both realized Wade had walked in with him at the same moment. Chloe wiped at her eyes and looked down.

When I glanced to Wade, he was smiling. He winked and lifted a bouquet of flowers. He pointed to me, then walked to Chloe.

"Hey, Chloe. Your Uncle Trevor told me you were here for dinner."

Her blue eyes turned big and bright as she stared at Wade.

"What a lucky coincidence for me. Since I had to pick Amelia up and all. But now I can give you your flowers."

Her mouth dropped open. "My...flowers?"

Oh, Lord. Could this man be any more perfect?

I had to place my hand over my chest. Wade's gesture was one of the sweetest things I'd ever seen. My grin spread from ear to ear, more evidence that I was enamored with this man.

"Yeah. It's 'give your best friend flowers' day today."

The way her little hands covered her mouth made my heart melt. I was pretty sure Paxton was on the verge of tears. My mother, too.

"Really?" Chloe asked as she jumped up and down. One peek at my parents proved they were both smiling. "I didn't know or I'd have gotten you some!"

Wade chuckled. "It's okay. It snuck up on me today. Good thing Trevor here told me."

I glanced at my brother. He walked over to Chloe and kissed her on the cheek. "How's it going, squirt?"

"It's goin', Uncle Trevor!"

My mother reached out to Chloe. "Let's put your beautiful flowers in some water. Shall we, Chloe?"

"Okay!" Chloe said as she hugged Wade and skipped off behind my mother to the sink.

Paxton kissed Wade on the cheek. "That was so sweet of you, Wade," she said in a soft voice. "Thank you for thinking of her feelings."

Wade flashed that handsome smile, his dimples on full display. "It was nothing, Paxton."

Steed reached out a hand. "It was everything, Wade. Trust me. We appreciate it."

Wade's cheeks turned pink. He turned my way and let his heated gaze move slowly over my body. I had on a long, flowing dress that hit above the floor and hugged my curves nicely. It was casual, yet still dressy enough if Wade was taking me out to dinner.

"You look beautiful," Wade said softly. He looked at me like everyone else in the room had vanished, and it was only the two of us.

"She always looks beautiful," my father added. "I take it you're the date, son?"

Wade nodded and reached across the island to shake my father's hand. "Yes, sir."

With a look that tried to scream *I'm scary*, my father crossed his arms over his chest. "Don't F-U-C-K this up, Wade."

Wade took a step back and swallowed hard.

"What did you spell, Granddaddy?" Chloe asked, bouncing back to Wade.

"Grown-up words, pumpkin," Steed said with a smile.

I took Wade's hand. "I think we should head out before another one of the Parker men threatens you."

Wade chuckled and laced his hand in mine, which caused my body to launch into a flurry of sensations. My pulse raced, my stomach fluttered, and my knees went weak.

Jesus. Get a hold of yourself, Amelia.

My chest rose and fell as I tried to act normal. If Wade holding my hand did this to me, I couldn't imagine what making love would feel like.

I peeked at Wade as he said goodbye to everyone, and found myself lost in him.

Oh, yes. Wade Adams held a power over me that left me both excited and scared to death.

CHAPTER 26

Amelia

I wasn't surprised to see Wade was a gentleman through and through. He led me out to his truck, held the door open, and helped lift me in. When he pulled the seat belt out and handed it to me, I playfully teased him.

"What? You're not going to buckle it for me?"

Wade's eyes turned dark as he took the belt and leaned over me in the truck. The feel of him pressed against my body instantly sent a throbbing pulse between my legs.

When he drew back, he flashed me the sexiest smile I'd ever seen. I was positive my heart was going to beat right on out of my chest.

"How do you do that?" I asked. My voice sounded breathy.

"Do what, darlin'?"

"You do something so simple and I turn to mush. Literally. My mind goes blank and my body acts like I'm fifteen again."

He slowly ran his tongue over his lips, and I was gone.

So. Gone.

He shut the door and he never did answer my question, which oddly enough, turned me on even more.

"Get a hold of yourself, Amelia Parker. This is not your first rodeo," I whispered while watching Wade round the front of his truck. And I swore he was talking to himself.

Once he got in, I took a deep breath. "So, where are we going?"

"I thought we would grab some dinner."

"Sounds like a plan. I'm starving."

He started up his truck and headed down the long driveway. We quickly fell into easy banter about work.

"So, how do you come up with all your stories?"

I smiled. "I've always loved telling stories. My mother said from the time I could form sentences I was telling her about my dreams."

Wade chuckled. "Do you only write romance?"

"No, I've written a few historical novels. I love historical romance. It's my favorite genre. Honestly, anything romance-related is my favorite to read and write."

"No paranormal?"

With a chuckle, I replied, "Some. Romance is it for me, and how do you even know paranormal is a genre?"

"I have my ways. Why is romance *it* for you?"

I shrugged. "I kind of lost my dreams of ever finding my Prince Charming, so I write about someone else finding theirs. It's why I make my heroes so swoon-worthy."

"Swoon-worthy?" Wade asked.

"Yeah, you know he sweeps the heroine off her feet. Lets her know it's okay to be saved every once in a while. That you don't always have to be strong. You can lean on someone else and not have to feel weak."

I felt the weight of his eyes staring at me.

"Guys feel that way, too, you know."

My head jerked to look at him. "You want to swoon?"

He laughed. "No, that's not what I meant. I mean, sometimes I don't feel very strong. There are nights I lie in bed and wish I had someone to talk through what a fucked-up day I had, or how much I miss my parents and sisters. Someone to lean on when shit goes sideways, you know? I imagine love to be a two-way street. You're both there for each other, not only when it's good times, but bad, as well. I've never experienced that type of love before."

I was breathless. Wade's raw honesty hit me square in the chest. I'd never had a man be so open with me. I remembered what he had said about his ex, Caroline, and how she left him after his family died and he sold the ranch.

"I thought I found love once," I said, my voice sounding sadder than it should. "He turned out to be a cheating bastard and what I thought was love was just me thinking we would be a good couple."

Shaking my head, I added, "I'm glad I saw the truth before it was too late."

"Sounds like we've both been burned by what we thought was love."

I focused back on him. "Yeah, I guess so."

Wade turned the truck down a road headed in the opposite direction of town.

"Where are we going?" I asked.

He grinned. "I told you, dinner."

A lightness settled in my chest as I felt my cheeks burn from my wide smile. "I have a feeling we're going on more of an adventure, Wade Adams. The only place this road leads is to the Hamilton family ranch and a make-out-slash-party-spot we all used to go to in high school."

Wade laughed. "What happened to the Hamilton family ranch?" he asked, peeking over at me with raised eyebrows.

"Hasn't had cattle on it in years. My father bought a good chunk of it after Mr. Hamilton took off with another woman and Mrs. Hamilton was left to run it. I went to school with the last Hamilton, Russ.

He didn't want to have anything to do with Oak Springs, the family ranch, nothing. After his father left, Russ hated everything that reminded him of his father. After high school, he told his mother to put it up for sale. She begged my father to buy it, but he couldn't ever get her to come down on the price. Trevor said she was asking for way more than what it was worth. It's been sitting on the market ever since. It's kind of sad. It's been in Mrs. Hamilton's family for years. There have always been rumors the family women were cursed."

"Wow. Why?"

I shrugged. "I don't know. I'll have to ask my mother about it. She grew up with Mrs. Hamilton."

"So, tell me about this make-out spot."

With a chuckle, I looked out the window. "It was really more of a party place. It's actually on a piece of land that the Hamilton's owned. It wasn't fenced in so whenever we wanted to have a party, that was where we went. We called it the lookout. For years kids went there to throw parties, and I'm pretty sure a few lost their virginity there!"

Wade and I laughed.

"My father told me when he was in high school they would go there. You used to be able to see the Frio River, that's why it was called the lookout. Over the years, trees grew up and blocked the view."

"Did the family know kids were using it to party?"

I frowned. "I don't know. I'm sure they did. Russ used to throw parties there all the time."

Wade passed the little dirt drive that led to the lookout. So, we weren't going there.

After a few miles, he pulled up to the gate at the Hamilton Ranch. The gate had been changed and a beautiful sandstone entrance was in place of the old rusted piping. I watched in awe as Wade pulled up like he owned the place.

"It did sell," Wade said as he punched in a code and the metal gate swung open. "I bought it."

My heart dropped and excitement filled my entire body. "Are you serious? You bought the Hamilton place?"

"Yep. After talking to Trevor and your dad, I decided to approach Mrs. Hamilton. Told her my story and that I was looking to start a new life. She dropped the price by nearly half. Turns out the day I called her she found out her ex-husband was getting married. She sold out of emotion, which sucks for her, but it was a win for me."

I was so taken with shock, countless questions poured out of me. "I can't believe it! Are you going to renovate? Will you live here full-time? Do you plan to ranch on it?"

He pulled through the gate and headed down the drive. "I'm going to open the ranch for your father's cattle to graze, but I've got a few other ideas I'd like to play around with."

I stared at Wade. "I think that's amazing. You must be pretty excited."

He nodded. "I am. I stumbled upon an area of the ranch I want to show you."

My heart fluttered. "I'd love that."

With a racing mind, I tried to figure out what in the world he was going to show me.

"The moment I saw it, I thought of your cabin."

A warm feeling pooled in my chest. "I love that old cabin. There is something about old buildings that I adore."

"I remembered you saying that, so I know you'll love this."

We drove down an old dirt road. Bluebonnets mixed with wildflowers, lining the sides of the road. It was beautiful and reminded me of a painting my mother had hanging up in her office.

"This is beautiful. I can't believe how many bluebonnets are still out with it being so late in April!" I stared out the window at the open field. "Wade, this is stunning!"

He chuckled. "I know. That field sold me on this place. Well, the field and that right there."

The truck came to a stop, and I gasped. My hands covered my mouth while I took in the sight.

"Oh. My. Gosh. Look at it." I opened the truck door and dashed out as fast as I could.

Spinning around, I looked at Wade. "How old is it?" I asked before turning to the old, stone, two-story house.

"Mrs. Hamilton said her great-grandparents built it. I guess the Hamilton family was one of the founding families of Oak Springs, along with your family, and the Hills."

"They were. I believe Russ's great-grandfather was the first town doctor."

"The house hasn't been lived in for years. Mrs. Hamilton said her great-grandfather moved out of the house and into a small cabin after his wife died. Said the memories were too much for him to take. So, this house sat empty. The trees and shrubs grew up around it, and Mrs. Hamilton said it was forbidden for any family member to live in the house. Something Dr. Hamilton wrote into his will."

My eyes widened as I stepped onto the porch. "You've got to be kidding me. Why would he do that?"

Wade's eyes turned sad, and he stared at the house. It was like a memory hit him.

He shook his head before looking at me. "Grief does weird things to you. Fills you with fear and doubt...and so much loneliness that you feel you might go crazy on any given day."

I walked up to him and took his hands. When our eyes met I was stunned for a brief moment. Wade looked defeated. "There is something far more beautiful here than grief, Wade."

"What's that?" he asked, his voice cracking.

"Hope. Excitement. The idea of bringing happiness to something that deserves it and longs for it."

In that moment, I wasn't talking about the house. I was talking about Wade, the incredible man who stood before me. Who put others ahead of himself and cared with his whole heart. Who had loved big and who had lost so much.

He dropped my hands and cupped my face, his thumbs left a burning path as they swept over my skin.

His eyes captured mine, and I knew in my heart there was something else I was talking about.

Us…and our love.

CHAPTER 27

Wade

My lips crashed against Amelia's. Her words tumbled in my heart, screaming a million and one different things as we got lost in our kiss. I wanted to do this every damn minute of the day.

I dropped my hands from her face and wrapped my arms around her. Lifting her up, I kissed her deeply, trying to fill her with the happiness that she had brought to me already.

When I slowly placed her back on the ground, I drew back. My breathing heavy, and my chest light.

Amelia swayed and grabbed my arms. "Jesus, what you do to me with your kisses, Wade Adams."

Grinning, I kissed her forehead. "I could say the same thing about you, Amelia Parker."

I loved hearing my name roll off her lips. I couldn't wait to hear it while I made love to her.

I took her hand in mine. "Want to see the inside?"

She nodded. "Is it safe to go in?"

"Yeah, I had an inspector check out the whole house. It has good bones. All it needs is a cleaning, painting, some wood replaced here and there. And air conditioning."

We made our way up the large, stone steps. The massive wraparound porch was amazing, and I could tell Amelia was being pulled in by the house.

"It's like something out of an old book. My mind is racing with stories right now!"

My stomach did a weird dip as I watched her take everything in. I loved seeing her excitement. I'd thought she would go nuts over the house, and I was right.

"Wait! I need a notebook."

She rushed down the steps to my truck. I wasn't surprised to see her pull a small notebook and pen out of her purse. She rushed back to me and wrote something. I glanced at it:

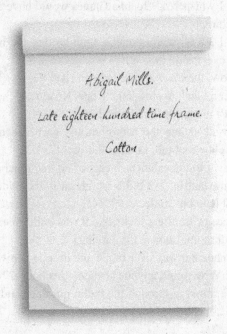

Abigail Mills.
Late eighteen hundred time frame.

Cotton

She took my hand. "Let's go inside. I'm dying to see it."

I unlocked the door, and we walked into a small hall. To our left, see-through book shelves led to the parlor, and a grand fireplace stood in the middle of the outside wall. We continued to another room.

"Must be a bedroom," I said as Amelia squeezed my hand.

We walked in, and she gasped. "Oh my! Look at this fireplace. This mantel. It's exquisite. Look at the tin on the ceilings, Wade! Look at the woodwork! It's all so amazing! How has it all stayed in such good shape?"

I smiled and squeezed her hand. "It is, isn't it? After I found the place, I asked Mrs. Hamilton. She said her mother told her never to go into the house. When she got older, she came in and fell in love. She's been having someone come once a month to clean and keep things in order."

"Wow!" I whispered. "Joanna Gaines would have a heart attack from all the shiplap!"

"Who?" I asked, while Amelia spun around the middle of the room, taking everything in.

"You know, the *Fixer Upper* lady on HGTV."

I gave her a blank expression. "Nope. No clue."

"It doesn't matter. Is that the bathroom?"

Amelia walked into the bathroom and gasped again. "Look at the porcelain claw foot tub. Look at this arch!"

I was drawn to the cabinets. Years of no one touching them and they were still beautiful. An old washtub sat in the middle of things, and I couldn't help but smile.

"This piece of furniture looks like it was built especially for this area of the bathroom. Look at the carvings."

Amelia made her way over to me and dropped down to examine it. "Stunning! Why would anyone abandon this house?"

We made our way through the bathroom door and into another bedroom. This one didn't have a fireplace.

"I wonder whose room this was," Amelia said.

"I'm sure I can try to find out some information from Mrs. Hamilton."

She simply nodded and walked into another living area.

"It's huge! I'm going to guess this was the sitting room. Wade, can you imagine this house filled with beautiful, antique furniture? Please, tell me you intend to bring it back to its glory days."

Laughing, I shrugged. "Sure. You might have to help me, though. Late eighteen-hundreds décor is not really my thing."

Her grin nearly knocked me off my feet. "I'd love to help! Let's see the kitchen."

We made our way into a large kitchen. There was really nothing to it. Cabinets, which were beautiful, an old farm sink, and a fireplace where I imagined they did the cooking.

"Look at this dining room! Holy shit! It could hold a table big enough to seat my whole family. It's huge."

Amelia ran her hand along the chair rail and barely touched the wallpaper. "I'm stunned this wallpaper has not fallen off with the humidity and heat after all these years."

"So am I."

"Let's keep going! This is exciting!"

We came to another room off the kitchen. "Butler's pantry, maybe?"

I shrugged again. We walked into another bedroom and I gasped.

"Holy shit," we said at the same time.

"Wade, this must have been the main bedchamber."

"Bedchamber?"

She shook her head. "Bedroom. Like the master bedroom." Amelia walked to a door and turned back to me.

"You don't think this is real gold, do you? The doorknobs and hardware?"

"Maybe gold-plated. I can't see even someone with a ton of money doing something so foolish."

She raised a brow. "You'd be surprised. Mrs. Hamilton's family is crazy rich, and she herself did the weirdest things with her money. The apple might not have fallen far from the tree."

Opening the door, Amelia stepped in…and screamed.

"What?" I asked, rushing into the bathroom. Amelia was down on her knees in front of an old bathtub. "Copper." Glancing up at me, she exclaimed, "They had a copper tub! Do you know how beautiful this will be when you get it cleaned?" Amelia jumped up. "We have to see what's upstairs! Come on!"

She grabbed my hand and nearly dragged me up the stairs. Then she threw open the door at the top and squealed. "This would make the most stunning writing room! Wade, it has a view of the river!"

We walked to the window. "And there's a rooftop porch," I added.

"Shut up!" Amelia shouted as she hit me in the stomach so hard I bent over.

Before I could get my breath back, she was on the deck, jumping.

"Lord, I hope the roof is okay," I mumbled while I made my way out the door.

Amelia spun around and ran into my arms. "Thank you for showing me this! I'm so excited for you."

I held onto her and felt something new—something I never dreamed I would feel. I wanted Amelia to live in this house with me…

For the rest of my life.

Holy shit. Where is this coming from?

We hadn't even known each other two months, and I was making plans about living together.

Forever.

When she drew back, I forced a smile. "You're welcome. I'm glad we got to see it together. Now, hold on, I need to go back to the truck. There's been a change of plans."

With a confused look, Amelia asked, "What kind of change?"

"Where we're eating dinner. I think this is the perfect spot."

Before she could say anything, I jogged back down the stairs to my truck. I grabbed the basket, cooler, and bag before I made my way up to the roof.

Amelia put her hands on her hips and tilted her head, giving me the cutest damn grin I'd ever seen. "A picnic? Wade, you planned a picnic?"

I nodded and set everything down. Before I knew it, Amelia had her arms wrapped around me and was kissing the living shit out of me. It didn't take me long to return the kiss.

Pulling her in close, I wrapped my hand around her neck and deepened the kiss, pressing my hard cock into her stomach so she knew what she was doing to me. A small moan slipped from her mouth, fueling the fire of our kiss.

When we finally had to stop for air, she peeked at me and smiled. My heart stilled as I stared into those beautiful blue eyes.

"That was some kiss," she managed to say. Her chest rose and fell with each breath.

"Just wait, darlin'. I plan on kissing you more. A lot more."

CHAPTER 28

Amelia

As if the high from touring the old house wasn't enough, Wade had to go and do something utterly romantic.

And that kiss. *My God,* that kiss.

Wade laid out the blanket as I watched. My fingertips moved lightly over my still-tingling lips.

"What's on the menu?" I asked, sinking down on the blanket and pulling my knees under me.

Wade opened the basket and pulled out two glass dishes. He grabbed the bag and took out paper plates, forks, knives, and napkins.

"You've done this before, Mr. Adams."

He laughed and shook his head. "Actually, a certain young lady gave me the idea when I was out walking her goat. She told me girls liked picnics. That her daddy takes her mommy on them all the time."

I grinned. "Don't you just love her? Chloe has brought so much joy to our family. I can't wait for the new baby!"

"I do adore Chloe. She is funny as hell. Jesus, the things that come out of her mouth."

I giggled in agreement. "If Steed only knew some of the things Chloe shared with us."

He stopped what he was doing. "Oh, tell me! She told me she walked into the room the other night and her daddy and mommy were wrestling in bed, but she shut the door cause her mommy had no clothes on. I almost died."

We both busted out laughing.

Wade shook his head. "I tried hinting to Steed to put some kind of warning system in the house that alerted them if Chloe got out of bed! He asked why he would do that. I had nothing to come back with. Nothing!"

My cheeks hurt from laughing so hard as he turned back to the picnic basket.

"I wasn't sure if you liked wine, so I brought the next best thing. Bud Light."

I reached for the beer and winked. "That's perfect. What's in the glass dishes?"

He peeked over at me. "A recipe Waylynn gave me."

With a raised brow, I replied, "Waylynn was in on this, too, huh?"

His grin had my heart melting. He pulled back the lid on the glass dish, and my mouth began to water.

"Ohmygawd. Waylynn's barbecue enchiladas! Wade, this is my favorite dish my sister makes!"

He chuckled. "I know. I asked her what I should make, and she gave me this recipe. Said it might win me some brownie points."

Lifting my brows, I replied, "You never know. Depends on how well you made it."

Wade put an enchilada on the plate. Handing it to me, he stopped and said, "If you don't like it, you have to promise me a do-over."

I reached for the plate. "Please, the fact that you cooked my favorite food, brought my favorite beer, and picked a romantic spot—trust me, it could taste like shit, and I'd still be swooning until I was senseless."

He stared at me as I took a bite. I closed my eyes and let the savory tastes of the barbeque sauce and cream cheese settle in. I chewed slowly, not wanting to let that first bite go.

When I opened my eyes, Wade was looking at me with wide, hopeful eyes. I let a small smile play across my face.

"Wade Adams, we are totally going to second base with this dish."

He tossed his head back and laughed. I smiled and got back to eating. Wade made a plate and we sat and ate while we talked about his plans for the future.

"A few months ago, if you were to tell me I'd be in Texas sitting on the roof of an old house talking about doing a major remodel, I'd say you were insane. I was in a bad place and your brother really pulled me out of it. I'm in his debt."

I set my empty plate down. "Do you use singing as an escape? I heard you singing the other night. Sounds carry far in the country, you know? You must have been on your porch."

My cheeks flushed with heat at the memory of Wade naked. That was a little secret I intended on keeping to myself.

He half-shrugged. "I guess I do. Sometimes."

"Have you always liked to sing?"

"Since I can remember. I used to sing in the choir at church. That made my mother happy," he said with a grin. "She thought I was destined to do something else besides run the ranch."

"Did she not like living on the ranch?"

"Oh, no, she loved it. But I think she thought my dream was to be onstage. It never was. Don't get me wrong, I love it. Doing it every now and then is one thing, but doing it for a living? I love ranching. The dirt, the animals, figuring how to make farming better. That's where my heart is. That's my true passion."

I chewed my lip before asking the next question. "Do you write your own songs?"

He nodded. "I've written some."

"Will you sing one to me someday?"

His eyes lit up and when they fell to my lips, I licked them. His stare quickly met mine again.

"I will."

"Promise me."

Wade reached over and took my hand. "I promise. Now, let's dance."

He stood and pulled me up with him. Through my laughter, I argued, "We don't have any music."

I should have known better when it came to Wade. He reached into his little bag of tricks and pulled out a Bose speaker. Connecting it to his phone, he set it on the edge of the wall. He searched for a song and smiled when he found the one.

He flashed me a sexy-as-hell grin and set his phone down, holding his hand out for me to take it. The second the music started I knew it was Frank Sinatra.

"Witchcraft" played, and I couldn't help but giggle. He pulled me against him, and we danced on the roof of the old house. My heart hammered. I'd never in my life been so happy.

I was falling in love with Wade Adams and that didn't scare me at all. It should have, but somehow I knew this man would guard my heart with his life.

Moving my mouth against his neck, I said, "If you were going for third base, you were successful, cowboy."

He pulled back and captured my eyes. "You bewitch me, Amelia. I can't stop thinking about you. I want you to know I want you."

His eyes closed and a beautiful smile appeared on his face.

"I *really* want you," he said, opening his eyes and looking at me again. "But our first time together isn't going to be fucking in the back of my truck or even on this roof. It's going to be special, because that's what you deserve. I want to make our first time together so magical it feels like our first time ever."

My throat bobbed as I swallowed hard. "I didn't think men thought about that kind of thing anymore. Making it special for the first time."

Wade ran his finger down the side of my face and along my jaw. "I do."

And there it was.

I was head over heels, no doubt about it, in love with Wade Adams, and he hadn't even made love to me.

"With Every Breath I Take" started, and I couldn't take it anymore. I looked up at him.

"Kiss me, Wade. Touch me. Please."

My voice was needy. It sounded strange, but I didn't care. I needed more. So much more. And it wasn't a need like the one I'd felt with Liam, or any other man. It was on such a different level. I longed to be with Wade. To feel his body against mine.

Framing my face with his hands, he kissed me slowly, perfectly. A blissfulness moved between us and I knew this was only the first of many moments this man would make my stomach drop and my head go dizzy.

He picked me up, carrying me over to the blanket. He gently set me down, moving the basket out of the way, and looked directly into my eyes.

"Lie back, darlin'."

My pulse raced. I'd never anticipated a man's touch like this before. When another Frank song started I was lost in the words and the feel of Wade's hand slowly moving up my leg.

"You're so beautiful, Amelia Parker."

Arching my back, I silently pleaded with him for more. His fingers lightly brushed over my panties, causing me to suck in a breath.

The romantic, old-fashioned music and his slow touch made it seem like what we were doing was forbidden. My body had never been so in tune to touch like this before.

Hot breath hit my neck, and my entire body shivered.

His fingers moved slightly under my panties, teasing me with what was to come. "Are you wet, darlin'?"

"Wade," I said, breathy. My mind was spinning, and my heart raced at a wild pace.

My legs spread wider as his hand dipped farther into my panties.

"Open your eyes. I want you looking at me when I push my fingers inside of you."

I popped my eyes open and found Wade's lips were inches from mine. His eyes blazed with a fire that had my stomach dipping. One quick brush over my lips, and he pushed his fingers in. I gasped, then quickly moaned in pleasure.

Wade smiled and pulled his fingers out, causing me to whimper in protest.

Then he brought them to his lips and slowly put them in his mouth. And I about died. He moaned and closed his eyes while slowly withdrawing his fingers.

"Amazing," he whispered.

Hottest. Moment. Of. My. Life.

His hand was back in my panties and my hips lifted with anticipation. This time he kissed me while pushing them back in.

His kiss coupled with his fingers moving inside me was pure heaven. It wasn't going to take me long to have an orgasm.

His palm pressed against my clit, and I was tossed over the edge. Pulling back, I cried out his name as I grabbed his shirt.

"Wade!"

His lips were on my neck, peppering it with hot kisses. "That's it, darlin'. Tell me how it feels."

"Oh. God. Feels so good."

His rhythm drove me to orgasm. It felt like it lasted forever. When I finally came down from the clouds, Wade was grinning.

"You're flushed, Ms. Parker."

I dropped my hold on his shirt and placed my hand over my cheek. "I am."

Wade moved over me, pushing my dress up so that I could wrap my legs around him. Pressing his hard-on into me, I arched my back and hissed, "Yes."

His mouth was on my neck, breathing into me. He ever-so-lightly placed kisses until his lips came up to my ear. "Do you think I could make you come again like this, darlin'?"

My breathing was labored as I pulled him closer to me. "You could probably make me come just by breathing on me."

He chuckled and began moving his hips, pressing what felt like a rather large cock right into my core. The friction from his jeans against my lace panties was delicious. I hadn't had a guy do this since high school. There was something so innocent, yet hot about it.

I grabbed the blanket as my orgasm grew. "Wade. I'm so close. I'm so close."

"God, darlin', I can't wait to sink my cock into your pussy."

And there it was.

The key to unlocking my next orgasm was Wade talking dirty.

Wade Adams talking dirty to me while dry humping me on the rooftop of the new house he bought.

Yep.

I cried out his name before he captured my moans with his mouth. If fooling around was getting me this crazy for him, I could not imagine what actual sex would be like.

When my body finally stopped shaking, Wade lifted off of me, still hovering inches from my body.

We stared at each other for the longest time before he broke the silence. "Jesus, I seriously just tested my willpower. You have no idea how much I wanted to take you. You're stunning when you come."

My face heated. "When do I get to see your face when you come?"

He narrowed his eyes. "Whenever you want, darlin'."

My hand made its way down the very visible bulge in his pants. Squeezing it, I whispered, "Tit for tat, Mr. Adams."

"Darlin, you better stop using words like 'tit' while you are rubbing on my dick or I'll be finished before you even get started," Wade said in a lust-filled daze.

I pushed his chest and made him roll onto his back.

My hands shook slightly while I unbuttoned his pants. I peeked up and noticed he was looking directly at me. Not watching my hands, but my face.

"I feel like a teenager about to see a dick for the first time," I said with a chuckle.

He smiled bigger and lifted his hips, throwing me off balance as I straddled him. Moving back a little, I unzipped his pants and instantly moaned at the sight.

Commando. Holy shit. He was commando.

Hot. As. Hell.

My teeth sank into my lip as he lifted his hips more and pushed his pants down, letting his very impressive cock free.

I licked my lips. I had fully intended on giving him a hand job, but this was a game changer. I usually hated giving head, rarely ever did it, but there was something about Wade that made it feel so right. Before I could give him a chance to say anything, I leaned down and took him in my mouth.

"Fuuuck! Amelia!" he cried out, reaching down to pull me off of him, his breathing instantly intensified. "Are you sure you want to do that?"

One small taste of him wasn't enough. I needed more. Nodding, I leaned back down, this time slowly working him into my mouth.

Running my tongue all over his cock. My other hand played gently with his balls, now nicely tucked up.

His hands went to my head, gently rubbing. I went faster, and he took a slightly firmer hold.

"Fucking hell. Jesus. Amelia. Oh, God. Yes."

Smiling, I went deeper, taking as much of him in as I could.

"Yes," he hissed. I could feel how his hips were fighting to not start pumping. I wrapped my hand along his shaft, working him with my hand and mouth while my other hand still fondled his balls.

"Amelia, pull back if you don't want me coming in your mouth!" Wade cried out.

Fuck that. I wanted everything. I sucked harder, and Wade let out a loud moan then cried out my name. His hot cum hit the back of my throat, and I swallowed while I kept working him until he stopped coming.

I slowly lifted my mouth away, taking the time to stop and lick the top of his cock. Wade's entire body shook, and he moaned again. Sitting up, I wiped my mouth and grinned.

That was the first blowjob I had actually enjoyed giving. And the first one where I'd swallowed the cum.

"That was fucking amazing. My God, woman!"

With a triumphant smile, I placed my hands on his chest and climbed a little more on him, settling against his still-hard cock.

He grinned wide, lifting his hips toward me, pressing himself against me.

"Fucking hell, sex with you is going to be amazing."

I leaned down and sucked his lip. "Don't make me wait long, Wade. I don't think I could take it, especially after what we've just done."

He lifted his brows. "Tit for tat, Ms. Parker."

I was on my back, and he was pulling my panties down before I could even respond.

Lifting up on my elbows, I watched as Wade kissed up the inside of my leg. My head dropped back and I let out a whimper as he slowly licked and pulled my clit into his mouth. Dropping back, I pushed my hands through his hair and let him take me to euphoria.

Wade and I sat against a tree, looking out over the Frio River. I sat between his legs, completely relaxed as my head rose and fell with each breath he took.

"So, was it the picnic or Frank that got me to third base?" Wade asked.

Grinning like a silly fool, I said, "Honestly? I'd have to say it was Frank. The old crooners have a way of making me swoon."

"There is that word again."

Lifting my head to glance at him, I asked, "What word? Swoon?"

The rumble in his chest vibrated through my body. "Yes."

"That's the romance writer in me. My readers expect to swoon because of the heroes I write. So, keep it up, cowboy. You're giving me good material."

He wrapped his arms around me tighter. "Is that so? Now I'm going to have to up my game if I'm going to be your next hero in one of your books."

I laughed. "Up your game? Wade, how could you possibly up your game?"

Wade turned me around. I wrapped my legs around him, and we sat face to face.

"Oh, I can up my game, darlin'."

Lifting my brows, a slow, evil smile spread across my face.

Oh, I'm going to reap the benefits from this little game.

"Really? Then I suggest you show me what else you've got."

His dimples appeared, and my stomach dipped.

Placing his finger on my chin, he drew my lips to his. "I think I'm going to like this game we're playing."

I wiggled my eyebrows. "So do I."

CHAPTER 29

Wade

The hot sun beat down as we gave the last goats their vaccinations. Lifting my hat, I wiped the sweat from my forehead. "Christ Almighty, it's hot."

Trevor and Steed laughed. "Welcome to Texas."

I shook my head at Trevor. "I went to college here for four years, or did you forget?"

He paused and then shook his head. "Damn. I did forget for a second."

Steed slapped his brother on the back. "I've missed the heat. I'm looking forward to a hot summer."

"I bet your wife isn't saying that," I said with a smirk.

With a shake of his head, he grunted. "No. She's not."

"When is she due?" I asked, grabbing my water and drinking it all in one gulp.

"July thirtieth."

Trevor grabbed a water and tossed it to Steed. "Damn. In the middle of the summer. Poor Paxton."

"I know. Chloe is trying to convince me we need to build a pool. I had to remind her that her grandparents have a pool. She countered by saying her poor mommy was going to be so big with her baby brother that she wasn't gonna wanna get in the car and drive to Granddaddy and Grammy's house. She's gonna wanna walk out the back door and there it is. Problem is, Paxton agrees with her."

Trevor and I exchanged glances before looking back at Steed. "You are in trouble with that little girl. I hope you know that."

He swallowed his water. "Don't I know."

"What do y'all say about heading out tonight? Just us guys hanging out and having a good time." Trevor asked.

"Cord's?" Steed asked.

Trevor shook his head. "Nah, there's a new place opened up outside of Bandera. Cord's wanted to check it out since it opened a couple of months ago. I say we all head there. It would be nice to find some new pussy."

I shook my head. "I'll go, but I'm not interested in hooking up with anyone."

I felt the heat from both of their stares.

"You don't say. You got a reason why you ain't interested in hooking up with anyone?"

With a grin, I replied, "I do. A pretty little redhead with the last name of Parker."

Steed grinned from ear to ear, as did Trevor. He reached over and placed a hand on my shoulder, giving it a light squeeze.

"Waylynn told us at breakfast that Amelia's been walking around with a goofy smile on her face."

I returned their grins. "She's an amazing woman. I've never felt this way about someone. Not even Caroline. Not even close."

Steed nodded. "I'm glad to hear that. Just take care of her heart. I really like you, Wade. You're good for the ranch, and I would hate to have all five Parker brothers kick your ass if you hurt our sister."

I laughed. "Trust me, you've all made that very clear. Including your dad. Besides, I have no intentions of letting Amelia Parker go anytime soon."

Trevor slapped the living shit out of my back. "Good. Good. I'm glad to hear that. I'd hate to have to cut your dick off and shove it down your throat and pull it out your ass."

"Wow. You really went there," Steed said with a hearty laugh.

Shaking my head, I felt my body tighten. "For fuck's sake, Trevor. What in the hell is wrong with you?" I asked as we started to get into the ranch truck.

"I'm just saying, Adams. That's my baby sister. And just so you know, once I find out y'all have slept together, I'm gonna have to kick your ass."

My eyes widened as I stopped at my door. "What the fuck for? You gave me your permission to date her."

He shrugged. "It's the principle. You know. It's expected of me."

"By who?"

Trevor pointed over to Steed. "My other brothers."

I shot my eyes over to Steed. He lifted his brows and frowned. "Yep. Afraid he's right. It's expected."

They both opened their doors and got in.

"Well, how do you know we haven't already slept together?"

They both stopped and got back out, and I knew I was fucked.

Trevor took a step closer, making me take two steps back. "Have you? Have you slept with my baby sister?"

"No!" I shouted. "And fuck, even if I did, do you think I'm going to tell you now?"

He pointed to me. "It don't matter if you don't sleep with her until your wedding night. Your ass is still getting kicked."

I felt the goofy ass smile hit my face. "You think she'd marry me?"

A look of horror washed over my best friend's face. "W-what?"

"You just said our wedding night. You see us getting married someday?"

Trevor stumbled over his words. "I mean, I guess I could see it. Hell, I don't know. We're late!"

He spun on his heels and jumped into the truck. I climbed into the back seat, and Steed turned to face me. "Well played, my friend. I don't think I've ever seen someone get Trevor to stumble on his own damn words."

Trevor hit the gas and took off toward the main barn. "Fuck you, Steed. And fuck you, too, Wade!"

Steed and I chuckled as Trevor turned on the radio, drowning us both out.

I stepped onto the porch of the cabin and peeked through the window. Amelia was sitting there, pen tapping against those beautiful lips. I knocked on the window, causing her to jump and look. A huge smile spread over her face as she quickly rushed to the door.

"Hey! What are you doing here?"

Before she could say another word, I pulled her to me and pressed my lips to hers. Amelia let out a moan and wrapped her arms around me. We were soon lost in the kiss and before I knew it, her legs were around my waist, and I was carrying her to the table.

"Wade," she panted, her hands slipping under my T-shirt. "I'm so horny."

Smiling, I worked my hand under her bra, pinching her nipple and bringing out a nice, long moan.

"You been writing naughty things, Ms. Adams?"

Her eyes caught mine. "Want to help me with a scene?"

Swallowing hard, I reached down to adjust my dick. "Hell yeah, I do."

Her tongue moved slowly across her lips. "I need to see a man's reaction to his girlfriend getting off in front of him."

"Jesus Christ. Are you trying to kill me?"

She slowly nodded while placing her hands on my chest. Giving me a push back, she slid off the table.

"Sit in that chair, cowboy."

I did as she asked.

Amelia moved to the sofa and pulled up the dress she was wearing to reveal a pair of blue lace panties. She slipped them off and dropped them onto the floor. My heart was going to fucking beat right out of my chest.

She sat down. "What should I do now, Wade? What would my hero want me to write?"

Where in the fuck is my voice?

"He'd, um..." I laughed. "Do you really want me to tell you what I'm wanting, Amelia? Cause I'll be honest with you. It's dirty as hell."

Her face turned red, and she nodded. "Tell me, Wade."

I took my cowboy hat off and set it on the floor. I couldn't believe I was going to do it, but if it was inspiration for her book, I'd gladly be tribute.

"Spread your legs so I can see your pussy."

She gasped at my use of the word pussy. By the way she licked her lips, I could tell she liked it.

"Like this?" she asked, slowly spreading her legs open.

"Yes."

Her finger went to her mouth as she gently bit down. "Now what?"

My dick was angry, pressed tightly against the fabric of my jeans, demanding to be let out.

"Slip your fingers inside. Work yourself."

Her chest rose and fell as she trailed her fingers up her thigh and slowly pushed them into her pussy. A hiss followed a moan.

"Jesus Christ," I whispered.

"Now what, Wade?" she asked as her voice turned heavy.

"Make yourself come."

She smiled. "Do you like watching me?"

I laughed. "If you could see how fucking hard my dick was you wouldn't need to ask."

"Take it out. Tit for tat, Mr. Adams."

Standing, I unzipped my pants and dropped them, allowing my dick to come out and play. Sitting, I slowly stroked my cock as I watched her move her fingers in and out of her wet pussy.

"Mmm, you are hard."

"If you're trying to test my willpower again, you're doing a hell of a job," I said, moving my hand slowly up and down my shaft.

"What do you want me to do now, cowboy?"

My mouth was getting dry. "Go faster. Touch your breasts."

Her smile grew bigger, and she increased her speed with one hand as she grabbed her tits with the other. Her head dropped back against the sofa, and she started groaning.

"I'm so close. God, it feels so good."

Fucking hell. This woman was everything. Sexy as shit, beautiful, funny, and did I mention sexy as shit? Watching her get herself off was one of the hottest things I'd ever seen.

"Are you close, Wade?"

My eyes were trained on that pussy. I wanted her. Fuck, I wanted her. Jumping up, I quickly made my way to her. Dropping to the floor, I grabbed her hips and pulled her to me, burying my face between her legs.

Amelia cried out as she dug her hands into my hair, pulling me close while she rocked her hips against my face.

"Wade! Oh, God. I'm coming! Oh, my gawd… Jesus…feels… so…good!"

Dropping my hand, I wrapped it around my dick and pumped hard and fast. Amelia's entire body shook as her orgasm rolled through her. I sucked her clit hard when my own orgasm came on strong, causing her to scream out again. The sound of her calling my name and the feel of her coming on my tongue had me coming in my hand.

When she begged me to stop, I drew back and looked into her eyes.

Her breathing was labored, but her eyes were on fire, and her smile was like nothing I'd ever seen before.

"Please, tell me you came, Wade."

With a chuckle, I kissed the side of her thigh. "Darlin', I came so damn hard I thought I was going to pass out."

With a giggle, she sat up. She placed her hands on the sides of my face. "That was the hottest moment of my life."

Relief swept over me. Hopefully all the fucking phone sex that asshole had her doing was now erased from her memory.

"It was for me, too, Amelia."

She kissed me on the lips and said, "Let's clean up!"

Watching her lead the way to the bathroom, I knew it was time to take things all the way. There was no way I could hold out much longer. I needed to feel Amelia Parker. Needed to make her mine.

CHAPTER 30

Wade

I raced through the door and slid to a stop. Melanie and John looked up at me.

"Well, good morning there, Wade. You in a hurry or something?" John asked.

"Yes! I've been trying to call Amelia, and she's not answering her phone. Is she still asleep?"

"No, she's down at the cabin. She went there last night to write since you and the boys went to check out the new bar in Bandera."

Damn it, I had forgotten she'd told me she would be there. "Okay! Thanks!"

I turned to leave as John called out, "Where's the fire, son?"

"April's in labor!" I cried as I rushed out the door.

Running to my truck, I quickly sent a text to Steed.

Me: *April's in labor. I know Chloe will want to see it.*

His response was almost immediate.

208

Steed: *We got the text. Thanks for telling Chloe about the text alert system, by the way.*

Laughing, I jumped into the truck and fired off another text.

Me: *Sure!*

I tossed my phone on the seat. It went off, and I glanced down to see Steed's reply.

Steed: *Asshole. I know you're laughing right now.*

I took off and drove down the old dirt road like a bat out of hell. I was familiar with the cabin. Amelia and I had been there a number of times. The last time I had pulled out all the stops and cooked her dinner. Fresh flowers covered every surface, and I made one of her favorite meals. Fish tacos. We spent the night in the cabin wrapped in each other's arms. The only way I could keep myself from making love to her was to be sure I didn't have any condoms. I knew neither one of us would break that rule.

When I finally pulled up, I raced down the path and into the cabin. Throwing the door open, I called out, "Amelia!"

She jumped and threw her cup of coffee straight into the air.

"Oh, my gawd and all the stars in heaven! What in the hell is wrong with you, Wade Adams? I just peed my pants!"

I looked down at her cute little pajamas. They were blue and white stripes. "You did?"

She reached down and picked up the mug that had somehow managed not to break. "Yes! Oh, my gosh. You scared the piss out of me, literally!"

"She's in labor!" I cried out.

Amelia dropped the mug again. "April?"

"Yes! You have no cell signal out here. I've been trying to call you! We have to go! Now! There are hooves!"

"What? OH, MY GOD, let me change my pants."

"There is no time!"

Turning to face me, she pulled her pajama bottoms and panties off. "I tinkled in my pants, Wade! There is time!" She slipped on yoga pants then ran to the table and grabbed her phone.

"Go! Go! Go!" she said as we rushed out of the cabin to my truck.

"Wade, drive fast! If I miss this birth I'm flying to New York and losing my shit on someone! Does that giraffe know how much of my writing time she has stolen? I *need* to see this birth!"

I hit the gas, and we took off.

"Can't you drive faster, you pansy ass? This isn't Driving Mrs. Daisy. Floor this bitch!"

"Stop yelling at me! You're making me nervous!" I cried out.

"I've got a signal! We've got a signal!"

"Yes!" I said, fist pumping the air.

"I didn't mean to call you a pansy ass!" she quickly said as she pulled up the website. "Oh, my God! Hooves. Legs! Wade, look!"

She shoved the phone in my face. I got one quick look then focused back on the road.

"Shit! Shit! Shit!" I said, pressing the gas down more.

"You might want to slow down," Amelia said.

Looking at her, I pinched my brows together. "You just told me to speed up."

Pointing, she shouted, "Dip."

I turned back, but it was too late. We were going airborne.

I hit the dip, and my truck flew off the road. Amelia screamed out like she was riding a damn bull.

"Yeehaw!"

The truck hit the road, jarring my teeth hard.

"Yeehaw? Was that fun?"

Amelia chuckled. "Hell yeah, that was fun. Mitchell was the only one of my brothers who had the guts to do that. Tripp tried it once and broke something on my father's truck. He was grounded for two months and none of the other boys ever tried it again."

I shook my head. "Oh, I'm sure I broke something."

Pulling into the driveway of the foreman's house, Amelia jumped out before the truck even came to a damn stop.

She rushed in through the front door and screamed.

"Did we miss—"

Clearly I hadn't calculated the steps because I tripped on the last one. My ass went down hard.

"Fuck!" I shouted, as I stood up and reached for my knee.

"Wade! Stop playing around. It's about to happen!"

I limped through the door and into the living room where Amelia was standing in front of the TV.

She glanced my way. "Why are you limping? What happened to your jeans?"

"Tripped. Last step. Fell hard."

Running over to me, she kissed me on the lips. "I'm sorry, baby. I'll make it better…after the baby's born!"

And like that, she was back in front of the TV.

"This is it! Here she comes!"

I stood next to her and took her hand in mine.

"I can't believe our April is having her baby," I said as I fought the tears in my eyes.

Holy shit. If Trevor saw me right now he'd give me hell.

"Wade! Oh, my gosh, we made it just in time! Look!"

We stared at the TV and watched as the baby giraffe was born. Tears streamed down Amelia's face. She sank to the ground and I followed her, pulling her to me while she leaned against my chest.

It must have been an hour before we actually stood up, continuing to watch the live feed.

Amelia let out a sigh. "That was the most amazing thing I've ever seen."

"I agree. And it's about damn time. I'm glad I pulled it up on the TV."

With a giggle, Amelia fell back on the sofa. "I'm exhausted. I feel like I gave birth to the calf. And I'm starved!"

"How about I make us breakfast?" I asked, heading into the kitchen.

Amelia got up and followed me. "I'll help."

"Do you need to get back to writing?"

Wrapping her arms around me, she let out a sexy moan. "Nope. I stayed up pretty late last night. Being at your old house really inspired me to put my current book down and write the historical one that was playing out in my head."

I placed my hands on her hips. "I'm glad. I can't wait to read it."

When she pulled her lower lip into her mouth, her eyes turned dark.

"Something on your mind?" I asked with a slight grin.

She nodded. "You. Me. *Fourth* base."

I gripped her hips tighter, drawing her closer to me. "I want you, too, Amelia. More than you know."

Her hands landed on my chest. "Then make love to me, Wade. I don't think I can stand to wait much longer."

Cupping her face in my hands, I gazed into her eyes, teasing. "Did watching that giraffe have a baby turn you on?"

As a slow smile grew over her face, I realized I was falling head over heels in love with Amelia.

"If I say yes?"

I picked her up, causing her to let out a gasp.

"Then who am I not to satisfy the woman I'm in love with?"

Amelia's eyes grew wide and her breath sharpened. Biting on her lip, she buried her head into my chest as I walked us into my bedroom. I had the room set up for tonight anyway. Tonight was going to be the night I made her mine. No reason not to bump it up a few hours.

I glanced around the room. "Keep your eyes shut, okay?"

"Why?" she asked.

"I was planning something special for tonight, so I need to make a few adjustments. I'm going to set you on the bed, but don't open your eyes." I ran the back of my hand down her cheek and whispered, "Promise me, darlin'."

Her body shivered as I caressed her. "I promise I won't look."

I lit the candles and pulled the gift box from the closet, gently setting it on the end of the bed. Shutting the blinds, I darkened the room. The candles gave off the perfect glow.

Pulling one of the red roses out of the vase, I walked back to her. I took her hand in mine and gently pulled her to her feet.

"Keep those eyes closed."

Amelia giggled and nodded.

Taking the rose, I ran it over her face, causing her take in a sharp breath.

"I know we haven't known each other for very long, but I knew the first moment you smiled at me that you were going to be the holder of my heart."

"Wade," Amelia whispered.

"Three months ago I never dreamed I'd be able to open my heart again, but being here with you and your family has taught me so much."

Her hands wound in my T-shirt.

"Open your eyes, Amelia."

The moment she did, our eyes met and she never looked away.

"These last couple of months with you have been the happiest times of my life. You've showed me it's okay to be happy, even while I'm still hurting from the loss of my family. You've proven that love gives us the strength we need to begin again. To take that leap of faith and spread our arms wide and let things fall where they fall. I thought I knew what love was until I kissed you for the first time. Ever since then I've been falling and let me tell you, it's been the best free fall of my life, Amelia Parker."

Tears fell from her beautiful blue eyes. Her lips pressed together as she continued to gaze up at me.

Amelia lifted her hand and wiped her tears away, then looked around the room for the first time. She gasped and covered her mouth, more tears quickly replacing the others.

"Oh, Wade! This is beautiful." Shaking her head, she took it all in then focused back on me.

When I took her hands in mine, she gave me the most breathtaking smile I'd ever seen. My knees shook and my heart felt like it was diving straight to the floor.

"I was so afraid of giving my heart away, and then you came along and I was even more scared," she said. "The things I feel for you leave me in awe every single day. I know now that what we share is a once-in-a-lifetime thing, and I don't care if someone says we couldn't possibly have fallen in love so fast, because I know I fell for you the first time I saw you dancing with Chloe. I can say without a doubt in my mind, my heart is yours, Wade Adams. I also wanted to say that waiting for this moment has meant more to me than you will ever know. It only proves to me what an amazing man you truly are."

My eyes stung with the threat of tears. We had both admitted to falling for each other, but were we ready to say the words?

Staring into those big, blue eyes, I had my answer, and I knew the exact moment when I wanted to tell her.

CHAPTER 31

Amelia

My heart pounded as Wade and I stood and gazed into one another's eyes.

I dropped my head to his chest and let out a chuckle. "I feel like a teenager about to have sex for the first time!"

Wade's laughter rolled over my body like a warm blanket, instantly making me relax.

His fingers brushed a piece of hair behind my ear. "You're so beautiful, Amelia. You take my breath away."

When his lips found the sensitive skin on my neck, I let out a long, soft moan.

"Wade. You're driving me crazy."

I could feel his smile as he peppered soft kisses along my neck. His hand laced into my hair and tugged it back, exposing more of my neck. When he ran his tongue over my skin it felt like a path of fire was left in its wake.

"Oh God," I gasped.

His hands moved to my shirt. He lifted it over my head and tossed it to the floor. My chest rose and fell, each breath heavy as I anticipated his next move.

I jumped when his finger traced the outline of my bra. Wade's thumbs rubbed over my nipples, a shot of pleasure racing to my core. I could feel my panties getting wetter. The hunger for this man grew with each second that ticked on his dresser clock.

"More!" I whispered.

He chuckled while unclasping my bra. It slipped down my arms to the floor.

The way his eyes took me in made me feel amazing. Licking his lips, he bent down, took my breast in his hand and sucked on my nipple. His other hand pinched and pulled at the other.

My body was on fire. The throbbing sensation between my legs grew, and if he didn't touch me soon I was going to have to touch myself.

My hands found his jeans and I promptly unbuttoned them. I was disappointed to find boxer briefs, but at the same time, knowing he was a little bit hidden from my touch fueled my desire.

Letting go of my breast, he moved to the other one, not giving it nearly enough attention like he did with the first one. Wade lifted his body and looked down into my eyes.

"Are you wet, Amelia?"

I nodded. "Yes. Yes."

A crooked smile slid across his face. "Let me find out for myself."

"Thank God," I whimpered as he pulled my yoga pants down. Kicking them to the side, I held my breath, awaiting what he had in store next.

Wade kneeled, lifted my leg and licked between my lips. I let out a small whimper as I pushed my hands into his hair and tugged his face closer to me.

"Yes. Oh, God. Wade, yes."

When he pulled away, I cried out in protest.

Wade stood and pulled his shirt over his head and pushed his jeans and boxers off. I knew he was trying to stay in control, but I also knew he wanted me as much as I wanted him.

He guided me to the bed and I sat, then crawled backwards, my breath insanely erratic.

Wade moved over me, cupping my face with his hands.

"You're so beautiful, darlin'. I will never be able to get enough of you. Never."

My head was spinning. From his romantic words to his mouth on my clit, the man drove me insane. I couldn't even imagine what him being inside of me would do.

His lips pressed against mine in the sweetest kiss. It wasn't rushed or hungry. No, this was classic Wade. Slow and determined. Innocent, yet utterly sexy. His hand moved over my body, touching and feeling his way around me while we kissed. There was magic in this man's touch. Wade's fingertips moving across my skin left me weak and needing so much more.

"Amelia, I cannot wait to make love to you."

I hadn't even realized my eyes were shut. I opened them to see him staring down at me. His breathing just as hard and fast as mine.

"Love me, Wade. Please."

He kissed me once more before leaning over and opening the side drawer of his nightstand. I watched him as he rolled a condom onto his impressively large dick. My body trembled. I'd never wanted to be with a man as much as I wanted to be with Wade. I couldn't even think of any other man I had ever been with.

Wade was it. The first man I'd truly given my heart to.

When he moved over me, I opened myself to him. I was positive we were both holding our breath.

Sliding his hand down my body, he softly pushed his fingers inside, preparing me for what I was sure would be the most amazing moment of my life.

Wade cradled my face within his hands as he positioned himself. The feel of him barely touching me sent my body into hyperawareness. Every breath he took, move he made, and word he whispered was multiplied by a hundred.

He slowly pushed into me, and our eyes met. What happened next was the most incredible thing I'd ever experienced.

"I love you."

We'd said it in unison, like we'd choreographed this moment.

Wade stopped moving, and we stared at each other before we started laughing.

"Oh, my gawd! We said it at the same time!" I giggled.

Wade shook his head and kissed me on the lips. "If that isn't a damn sign, I don't know what is!"

Wrapping my arms around his neck, I pulled him into me with my legs.

"It feels like I've been waiting for this moment my entire life. I've been waiting for you, Wade."

A smile spread across his face and his eyes burned with passion. "I've been waiting for you, too, Amelia. You're the answer to my prayers."

My breath caught. When I looked into his eyes every fear and doubt quickly vanished. Placing my hand on the side of his face, I whispered, "Make love to me."

With a wink and another kiss on the mouth, Wade replied, "Yes, ma'am."

It was both pleasure and pain. The feel of him slowly sliding into my body was one of the most pleasurable moments of my life. What was painful was how much I needed him. I needed him to fill me deeper. Stay inside of me all night. The feeling of us as one was so powerful it caused every nerve in my body to light with fire.

"Jesus, Amelia. You feel so damn good."

My fingers moved lightly over his back as Wade reached under me, pulling my ass toward him so he could get deeper, fill me more. He moved in and out of my body in the most delicious way.

"I'm not going to last very long, darlin'."

"Feels so amazing. I don't want this to end," I panted. I wanted him to take his time, yet I wanted to feel more from him.

Our mouths crashed together while Wade moved slowly.

"This going slow is killing me."

Smiling, I let out a chuckle. "Same here."

He pushed in deep, his body flush against mine.

"Wade, faster. Please, go faster."

"Thank fuck. I need more of you," he grunted while he pulled out and slammed into me so hard and fast I cried out.

"Yes!"

"You like that, darlin'? Are you getting close?"

"Oh God," I panted.

Our bodies were covered in sweat as we became lost in one another, our hips meeting thrust for thrust. My orgasm was beginning to build, and I could feel it in my toes.

"Wade!" I cried.

"That's it, baby. I can feel you squeezing my dick. I'm so close, Amelia."

He pushed in and let out a growl from the back of his throat, sending me into sweet oblivion.

"I'm going to come. Oh God, yes, I'm coming!" I cried out, and my entire body shook as stars danced behind my eyes. I could feel Wade grow bigger.

"Amelia," he groaned out. "That's it, baby. You feel so good falling apart with me inside you."

Moving his hands under me, he grabbed my ass and pushed in deeper, sending me diving off the cliff into another round of utter bliss.

It felt like it lasted forever.

"Look at me, Amelia," Wade said as he pushed deeper.

My eyes opened, and I felt like I was floating down from heaven.

I'd never experienced sex like this. It was beyond amazing.

No. This wasn't sex. This was Wade making love to me.

"I'm going to come, darlin'."

I grabbed his arms and arched my back as we fell together.

Wade's fingers moved across my arm as we lay on his bed. After discarding the condom, Wade brought in a warm washcloth and cleaned me off. It was the sweetest thing a man had ever done for me after we'd been together. Then he crawled back into his bed and held me.

"I've never experienced anything like what we just shared," I said, breaking the silence.

He placed a soft kiss on my shoulder. "I feel the same way. It felt like I couldn't get deep enough. Close enough. I wanted to crawl into your body."

I smiled. "Do you think it will always feel like that?"

He let out a chuckle, "Yes."

Rolling over to look at him, I lifted a brow. "Really? You think when we're sixty years old and having hot sex in the rocking chair it will feel the same way? Because that was the best moment of my life."

He ran his finger along my jaw. "I think it will be even better because that'll be years of us learning each other's bodies, and all that practice makes perfect, right? I've fallen in love with you, Amelia Parker, and now my life's mission is to make sure every time we make love it's magical."

My lips pressed tightly together. I fought to keep my tears at bay, but lost. A single tear trailed down my cheek.

"Happy tear?" Wade asked, wiping it away with his thumb.

I nodded. "I'm going to have such great material for my books with you around."

His eyes widened in shock before we both laughed. Flipping me onto my back, Wade reached for another condom. "I guess it's time to show you my wild side then, huh?"

Giving him my sexiest smile, I replied, "Bring it, cowboy."

CHAPTER 32

Amelia

Laughter came from the kitchen as I walked in through the back door.

"There she is!" my mother said.

I scanned the room to find my mother, Paxton, Waylynn, Corina, and my best friend from high school, Jen.

"Wow. Are we having a secret women's meeting or something?" I asked, setting my workbag on the island.

Waylynn and Paxton both stared like I had something on me. With an evil little smirk, Waylynn asked, "Where have you been, little sis?"

With a half shrug, I replied, "Working. Watching April have her calf."

"Who?" Jen asked as I gave her a quick hug and kiss on the cheek.

"It's a giraffe. What are you doing here?"

She held up her hand. "I'm engaged!"

My mouth fell open as I stared at the diamond on her finger. "Martin?" I finally managed to ask.

"Yes! I'm getting married. I came over to ask if you would be in the wedding."

She pulled me into a hug, and I looked over to Paxton and Waylynn. Both were attempting not to laugh.

I took a step back. "Wait, Jen, you just started, um, dating. You don't think this is too soon? To get married?"

"No. We've been attracted to each other since high school. Even you said we've always flirted."

Taking Jen by the arm, I pulled her out of the kitchen and into the dining room.

"Jen, listen. It's probably not too soon, but you said yourself you were worried Martin might be having sex with other women. Are you not concerned about that anymore?"

She rolled her eyes. "Why would you bring that up, Meli?"

"Because! It's a valuable thing to bring up. Do you not feel that way anymore?"

Not looking at me, she stared at the ground. "No. I'm not worried about it anymore."

"Look me in the eyes and tell me you're not the least bit worried Martin might cheat on you."

Her head shot up. "We can't all have a Steed Parker or a Wade Adams."

It felt like she had slapped me across the face. I took a step back. "What the hell does that mean, and how did you know Wade and I were together?"

Shaking her head, she turned to leave. "Never mind. Forget I even came here."

I forced her to stop. "Now hold on one second. You can't be running your mouth off like that and then turn to leave. First off, Paxton and Steed had their own set of problems before things worked out. Plus, they'd dated for years. And as far as Wade goes, you don't know anything about our relationship."

"You're datin' him. It's all over town how the Parker princess captured the prince."

Snarling, I pinched my brows. "What in the fuck? Did you just make that shit up because I know no one has said that, and if they have I want names. I'm kicking some ass!"

"Whatever. I'm so sick of watching everyone else get the guy. I want the guy for once! I knew that first day you came walking into the bar and Wade stopped talking to me just to stare at you that he had a thing for you. It's never going to change for me. I'll always be the girl who gets the *okay* guy. Well, Martin is more than okay. He's hot, he has a big dick, he knows how to use it, and he loves me!"

"I really hope for your sake my mother did not hear you say that."

Her face turned red. Closing her eyes, she slowly took in a breath and let it out. "Amelia, I'm happy. Can you not just be happy for me?"

My heart dropped, and in that moment I totally got it. "If you're sure this is the right thing to do, I'll be there for you. Hell, I'll even throw you the shower."

Jen's eyes lit up. "Really? And you won't mention Martin being unfaithful again?"

Ugh.

I bit the inside of my cheek. "I promise I won't ever mention it again."

But it will happen. And you'll be on my doorstep crying about it.

Jen hugged me. "Thank you, Amelia! Thank you so much!"

We laced our arms together and walked back into the kitchen. Jen wore a huge smile. "We were just talking about the wedding and all of that."

Everyone in the room gave her a polite smile, but I knew damn well they'd heard the whole showdown. Noises carry far in the country, and all.

"Well, I best be going. I've got to ask a few other friends. Bye, y'all!"

"Bye," everyone called out as I walked her through the house and to her car.

"Let's plan a weddin' meeting soon. We have lots to go over," Jen said. She slipped into her car, rolled the window down, and called out, "See ya around, Meli!"

I watched her drive off. A sick feeling settled in my chest because I knew she was headed for heartache. The front door closed behind me, and I heard the girls walking my way.

"Does she have any idea she is marrying the biggest manwhore of them all, Meli?" Paxton asked.

I nodded. "She knows."

"And she's not worried?"

I shrugged. "I guess she's willing to ignore it. Maybe he's changed."

Waylynn pushed open the screen door. "He hasn't. Trust me. I can't tell you how many times he tried to feel me up at my welcome home party."

I groaned. "Oh, God. What do I do? I promised her I'd never bring it up again, but I know he is going to end up hurting her."

Waylynn sighed before saying, "You don't do anything. Jen is not stupid. She damn well knows what she's getting into and if that's the door she wants to walk through, you have to let her walk through it. Hopefully when she reaches the next one, she'll know if she should go through it or not."

I exhaled loudly.

"But honestly, who cares about Jen and Martin? I want to hear all about it!" Waylynn gushed, grabbing my hand to pull me to the porch swing.

"What are you talking about?"

Paxton and Waylynn glanced at each other and then back to me. "Aww, that's cute, Meli, but you trying to pull off the whole innocent thing is not working," Waylynn said. "Spill it. Was he big?"

"Did you come the first time?" Paxton asked as Corina chuckled from behind her. My eyes shot up to Corina.

"Why are *you* laughing?" I asked.

She attempted to remove her smile but couldn't. "No reason."

"Don't veer off the subject," Waylynn said, grabbing my chin with her hand and making me look at her. "Was it good?

How in the hell do they know Wade and I made love?

"Was what good?" I asked.

Giving me the stink eye, Waylynn leaned in closer. "Girl, don't try to outwit the master. You had sex. I saw it on your face the second you walked through that door."

"So did I!" Paxton said, clapping.

I let out a nervous chuckle. "Are you insane? You can't tell if I've had sex by the expression on my face."

All three of them looked at me and then lost it laughing.

"Seriously, Amelia? I don't know you all that well, and even *I* could tell the second you walked in. Your face is glowing," Corina said with a grin.

"Glowing!" Paxton repeated.

"And that smile!" Waylynn said, giving me a slight push. "Baby sister, I've never seen you smile like that. You just had sex. Hot, amazing sex."

A blush rose to my face.

"You did! Ohmygawd!" Paxton squealed.

I shook my head and stared at Paxton. "What in the hell is wrong with you, Paxton? You're acting like a teenager!"

Rubbing her stomach, she took a deep breath and sat down in a rocking chair. "I don't know. It's like this pregnancy is making me stupid or something. It's weird."

Grinning, I reached for her hand. "You look beautiful. I hope Steed tells you that."

The way she smiled made my heart melt. "He does. At least three times a day. Every single morning when I wake up, and every evening when I'm standing there brushing my teeth. Your brother is amazing."

We all sighed. Well, all of us but Waylynn. She made a gagging sound. "Whatever. I want to know details. Come on, Meli. It's been so long since I've had amazing sex. I think I forgot what sex even is."

"Same here," Corina said. All of our heads snapped over to her.

"*Really*?" Waylynn said, pulling Corina down in the rocker next to Paxton.

"Oh, Lord. Waylynn, don't scare her. She's the best first grade teacher we have." Paxton said.

Shooting Paxton a smirk, Waylynn replied, "I'm only curious, that's all."

She focused back on Corina. Even I leaned in, waiting to see what my sister would hit the poor girl with. "You and Tripp didn't have sex often?"

Corina let out a chuckle. "We never had sex."

"What?" Waylynn and I both said at once. Paxton nodded like she already knew this information. I was going to have a bone to pick with my sister-in-law after this.

"Why not?" Waylynn asked.

Corina looked between all of us. "It never felt…right."

"That's cuz you had a taste of Mitchell." The moment after Paxton said it, she slapped her hands over her mouth and closed her eyes.

"Paxton!" Corina shouted.

Waylynn rubbed her hands together. "Hell's bells, this shit just got good."

I got up and went over to Corina. "Wait. You slept with Mitchell? Oh, my God! When?"

She chewed on her lip. "Um, last fall. It was sort of a one-night stand."

Waylynn shook her head. "Corina, you had a fling with Mitchell and then dated Tripp? You whore!"

Both Waylynn and I giggled as Paxton pointed at us.

"Stop that, both of you. Corina, she doesn't mean that. Tell them what happened."

Waylynn waved her hands, trying to stop giggling. "I was kidding. I'm sorry. Tell us what happened."

The poor girl wrung her hands. "Well, Paxton and I were at Cord's Place and Mitchell asked me to dance. We spent the whole evening drinking and dancing, and I have to be honest, I'd never had so much fun."

Motioning with her hands for Corina to keep going, Waylynn said, "Okay, get to the part where y'all had sex!"

Corina took a deep breath. "Mitchell asked to take me home so he knew I got there safe, and I invited him in for one more drink and before I knew it we were…we were…"

All three of us leaned in closer. "You were what?" Paxton asked.

"Oh, cheese and crackers, Paxton! You already know. He fucked me senseless. More than once."

Waylynn and I gasped.

"How in the hell can you say cheese and crackers and then 'he fucked me senseless' and make it all sound so innocent?" I asked.

Corina grinned and shrugged. "I don't know."

"Okay, so if y'all had amazing sex, what happened?" I asked. "How did you end up with Tripp?"

When she looked over at Paxton, I couldn't help the way my chest tightened. Her eyes looked so sad. I peeked at Waylynn; from the expression on her face, I knew she saw it, too.

Reaching for Corina's hands, Waylynn said, "I'm going to kick Mitchell's ass if he hurt you."

When I saw the tears forming, I asked, "What did he do?"

She dropped her head and stared at the floor. "Nothing. He pretty much acted like it never happened. He never called. When Paxton said your brothers didn't do serious, I didn't want to believe her. It didn't take me long to figure out Tripp only asked me out because Mitchell was interested in me. I never told Tripp what happened, but he seemed to know already. I think he knew my heart wasn't in the relationship. His wasn't, either. We had a ton of fun hanging out together, and he's a great friend."

"That's why y'all broke up but still hung out?" I asked.

"Yeah. I mean, I adore Tripp. He's a great guy, and I was honest and told him how I felt about Mitchell."

"What did he say?" I asked.

"He said he understood, and that we were better off as friends, which I agreed with. I honestly think that man is in love with another woman."

"Harley," the three of us said.

"Who?" Corina asked.

I chuckled. "That is a story for girls' night."

Waylynn stood, her hands on her hips. "Wait a minute! Somehow we lost track of our interrogation! Back to you and Wade having sex!"

"What?" Two booming voices said in unison, making us jump.

My heart froze. Trevor and Cord were standing on the front porch.

"I'm gonna beat his ass," Trevor said, spinning on his cowboy boots and marching to his truck, Cord two steps behind.

"Oh, shit," Waylynn, Paxton, and I whispered at once.

"What are they going to do?" Corina asked.

Waylynn shook her head. "It's probably best we don't know."

CHAPTER 33

Wade

Cord placed the beer on the bar. "You sure you don't want to sing?"

I shook my head. "Nope."

He frowned. "Come on, Wade. You ain't still sore about Trevor hitting you, are you? It was over a month ago."

Rubbing my jaw, I shot Trevor a dirty look, only to have him laugh his ass off. "My jaw hurts too much to sing."

Warm arms wrapped around my waist. "Hey there, handsome."

I spun on the stool and grinned at Amelia. Goddamn, if she wasn't the prettiest thing ever. These last few months had been the happiest of my life. I'd never dreamed I could be this happy.

"Hey." She leaned toward me, rubbing her hand dangerously close to my cock as she placed a soft kiss on my lips. Moving over to my ear, she whispered, "I'm so in need of a good orgasm."

I couldn't help the smile that spread over my face.

"Son-of-a-bitch. If my baby sister is talking dirty to you, you best put a stop to that shit right now."

Ignoring Trevor, I pulled her between my legs. "What should we do about that?"

Her teeth snagged the corner of her lip while her eyes grew dark. "We could sneak off. I've never had sex in my brother's bar."

I threw my head back and laughed. "And darlin', you're never gonna. I kind of want to keep my dick attached to my body."

She pouted cutely.

"Oh, hell no, Amelia Parker," Cord said. "No giving him pouty lips. Fuck. No. I know that look. You take this shit somewhere else. That will never happen in my bar!"

Amelia lifted her eyes to stare at Cord. Giving him a wink, she said, "How do you know it hasn't already?"

I jumped off the stool, getting between Amelia's back and Cord. I held up my hands. "It has not! I swear to you."

Cord pointed to me. "Don't forget, I know people! I will have Mitchell arrest your ass!"

Giving him a thumbs up, I threw some money on the bar and took Amelia's hand. "Come on, troublemaker. Do you want to see me with a black eye again?"

"I'm still mad you let them hit you, Wade. I'm an adult and they don't get to say who I can and cannot be with."

Making our way through the bar, I lifted my hand and waved goodbye to Mitchell. He was talking to a girl with dark hair. He waved, but I could tell he wanted to be anywhere other than where he was.

Once we got to my truck, I turned to Amelia. "I thought Mitchell liked Corina?"

Her eyes nearly popped out of her head. "He does?"

"Doesn't he?"

"I don't know! Does he?"

I shook my head. "Whatever. Come on, I've got something to show you."

"Your naked body on top of mine?"

Laughing, I took her hand. "You're in a mood this evening."

She sighed. "I had to listen to Paxton and Waylynn talk about baby shower decorations. I fell asleep and had a crazy hot dream about us in the shower."

"I've got an idea," I said, heading toward the land I'd bought a few months back.

"Where are we going?" Amelia asked.

With a wink, I replied, "You'll see soon enough."

The second I pulled down the overgrown road, Amelia started laughing.

"You naughty boy," she purred. Her hand moved over my leg to cup my already-hard dick.

I parked and undid my pants, shoving them down enough to get my cock out.

"Glove box, condom," I said as I fumbled trying to get her dress up.

"Here," Amelia panted as she pulled her panties off and tossed them in the backseat. "Let me put it on."

I handed the condom back. Amelia's hands trembled as she ripped open the package and took it out.

Reaching for her hands, I asked, "Hey, why are your hands shaking?"

She chuckled. "I have no idea! I guess I'm excited."

A wide grin covered my face. "Well, hell, if that doesn't make a guy feel good."

She slapped me on the chest, then grabbed my cock and stroked it a few times. Damn, this girl knew how to work me up. I craved her touch in some form or fashion twenty-four hours a day.

"Amelia, if you don't crawl on top of me soon, I'm going to come in your hand."

Quickly rolling the condom on, Amelia positioned herself over me. I reached between her legs and pushed my finger in, letting out a deep growl from the back of my throat when I felt how wet she was.

"I'm ready, cowboy."

Guiding her hips over me, I reached up and sucked her lip into my mouth. We both moaned when she sank all the way down on me.

"Fucking hell," I said as she rocked her hips. "God, you feel so good, darlin'."

Her long, red hair was hanging down while she moved over my cock. I reached for a handful of hair and gently pulled her head back, capturing her eyes with mine. "Amelia, you own me. Do you know that?"

With a nod, she pressed her lips to mine. She spoke between soft kisses. "You own my heart. My body. My love. You own me."

Taking her ass in my hands, I pulled her closer, causing us both to gasp at the incredible way I filled her body.

"Wade, I'm going to come," she whispered against my lips.

"Come for me, darlin'."

Amelia's head dropped back, and she let out the sweetest whimpers while she fell apart. Moving my hips faster, I felt my own orgasm build up. What I wouldn't give to feel her without a fucking condom.

Someday soon. We'd talked about it and decided Amelia would get on the pill and we'd continue to use a condom for a bit longer, just as a safety precaution. But, fuck all, I was counting down the days to when I could ride my cowgirl bareback.

Damn. The feel of her against my bare cock. I couldn't wait.

The thought alone pushed me over the edge, and I let out a long moan as I came so hard I swore I saw stars.

When we finally stopped moving, my cock twitched inside her.

"I've never felt this happy before in my entire life," she whispered against my lips.

Lacing my fingers in her hair, I held her head in my hands and stared into those beautiful blue eyes.

"Neither have I, darlin'. This is just the beginning."

Her smile made my chest tighten. I knew deep in my heart that nothing would ever pull us apart. This was the happiness we had both longed for. There wouldn't be a day that went by where I didn't thank God for the blessing of Amelia's love.

The sweat from my brow burned my eyes as we threw the hay bales onto the back of the trailer.

"Fucking hell. It's hotter than a pair of balls in skinny jeans," Trevor said.

We all stopped and stared at him.

"What in the hell did you just say?" Mitchell asked.

"I said—"

Tripp held up his hands. "Dude, don't repeat it. Please."

Cord handed everyone water and asked, "Steed, you getting excited?

I glanced over to Steed. Judging by the smile on his face, there was no doubt that he was beyond excited.

"I can't believe in a little over a month I'm going to be a dad again."

"Y'all pick out any names for the little guy?" Tripp asked.

"We've got a few ideas. Of course, Chloe thinks we need to name the baby after her goat, Patches."

Everyone laughed.

Trevor sat down on the trailer. "So, Wade, tell us what life is like for you."

My eyes scanned across all five Parker brothers. Each of them staring, waiting for me to fuck up.

"Wonderful. I don't think I've ever been this happy."

They all smiled.

Thank God. Right answer.

Mitchell grinned. "I don't think I've ever seen Amelia so happy. All we ask is that you treat her right, dude. I'm happy to see my sister is in love."

I nodded. "I do love her. I want y'all to know that. I've never loved anyone like I love Amelia. She's my everything."

Trevor slapped me on the back. "I had no doubt you would make her happy."

Cord stood up and groaned. "Shit, my gloves have a hole in them. Trevor, you got extras?"

"I've got some in the backseat," I said, motioning toward my truck.

"Thanks," Cord said.

Tripp stood and looked west. "Damn, those clouds are building. Looks like another storm is brewing."

"Shit, if we get any more rain, the river's gonna crest over the bank," Trevor said.

I rubbed the cold bottle of water against the back of my neck.

"Ah, Wade? You mind stepping over here?" Cord asked.

"You can't find the gloves?" I asked, making my way to him. He wore a pissed-off look.

"What's wrong?" I asked.

He pointed. "Dude, you better hope those are my sister's. Then again, you better hope they're not."

Furrowing my brows, I said, "What in the hell are you talking about?"

He grabbed my T-shirt and pulled me around the door, pointed to Amelia's panties.

The memory of us fucking in the truck hit me, and I couldn't help but smile.

"Dude, I know you are not smiling about this."

I dropped my smile and reached for the panties, shoving them into my pocket. Turning to Cord, I said, "They're your sister's. And I smile because she makes me happy. Would you rather her be with some asshole who uses her and then moves on to the next girl? I love your sister, Cord, and, yes, we have sex. I had sisters, and I can imagine that pisses you off. But y'all have to stop threatening me. I'm gonna be honest with you, I plan on asking Amelia to marry me some day so you better get used to the idea that we're together in that way."

Cord's mouth dropped open.

"Dude, I respect the hell out of you for standing up to me. You're right, Amelia is an adult, and we need to realize that she isn't walking around wearing a chastity belt."

"Thank you."

He pointed at me. "Next time, though, y'all pick up after you do the deed. Christ Almighty, I didn't need to see that."

Cord walked off, mumbling something under his breath.

A crack of thunder rumbled in the distance.

"Let's go! We need to get this hay up to the barn before another storm hits," Trevor called out as he reached for a bale and tossed it up on the trailer.

Tripp climbed into the ranch truck as the rest of us loaded up the hay. The breeze coming in from the approaching storm felt nice and actually made us work a little faster.

After everything was loaded, we headed to the barn and unloaded it all.

"Y'all getting hungry?" Waylynn asked.

Tripp wiped his brow. "Hell, yeah. Mom got something going?"

"Yep. Roast, veggies, fresh bread that Chloe helped her make. Oh, and Aunt Vi's made her sweet potato soufflé. I'm pretty sure there is whiskey in it, though."

Steed jumped off the pile of hay and fist pumped the air. "Yes! Damn, I love that stuff."

"Come on, that storm's coming in and from what the weather is saying, it's gonna be bad. Farther up the river they've gotten five inches of rain already. We're under a tornado watch."

I turned to Trevor. "Some of the horses are out in the north pasture. We should bring them in, at least the mares and foals."

He nodded and rubbed the back of his neck in a nervous way.

"Wade and I will ride out and gather them up. We won't be long," Trevor announced.

"I'll go with you," Mitchell said.

"You need any more help, Trev?" Steed asked.

He shook his head. "Nah, the three of us can get it. Just don't eat all the damn food."

CHAPTER 34

Wade

The rain was coming down so hard it stung my face as I rode alongside Trevor and Mitchell.

Trevor pointed and shouted, "There they are! Get them all tied on the lead and bring them in."

We followed him over to the group of horses. The lightning was insane. I don't think I'd ever seen the sky light up so much. Every time the thunder cracked, a foal would try to take off.

"Is that it?" Mitchell asked, ducking when lightning hit close by.

"Fucking hell. We need to get back. I can hear the river coming up."

We turned to see the Frio River swollen over its banks.

"It's flooding fast. Let's get out of here," Trevor said. He kicked his horse and we started trotting back at a slow enough pace that the foals could keep up.

Mitchell rode to the side, and I rode in the back. Looking to my left, I saw a foal caught in the water.

I quickly caught up to Mitchell. "There's one left behind. I'm going for her."

He turned and looked over his shoulder. "Fuck! The river's coming up too fast, Wade."

"I'll rope her in. Just keep going."

"Wade! Wade!" Mitchell called after me, but I kept heading to the foal.

"Just keep going! I'll catch up!" I yelled back.

Getting my rope ready, I swung it a few times and got it over her head. Tying it around the horn of my saddle, I kicked for Marley to back up and pull the foal out of the water. Once I got her out, I jumped down and checked her. Poor thing was so exhausted from trying to swim. She could hardly move.

"Come on, baby. Marley will carry you back."

Lightning hit a tree causing me and the horses to jump. The last thing I heard was the sound of rushing water coming from somewhere I couldn't see.

CHAPTER 35

Amelia

I stood on the back porch waiting for any sign of him. My chest felt so tight I could hardly breathe.

"Amelia, come inside. The lightning is bad."

Shaking my head, I replied, "He's out in this, Daddy. I'm not coming in until he is standing in front of me."

My father's warm hands squeezed my shoulders. "He's fine, sweetheart. He may just be down at the barn, not wanting to get out in this to come up to the house."

With a nod, I replied, "Probably."

In my heart I knew he wasn't at the barn. Something was wrong. Terribly wrong, and I couldn't shake the awful feeling.

Trevor walked out and stood next to me. "I'm going to drive down to the barn and see if he's there."

I turned to my brother, hugging him tight. "Thank you, Trevor! Please bring him back up here. Please."

I knew he could hear the desperation in my voice. When I stepped back, he looked me in the eyes. "I will, Meli. I will."

Mitchell was now next to Trevor. "I'm coming with you."

My hands covered my mouth as I watched them dash out into the pouring rain and into the ranch truck.

Someone reached for my hand. I turned to find Chloe smiling up at me.

"He's okay, Aunt Meli. He probably didn't want to leave all the baby horses in this storm."

My chin trembled, and I fought to keep my fear down. I dropped down to look her in the eyes and grinned. "I think you're right. If I know Wade, he's singing them all a song right now so they won't be scared."

Chloe's eyes lit up. "Yes! I bet he is. I'm gonna go draw him a picture for when he gets back."

I kissed her forehead. "Yes! That's a wonderful idea, pumpkin," I said, forcing the words.

Chloe dashed back into the house. I sat on the porch, pulled my knees to my chest and closed my eyes. My father was still there, standing next to me.

"Amelia, come back into the house."

His stern voice made me stand and mindlessly follow. I sat on the love seat in the family room and watched as Chloe drew a picture for Wade.

An hour passed, and Trevor and Mitchell hadn't returned. Now I was worried about them. Cord paced back and forth before he stopped at the window.

"They're back."

I jumped up and ran past everyone, into the kitchen. Mitchell and Trevor walked in, but Wade wasn't with them. The looks on their faces told me something was terribly wrong. Mitchell immediately took out his work cell.

"Pax, why don't you take Chloe into the living room," Steed said.

"Come on, pumpkin, let's go see if we can beat Aunt Vi again."

I couldn't bear the thought of looking at Chloe. She was smart enough to know she was being sent away for a reason.

Trevor held his cowboy hat in his hands. The water dripped off him and onto the floor. Mitchell took a deep breath, and I knew that for as long as I lived I would never forget the look on his face.

Tears formed in my eyes and rolled down my cheeks. "Where is he?"

Mitchell placed his hands on my arms. I could see the fear in his eyes and it caused my entire body to shake.

"He wasn't at the barn, but Marley came running up. Wade wasn't riding her."

My hands covered my mouth. "What? What do you mean, he wasn't riding her?"

Trevor sat down and buried his face in his hands.

"We tried to drive to the north pasture but the entire area is flooded. There's no sign of Wade anywhere. We think…he might… he may have gotten…"

He closed his eyes and took a deep breath.

I shook my head and dropped my hands. "Don't you dare say it, Mitchell Parker! Don't you dare say it!" My body trembled even harder, hysteria overtaking me. My knees gave out, and Mitchell caught me. He brought me over to a chair.

Tears streamed as I felt my mother's arms around me. Leaning against her, I looked at my brother with pleading eyes. "Please, don't say it, Mitchell. Please."

A tear trailed down his cheek. I watched it until he reached up and brushed it away.

"Amelia, I'm so sorry, baby, but the flood waters might have taken him by surprise. I've already called it in, and we're going to start searching."

Shaking my head frantically, I cried, "No! No!"

My mother pulled me against her. I buried my face into her chest and screamed Wade's name. "God, please don't do this to us!"

All I remember after that was blackness overtaking me as I leaned against my mom for support.

Twenty-four hours later...

I sat on the roof of the old house Wade had bought, staring over the still-flooded Frio River. Each breath hurt more than the last.

He wasn't gone. I felt it in my heart.

Paxton walked up and handed me a blanket. I forced a half smile and wrapped it around my shoulders.

Steed had brought a chair for Paxton to sit in. I sat on the same blanket Wade had used for our first picnic.

"He's stuck somewhere, hurt," I said with a trembling voice. "He just can't get back to us. That's all. He's...he's not...he's not gone, Paxton. He promised me he would never leave me. He's not gone!"

I felt someone sit next to me, and opened my eyes to see Corina. She took my hands. Her smile was hopeful. "Believe what's in your heart, Amelia. Reach out to him. *Help* him find his way home."

I could hardly see her through my blurry eyes. "You think he's okay?"

She nodded. "A love like what y'all have is strong. I know Wade, and I know he would fight with everything he has to come back to you. Don't. Give. Up."

"I won't," I said, my voice sounding weak. "I won't."

Corina pulled me to her and let me cry as she ran her hand over my head. "Shh, it's going to be okay."

Paxton squeezed my shoulder. "She's right, Meli. Don't give up."

I wasn't sure how long we sat on that roof. Steed insisted Paxton leave to get something to eat. Corina asked Steed to have one of the boys bring food to me. She totally understood why I needed to be here. She never once told me to give up hope. In fact, she did the opposite. She kept insisting Wade was fine.

The sound of footsteps caused me to open my eyes. I was still on the blanket, but my head was resting on Corina's lap as she played with my hair. Mitchell bent down and gave me a weak smile.

"Hey, I brought y'all some food. Will you eat something for me, Meli?"

"Of course she will," Corina said. "She'll need her strength to hug Wade when he gets back."

Mitchell's eyes darted over to Corina. "May I speak with you, please?"

I sat up and took the food from Mitchell as Corina followed him. They stopped not far from where I stood. I couldn't take my eyes off of them. Mitchell seemed angry. Maybe he felt like she was giving me false hope.

I took a bite of sandwich and turned my focus back on the river. The sun was beginning to set and the clouds were a beautiful orange and pink, so different from yesterday's storm-filled sky. I glanced back to Corina. She looked upset. I made my way closer to where she stood with Mitchell.

"I can't help it that you don't believe in love, Mitchell Parker. I do! And I'm going to be by her side until Wade walks through that door!"

"If he got swept away by the flood waters there is a good chance he may not have survived, Corina."

My eyes closed. A visual of my Wade being swept away hit me and I squeezed my eyes tight.

"He's not gone," I whispered. "He promised me, Mitchell."

"Amelia, sweetheart. I know how much Wade loves you. I want to believe he's not gone, too, but you have to realize there is a chance he might not have made it."

"Mitchell!" Corina gasped.

"Stay out of this, Corina. It's none of your business."

I sucked in a breath, and pushed my brother away from me. "Don't you dare say that to her. She's been here for me. She's my friend and you cannot push her away. It's your own damn guilt talking, Mitchell! You let him go after that foal! You didn't try and stop him! You haven't found him! You're supposed to be able to find him! You promised you'd bring him back to me and you lied. You. Lied. To. Me."

A look of horror moved over my brother's face. "What?"

"Go away, Mitchell. I don't want you here."

"Amelia, I'm only…"

"Go away!" I shouted.

My brother stepped back like I'd slapped him, looking between Corina and me. His shoulders slumped, and he slowly turned to leave. Corina walked after him, pulling him to a stop.

"Mitchell," she said softly.

He stopped. "I'm sorry I said that to you. Please, don't leave her alone. I'll bring back some cots if she refuses to leave."

When I heard his footsteps going down the stairs, I faced Corina. We both were hanging onto the dream that Wade would come back, but we also knew that what Mitchell had said was possibly true.

Corina walked over to me quickly. She took me in her arms and let me cry.

This time she didn't tell me everything was going to be okay. I knew in that moment that neither of us could be sure what the future held.

CHAPTER 36

Amelia

Corina and I sat on the roof until the last orange cloud turned dark.

"We should probably head back to the house," I said, standing.

Corina reached for her phone and sent a text off before she helped me fold up the blanket.

"Just leave the chair," I said, sounding defeated.

Using a flashlight that Mitchell had left, Corina led the way down the steps. My heart felt as if it was being ripped out piece by piece while we made our way through the house, down the steps, and to Corina's car.

She opened the passenger door for me. Before getting in, I looked at her.

"Why are you here? Doing this for me?"

Her lips pressed together. "My father died when I was young, very young. But I remember seeing my mother sit in a rocking chair for days. Her heart was so broken and no one was there for her. I was, but I was so young I don't think I truly understood her pain. I know if it was me and the man I loved was lost out there, I'd want someone next to me. Just to know they were there if I needed them."

My eyes filled with tears. "I see why Paxton adores you. I'll never forget your kindness, Corina. Never."

She gave me a sweet smile. "I'm not giving up hope. I don't think you should either. What does your heart tell you?"

I swallowed hard and tried to speak between sobs. "I don't know. It's too broken."

Corina took me in her arms and gave me a good hug. "Let's get you home to your family."

It looked like every single light was on in the house. I was positive all of my brothers were staying here tonight.

"Why don't you stay the night?" I asked as Corina and I walked up the steps to the front door.

"Oh, I don't have anything to sleep in, and I wouldn't want to be a burden."

I laced my arm with hers. "You can borrow something of mine, and we have plenty of room. I would really love it if you would stay."

She nodded. "Okay. I'll stay."

"Stay where?"

We both turned to see Mitchell standing at the door. "Here. I've asked Corina to stay the night. Would you let Mom know? We're going up to my room to get her something to wear."

My brother's eyes lit up. He glanced at Corina and smiled before heading into the house. No one was in the main living room so we were able to get upstairs unnoticed.

Flipping through my drawers, I found a set of sleepwear I hadn't even taken the tags off yet.

"Are these okay?" I held up the sleeveless, navy blue shirt and matching Capri pajama pants.

"Yes. Thank you so much."

"You can use my bathroom. I've got shampoo and everything. The guest room is right next door to me. On the other side is Mitchell's room."

I wiggled my brows, and she shook her head at me. "Don't even go there. I'm here for you, not him. Now, why don't you hop in the shower and get ready for bed. You need sleep, Amelia."

I nodded in agreement, stopping when my mother walked into my room.

"You're home. Do you need something to eat?"

"No. I'm tired, and I think I'll take a quick shower and head to bed. Did Mitchell tell you Corina was staying the night?"

My mother nodded and glanced over to Corina. "I've got the bed turned down for you, sweetheart. If you need anything, you'll let me or John know?"

"Yes, of course. Thank you for letting me stay."

My mother walked over to Corina, kissed her cheek, and whispered something.

I grabbed my phone and headed into the shower. I spent the next thirty minutes standing under steaming hot water crying until I had no tears left to cry

I would never leave you, darlin'.

The memory of Wade's voice made my body tremble.

I'm coming, Amelia. I'm coming.

My eyes snapped open, and I fought to catch my breath.

I glanced over to the clock to find it was just after five in the morning.

My door opened and I sat straight up in bed. The light in the hall was on, illuminating Corina as she walked into my room. She ran over and jumped on my bed.

"Get up! Amelia, get up! Mitchell has Wade!"

My head was spinning. "What? Mitchell's sleeping."

She shook her head. "After you fell asleep he left again and went to help with the search party along with Tripp, Cord, and Steed. He got a call on his radio. Wade is okay! Mitchell is bringing him here as we speak!"

I stared at her in disbelief. Afraid to believe her words.

"He's okay?" Tears streamed down my face. My heart raced as I waited for her to answer.

She took my hands in hers and stood, pulling me up. "Yes! He was able to find his way to a house! No one was home, and he had no idea where he was. The flood waters took him about forty miles downstream. Wade told Mitchell he had no clothes on. Everything had been stripped off of him. He managed to find something to wrap around himself and he slept on the porch until someone finally came home! They gave him clothes and fed him and the foal. They tried your cell and Trevor's, then the police. They patched the call through to Mitchell!"

I reached for my phone. "Oh my God! I forgot to plug it in! How could I forget to plug it in?"

I felt sick to my stomach. Wade had tried to call me, and I wasn't there for him.

Corina took my face in her hands. "Don't. He's okay. He's on his way back to you. Smile! Jump up and down! Scream, do something!"

I reached up and took her hands. We both started jumping around my bed like silly schoolgirls. Paxton walked in, her hands on her stomach.

"What are you two doing? You're going to wake up Chloe!"

"Wade's okay!" I yelled out. "He's okay!"

Paxton covered her mouth and screamed. "I'd climb up there and jump with y'all if I wasn't so pregnant."

Corina and I jumped off the bed and took Paxton's hands. We danced around the room, laughing and crying.

"He's here! He's here!" my mother cried out, running into my room. "Mitchell is pulling down the driveway now."

I raced past everyone.

"Slow down, Amelia Parker, or you'll break your neck!" my father cried out from the bottom of the stairs.

I giggled and jumped down the last three steps. I threw the door open and came to a stop on the porch. The passenger side door of Mitchell's patrol car opened and Wade stepped out.

Crying out his name, I ran down the steps. He had a huge smile on his poor, cut and bruised face. I was running as fast as I could, aiming to slam into Wade's body, when Trevor grabbed me.

"Whoa, hold on there, Meli. He has broken ribs."

I sucked in a breath. "Oh, my God! Wade!"

Trevor slowly set me down. "I know you want to attack him, but he's in bad shape."

"I'll be gentle, I swear. I just need to touch him, feel him, to know this isn't a dream."

Trevor let me go and I walked up to Wade. His entire face was covered in scrapes and cuts.

"Oh, God," I said, placing my hands on his beautiful face. "You're here. You didn't leave me."

Wade closed his eyes for a second before opening them and looking at me. It was still dark out, but I could see those breathtaking grays. "I'm so sorry you've been through hell."

Reaching up on my toes, I gently kissed him. "I love you. I love you so much. I'm so sorry this happened to you."

His hand wrapped around my waist and pulled me to him. "I survived because of you, darlin'. You were the reason I kept fighting."

I buried my face into his chest. "You're home. Thank you, God, for bringing him home to me."

CHAPTER 37

Wade

I couldn't breathe. My body had never hurt so bad. The water rushed all around me as I tried like hell to hold the horse and keep my head above the water.

"Wade! Don't leave me. You're leaving me!"

I forced myself to swim to her voice. "I'm not leaving you, Amelia! I'm here!" I screamed, climbing out of the water.

"Wade! Wade, help me!"

Turning, I watched in horror as my sister was swept away by the flood waters.

"No! Grace, no!"

Sitting up in bed, I grabbed at my chest and sucked in a deep breath.

"Wade, are you okay?"

The feel of Amelia's hand on my arm calmed me, the nightmare slipping from my mind. Or at least, I pretended it did.

"Yeah, just a bad dream," I mumbled.

Her blue eyes looked so sad. "Do you want to talk about it?"

Forcing a smile, I placed my hand on the side of her face. "I'm okay, darlin'. I promise."

Her eyes closed, and I knew she wanted to say something else, but she didn't. Pulling her to me, I held her tightly while she drifted back to sleep. I spent the rest of the night with my eyes fixed on one spot, forcing myself not to fall asleep.

I heard muffled talking as I sat on the back porch and stared out. The last few weeks had been hell. I was ready to put it behind me, if only my mind would let me.

"Mind if I sit with you?" Mitchell asked as he took a seat in the rocker next to me.

"Not at all. Bored with the baby shower?"

He let out a gruff laugh. "I'm happy for Steed and Paxton, but I'm going to kill my sisters for coming up with this whole co-ed shower shit."

"Yeah, Amelia's been pretty excited. I feel bad they put it off because of me."

Mitchell tipped his beer back and waved off his hand. "Don't be. It's keeping Paxton's mind off of things, and she isn't due for another couple weeks."

I finished my beer and set it on the table. "Can't believe it's almost the end of July."

"Wade, if you need to talk, you know I'm here, right?" Mitchell asked.

I felt the anger building as I turned to face him. "What did Amelia say to you?"

He looked at me. "Nothing. She hasn't said a word, at least not to me."

I sighed and sat back in the chair. I needed to let this damn anger go.

"Wade, I'm a cop. I see people dealing with post-traumatic stress all the time. Hell, I've had to deal with it myself. It's okay to talk to someone. Have you talked to Amelia at least?"

"No. She's worried, though." I pushed my hand through my hair and squeezed my eyes shut for a few seconds.

"I hate that I'm worrying her, Mitchell. It's just, every single time I close my eyes I relive it. I thought I was never going to see her again and the idea of leaving her heartbroken nearly broke me. It was the only thing that kept me fighting. I refused to let someone tell her I was dead."

"You didn't want to break her heart, but don't you think you're doing that now by not letting her in? Not letting her help you deal with what you went through?"

I nodded, knowing he was right. We sat for a few minutes in silence.

"I was so fucking scared. The water came out of nowhere and swept me off my feet. It wasn't even that deep, but I couldn't win against the force. Somehow I was able to stay out of the main river. Someone up above was watching out for me. I truly believe not getting swept into the middle saved my life."

"I can't imagine what it was like. And you kept a hold of that damn foal the entire time!"

With a chuckle, I replied, "Poor thing. How's she doing? I haven't seen her in a week."

"Vet said she's healing up nicely. I don't know how you did it, dude, but you saved that horse's life."

"I know she belongs to the ranch, but I'd love to have her. We kind of have a…bond."

Mitchell laughed. "I'll say. The vet says when you stop by she perks up."

"Yeah, well, she is a miracle, as well. She honestly should have died. How I was able to hold on to her in the water or have her lay next to me on that porch for so long, I'll never know. I think we both saved the other one's life, if I'm being honest. I had Amelia to live for but this little horse was depending on me just as much as I needed her."

"Amelia's been to see her almost every day. Vet said she actually sat in the stall with both the filly and the mom and wrote for a few hours."

I smiled. "Sounds like her."

"She loves you, Wade. Don't shut her out."

I knew Mitchell was right. "I know, man. I won't."

We sat for a few more minutes in silence until I turned to Mitchell. "What's going on with you and Corina?"

His head snapped to me. "What?"

"You like her. She likes you. What in the hell is wrong with the two of you?"

Fear filled his eyes. "I do like her. A lot. Matter of fact, I can't stop thinking about her. Her smile. Her laugh. The way her cheeks flush when…"

His voice trailed off, and we both let out a chuckle. "So, what's holding you back? I mean, first it was Tripp, but they haven't dated in months. Aren't you worried she'll get tired of waiting for you to get off your ass and ask her out?"

"Way to get right to it, Wade."

I shrugged. "Hey, I'm just shooting straight like you've done with me. All I'm saying is if you wait too long, she's going to move on."

He scrubbed his hands down his face. "Christ, I know. I'm not sure if I'm the settling down kind of guy. I mean, I can't tell you the last time I was actually with a girl. I've fooled around with some, but I've only slept with one other girl since that night last fall when I was with Corina."

"Damn, you're already practically settled down. You do know it's mid-July, right?"

Laughing, he rubbed the back of his neck. "I don't know. The girl oozes innocence, and I'm not exactly squeaky clean when it comes to sleeping around. I've got a pretty dangerous job. How do I know if she wants to worry like that? She probably wants kids right away. That is something I'm not interested in right now."

"At all? And have you asked her or are you just assuming she wants kids right away?" I asked in a surprised tone.

"I don't know... I don't see myself like Steed. Don't get me wrong, I'd do anything for Chloe. I love that little girl, but one of my own? Hell, no. And, no, I haven't asked her, but all chicks want kids."

Mitchell looked away, and I knew he was struggling with what his head was saying and what his heart was feeling.

"Hey! Here y'all are. You're missing the fun," Amelia said. "More people just showed up so now we have enough to play the couples' game Waylynn wanted to play.

Mitchell groaned as he stood. "Jesus Christ, Amelia. Games? No one likes to play games."

She shot him a dirty look. "You don't like to play games, but everyone else does. Come on, Waylynn needs a partner, and we have enough now that Corina and Philip showed up."

I nearly ran into Mitchell as he came to an abrupt stop. "Who's Philip?"

Amelia glanced at me and then back to Mitchell. "The guy Corina's with."

Oh, hell.

"She's...she's dating someone?"

Her eyes darted over to me, then back to Mitchell. "Um, I don't know, I guess they've gone out a few times. I'm not sure how serious it is or anything. They might just be friends."

Mitchell walked right past Amelia. I stopped next to her, leaning down to kiss her cheek. "I was just telling him if he waited too long with Corina, she was going to move on."

"Ugh! Why is he being so stubborn? Why can't men just be open with their feelings? Drives me nuts."

When she started to head back into the house, I reached for her hand and pulled her back to me. Mitchell was right. I needed to let her in. I owed it to her.

"I'm sorry I've been distant. The last few weeks have been hard, and I thought I could handle it on my own."

Amelia's lips pressed tightly together. She waited for me to keep going, so I did.

"I keep re-living what happened to me. Sometimes I'm afraid to close my eyes at night. Something as simple as your parents' pool water falling over the edge of the hot tub can trigger it, and I can't even begin to tell you what it does to me. I feel like I can't breathe, and it scares the living shit out of me. I'm sorry I didn't tell you sooner, darlin'. Guess I didn't want you to think I couldn't handle things on my own."

Her mouth fell open. "Wade Adams, this thing we have between us." She used her finger to point back and forth. "This is a partnership. During the good and the bad. I know you've been waking up having nightmares, and I suspected there were some other things you were dealing with, as well. I didn't want to push you, but I've already done some research and...well..."

She closed her eyes and shook her head.

Tugging her hand to make her look at me, I said, "Hey, I'm talking to you. You talk to me."

Amelia chewed on her lip. "I'm wondering if the accident didn't also bring out some feelings from your parents' and sisters' death. The other night, you were having a nightmare and you called out your sister's name."

My heart felt like it jumped to my throat. "I did?"

She nodded and reached for my hands. "I also think you holding onto that foal the entire time was your subconscious way of trying to save your family. In that moment, that baby foal was your family and you weren't letting go."

A sense of calm and clarity overtook me. Amelia had no idea what she'd just given me in those few words.

"You need to know that no matter what, I'm here by your side. If you want to talk to me, or my father, the pastor, a therapist… I will be there by your side. One hundred percent."

How in the hell did I get so lucky with this girl?

"You amaze me, Amelia Parker."

The left side of her mouth rose. "Oh, yeah? I bet I can do a few other things later tonight to amaze you."

"You're on."

I took her hand, and we made our way back into the house. Waylynn was walking back in from the main living room with a frown.

"Hey, what's wrong?" Amelia asked.

Waylynn looked at her sister and shook her head. "Mitchell stormed out of here. He left. Walked over to Steed and Paxton and told them he had to get to work and left! I know damn well he is not on call."

My eyes shot across the room to the real reason Mitchell left Steed and Paxton's baby shower.

Corina and her date, Philip.

CHAPTER 38

Amelia

The heat from the August sun was beating down as I carried the cans of paint into the house. Wade had found an outlet to help with his stress: remodeling the old house. It also helped that he'd started to see a therapist once a week. In a few short weeks, I'd seen such a change in him. The nightmares were slowing down, and Wade had actually gotten into the pool with me yesterday.

"The entire house has been rewired," Wade said as he gave my folks and Aunt Vi the tour.

"Lord, I'm seeing some parties we can have at this house!" Vi said.

Wade and my father rushed over to take the five-gallon cans of paint out of my hands.

Vi was going from room to room. "You could rent this out as an event venue. Can you imagine weddings in this place? Oh, how I love Texas! John, I must find a house so I can officially move here."

My father pulled his head back. "You haven't officially moved here, Vi?"

She looked at him like he had lost his mind. "Of course not. I still need to sell my house in California."

"So, that storage unit we bought and stored all of your stuff in, you living in my house for the last five months, that's not you moving to Texas, Vi?"

Vi let out a roar of laughter. "Hell, no. That was me dipping my toes into the water to see how I liked it."

The smile on my mother's face said it all. Aunt Vi was a hoot and I knew my parents loved having her in their house, but they were ready for Vi to move on and settle down in her own home.

Wade and I exchanged glances. "Actually, we were thinking we would live in this house and rent out the main house. It's huge. The perfect house to throw garden parties, tea parties. Any kind of party you could think of."

Vi's eyes grew wide. "You don't say? You know I don't want to buy. This girl doesn't want to be tied down. You never know when I'll meet a man." She wiggled her brows and my father groaned.

"It's for rent! It would be perfect for you, Aunt Vi!"

She tapped her finger on her chin. "Well, let me think about it."

"It has a wine cellar and an enclosed area around the pool. Perfect for pool parties."

An almost evil smile grew across my aunt's face. "You had me at wine cellar and skinny-dipping parties."

I chuckled. "I didn't say anything about skinny dipping!"

She winked, and my father quickly said, "So, it's settled. Vi's renting the main house on Wade's property to have her little orgy parties."

"Oh, John!" my mother said, hitting him in the stomach.

"You're just jealous, little brother," Aunt Vi said.

Lifting his brows, my father said, "Yeah. Okay, Vi. Let's go with that. That's exactly what I am, my green-eyed monster rearing its ugly head over a bunch of old farts running around naked and jumping into a pool. No, thank you. Come on, Wade. Finish showing us the house and we'll head on back and have lunch."

"Daddy, I've got a lot of painting to do, and the girl who is going to wallpaper the parlor is coming tomorrow. I need to have the trim finished."

My father gave me a look that said I wasn't going to win, I sighed. "Fine, but then Wade and I are coming back over here and he gets the rest of the week off!"

"You want me to give him the week off just so you'll come have lunch with us?" my father asked with a half-hearted laugh.

"The faster the house gets done, the faster I move out."

"That brings us that much closer to an empty house," he said aloud. "Meli, between you and Vi moving on, you just made yourself a deal."

After the tour, we headed back outside. My mother stopped me behind everyone else. She pushed me out at arm's length while she scanned me and grinned like a fool.

"Being in love looks good on you, Amelia Renee."

I could feel my cheeks heating. "It feels good."

"How is Wade doing?"

Peeking at where the other three were walking across the lawn, I said, "He's doing really good. In a way, the flood has helped him."

She pinched her brows. "How?"

"Well, I think it brought to the forefront some underlying issues Wade was trying to bury and not deal with."

"His family?" she asked, sadness in her eyes.

I nodded.

My mother hooked her arm with mine and started walking. "I'm glad he listened and talked with someone," she said.

"Me, too."

"And I'm very glad you came up with the idea of Vi moving into the main house. I love her, but Lord, she is driving me to drink. I told your daddy I wasn't sure how much more I could take."

Giggling, we crossed the front porch. "Just think, now all you have to do is get rid of Waylynn, and you and Daddy can have your own little private naked party in an empty house."

She grinned. "Bring on the Viagra! Oh, who am I kidding. Your father doesn't need that. He's still a young stud."

I shrieked and covered my ears. "Mom, really? Now I've got the visual. Yuck!" I gagged a few times and my mother laughed her ass off as she walked toward their truck.

"What's wrong?" Wade asked, holding open the passenger side door to his truck.

"My mother just told me my father was a young stallion who could still get it up without Viagra."

Horror moved over his face as Wade glanced at my father. "You could've taken that with you to the grave, darlin'."

He took my hand and helped me up into the truck. I grabbed his T-shirt and pulled him to me. I gave him a quick kiss on the lips and said, "If I have to live in this nightmare, I need company."

When we reached my parents' house we pulled around back and parked behind my father. The first thing I saw was Chloe with Patches.

"Why does Chloe have Patches tied up to the tree?" I asked.

Wade opened his door. "I'm not sure."

Jumping out of the truck, we headed over toward Chloe. She looked up and flashed us—well, Wade—a huge smile.

"Wade!" Running right past me, she jumped into his arms.

"Your ribs, Wade!" I said.

He lifted Chloe and did a little spin while she cried out in glee.

"Aww, this little girl weighs nothing! Besides, they're almost all healed up."

"Chloe, sweetie, why is Patches tied up?" I asked.

"She's tied up 'cause she ate Grammy's flowers so I had to put her in time out. Mommy's here with Aunt Waylynn picking out colors for Aunt Waylynn's dance studio."

My mouth fell open. "Oh, hell no."

"Oh, hell no!" Chloe repeated.

"No, shit. Chloe don't say that!"

"Don't say *shit* or *hell*?"

Wade attempted to hide his smile.

"Don't say either."

Chloe tilted her head. "But you said them both. If you said them, why can't I say them?"

"Fuck," I whispered as I looked away. Of course, it was still loud enough for my niece to hear.

"Hell! Shit! Fuck!"

"Chloe Lynn Parker! You do not say those words!" I said sternly as Wade put Chloe down and started toward the main barn.

"I see your shoulders moving, Wade Adams! You're going to abandon me like this?"

Wade lifted his hand. "I see Trevor! Got to ask him…a question."

"You're a terrible boyfriend, Wade Adams. I can hear you laughing!"

"Hell, shit, fuck!" Chloe shouted.

I spun around and pointed to Chloe. "Now you listen here, young lady. You are old enough to know that those are bad words. Adult bad words."

"How come you can use them?"

I opened my mouth to speak and nothing came out at first. I looked for my parents but they must have already gone into the house.

"I'm an adult. That's why." My hands landed on my hips. I was positive I looked and sounded more like a child than an adult.

"But if they're bad words, how come you say them, Aunt Meli?"

Nothing. I had nothing.

"Go get Patches, and we'll bring her down to the barn."

"You didn't say how come you can say bad words."

Bending down, I looked directly in her eyes. "I didn't answer you because I don't have a good reason. You're right. They are bad words, and I shouldn't be using them. It's just sometimes, adults get angry or super excited and they use bad words to express how they feel."

She crinkled her nose. "Why?"

I shrugged. "I don't know, but I'm sorry. Now, I don't want you using those words, young lady. One reason is your father would be very upset with me if he knew you learned such bad words from me. The other reason is it's not a polite way to speak."

She nodded.

"So, it's our secret and you promise to never say them again, right?"

Chloe crossed her heart "I promise!"

"Good! Now let's get Patches to the barn and see what your Aunt Waylynn and mommy are up to."

"Okay!" Chloe said, skipping over to Patches. "She wasn't really tied around the tree! I tricked her!"

I held Chloe's hand as we made our way to the barn. Trevor and Wade were in Trevor's office talking about what type of grass to plant in the south pasture. Chloe and I put Patches in her stall, fed her some grain, and made our way up to the house.

The moment we walked into the kitchen, I noticed Paxton's face. Something was off. Poor thing was two weeks overdue and the doctor was finally going to induce her tomorrow.

"Hey, what's up, y'all?" I asked.

Waylynn looked up at us with her hair a complete mess and her mascara smudged under her eyes. Chloe and I both jumped. "Oh, my

God!" I shouted. "What's wrong? You look like hel…um. You look bad."

Good save!

Giving me the middle finger, Waylynn said, "I can't decide on colors."

I sat at the table and pulled the swatches closer. "Okay, we'll narrow it down to two you like."

"She can't," Paxton said, sounding exhausted. "She has it narrowed down to ten."

My eyes shot up. "Ten!"

Paxton frowned and slowly nodded. "Yep. Ten."

I glared at Waylynn. "You're making our poor sister-in-law sit here and deal with this shiiii…um…stuff?"

I glanced over to Chloe who was sitting next to Paxton, smiling all innocently.

"I'm narrowing it down to three and you'll pick," I said to Waylynn.

"What!" my sister gasped. "But!"

Holding up my hand, I said, "No! This is what we are doing. Waylynn, these are all green. Just different shades."

"Aunt Waylynn, can I take dance lessons from you?" Chloe asked.

Taking Chloe's hand, Waylynn said, "Of course, you can! You'll be my first student!"

"Yay!" Chloe jumped out of her seat and hugged Waylynn.

Staring at the paint samples, I picked the three I thought would look best with the natural light and the wood tones in the studio. I slid them over to Waylynn.

"There. Pick one."

"Where were you the last two hours?" Paxton asked. Exhaustion had clearly overtaken her a long time ago.

"Two hours?" I asked, stunned.

"Let's see. This green might be a bit too light. This one looks more like a sage. I'm kind of thinking I like this one. Yeah. This is the one."

"Are you freaking kidding me right now, Waylynn?" Paxton said. "That is the very first color I picked out and said would be perfect!"

Waylynn looked at the paint sample and then Paxton. "It is? Are you sure?"

Letting out a frustrated growl, Paxton stood and headed to the sink. "You need help, Waylynn Parker!"

"Is that your color, Aunt Waylynn?" Chloe asked.

Waylynn was staring at it, and I knew if she contemplated too long she'd pick something else.

I grabbed it from her hand. "That's the color. Bam. Decision made."

Waylynn stared at the card in my hand and made a face. "I don't know. Maybe I should look at blue."

"No!" Paxton cried out. "Please. Don't. Look. At. Blue. For the love of God, just go with that color…ohhh. Oh, wow." Paxton bent over as best as a full-term pregnant woman could bend.

Waylynn held up her hands and stood. "Fine. Fine. If you like the color that much I'll go with it."

"Oh, dear God."

Waylynn huffed. "Okay, Paxton, I think you're overreacting. I get that was the first color you picked, but it's a big decision."

Paxton held onto her stomach and started taking deep breaths. I jumped up.

"Is this it? Is it time?" I screamed, and Waylynn spilled the coffee she was pouring.

My mother came running into the kitchen, nearly knocking Waylynn over. "It's time?"

"Where in the heck did you come from?" Waylynn asked laughing. "You appeared out of thin air."

"Dining room, dusting the china cabinet," my mother said without looking at Waylynn. She rushed over to Paxton. "Honey, are you okay?"

Paxton looked at all of us, a tinge of fear in her eyes. "I had a contraction!"

We started jumping up and down. Chloe was cupping her hands on Paxton's swollen belly and saying something to her baby brother.

"This is it! This is it! Steed!" I screamed. "Steed!"

I grabbed Chloe's hand. "It's baby time! Your baby brother is coming!" I shouted as we ran through the house. I pushed open Steed's office door to find him and my father sitting at his desk.

"Steed!"

"Daddy!"

He jumped up. "Is it time?"

I jumped. Then Chloe jumped. "Yes! Yes! It's time!" I cried out.

"I'm so happy! Hell! Shit! Fuck! My baby brother is coming!" Chloe cried out as she ran in circles around the desk.

Coming to a sudden stop, I covered my mouth with my hands. Chloe kept repeating over and over how happy she was and throwing those curses in at the end. Steed looked stunned as he watched his six-year-old daughter run around his office yelling obscenities.

My father walked over to me. "I'm going to guess this was your work, Amelia?"

Nodding, I replied, "Yes, sir."

He rocked on his heels a few times and said, "Thought so."

CHAPTER 39

Wade

Trevor's cell went off at the same time mine did.

We both read the text.

Steed: *It's time! We have a baby coming!*

Looking at each other, we both said, "Holy shit!"

We took off running at the same time, and I cried out, "I'll drive!"

We smacked into each other so hard, it knocked us on our asses.

"What in the fuck, Adams!" Trevor cried.

"You ran into me! The plan was for me to drive!"

"Oh, hell no. You are not driving my nephew."

My jaw dropped to the ground. "Why not?"

"I'll drive. That way there's no chance my sister's panties will be in the backseat."

I followed Trevor out of the barn.

"That was months ago! Why can't Cord let that drop?"

"I'm driving," Trevor repeated.

I picked up my pace, jogging back to the house. "No, I've been assigned by your dad to drive."

"My dad wasn't thinking straight."

Trevor and I ran to the house, pushing and shoving. I was able to trip him up, causing him to tumble to the ground. I glanced back and laughed, only to trip over something and hit the ground myself. It felt like I had cracked one of my healed ribs.

"Damn it!" I cried out. Trevor jumped over me as he ran by.

"What's the matter? Hurt a rib?" He called out as he ran backwards laughing. I pointed to the gate that was coming up. The one that went around the entire pool.

The next thing I knew, Trevor flipped over the fence and landed on the other side, but not before he stumbled and barely caught himself before falling into the pool.

Once he got his balance he raised his hands in victory. Walking up to him, I gave him a small push. Into the pool he went. Standing over him, I said, "Bummer. Looks like I'm driving."

"I'll get you for this, Wade Adams! You asshole!"

The entire Parker family, along with Paxton's parents, April and David, sat in the waiting room.

Amelia and I sat in the corner coloring with Chloe. She surprised the hell out of me by saying, "When we have a baby, let's not do this with the whole family camping out waiting."

I stared at her, feeling the *holy shit* expression form on my face.

Oh, hell. Amelia is bringing up the "B" word.

My heart raced, and I wasn't sure if I was excited at the idea or completely freaked out by it.

Little Chloe jumped up. "You're having a baby, Aunt Meli?"

Gasps filled the waiting room.

Amelia shook her head and waved her hands around. "What? No!"

Trevor and Cord shot me what appeared to be death rays from their eyes while Tripp and Mitchell looked on in horror...as if some poor girls had just told them *they* were about to be dads.

Tears filled Melanie's eyes as she said, "Amelia!"

Waylynn groaned. "Oh, nice. I'll be *forty* by the time I have a damn kid."

"Damn kid!" Chloe practically shouted.

Amelia gasped and looked at Chloe, giving her the best stern mom look she could. "Chloe Lynn, what did I tell you about swearing?"

She motioned like she was zipping her lips. Amelia rolled her eyes and looked around the room. "I'm not pregnant, so you two over there, stow the evil eyes." Pointing to Chloe, she said, "You and I need to have to have a serious girl-to-girl talk about this repeating everything you hear."

Chloe's little mouth opened, and Amelia lifted her hand. "No! Don't even, you little stinker!"

She giggled and went back to coloring as if her little outburst hadn't tilted the world on its axis.

John clutched his chest and looked toward the ceiling, whispering, "Thank you!"

Hands on her hips, Amelia snarled. "Well, it's nice to get a preview of how everyone will feel. The only one I've got on my side is Aunt Vi and that's because she's passed out!"

Tripp walked over to his sister, giving her a kiss on the forehead. "Amelia, you're the baby, and you'll always be the baby. When the time comes, everyone will be thrilled."

With a defeated sigh, she flopped back down in her seat.

Amelia glanced my way. I was positive I had a goofy-as-hell look on my face. Taking her hand in mine, I kissed the back of it.

"When that day comes you'll have made me the happiest man on Earth, Amelia."

Her eyes pooled with tears. "I hope I didn't spook you. I wasn't meaning right away or anything."

I pulled her up and winked at her before saying, "We're heading out for some fresh air. Anyone care to join us?"

"No, thank you" and "enjoy the air" came from around the waiting room, so Amelia and I headed to the elevator. The moment the doors shut, I pressed myself against her, kissing her like I hadn't seen her in months.

Wrapping her arms around my neck, Amelia let out a moan. The elevator came to a stop and we broke apart, both of us breathing like we had just run a marathon.

"Good afternoon," an older woman said as she stepped into the elevator.

"Afternoon," we both said. I tipped my baseball cap at the lady. When the doors opened and we stepped out, I practically pulled Amelia through the lobby of the hospital.

With a giggle, she asked, "Where are we going?"

I stepped outside and started across the street to the Holiday Inn Express.

"Wade Adams! You want to go have sex while Paxton's having a baby?"

I replied, "Yes. Yes, I do."

She did a little hop and said, "Okay!"

We stood in the lobby and waited while the young woman at the counter checked us in. I kept glancing at the door, waiting for Cord and Trevor to come rushing in like they had a tracking device on me.

"They think we're out walking around," Amelia said, squeezing my arm.

The young woman stopped typing and peeked at us with a smile.

I replied, "I know."

"So, you better be quick!" Amelia added.

Clearing her throat, the young girl said, "Right, well, here is your room card. I'd explain where the pool and other amenities of the hotel are but it sounds like you aren't going to be using those. So, um, enjoy your stay."

The poor girl's face turned bright red when I took the card and said, "We will. There's no doubt about that."

I guided Amelia to the elevator. Hitting me on the stomach, she whispered, "That was mean. You made her blush."

I kissed her on the top of the head, and we stepped through the doors. "Made you blush, as well."

We barely got into the room before our hands were fumbling with our pants. The way this woman made me feel was unreal. I couldn't get enough of her.

"Damn it, Amelia. I need to be inside you."

She nodded, tugging my pants to get them off my legs, nearly falling in the process.

Her bra was still on as she crawled onto the bed and moved up toward the headboard.

"Your socks are still on," she said with a chuckle.

"My feet are cold."

Laughing, she dropped onto the pillow. I could tell she was waiting for the delicious moment when I slipped inside of her, and we were lost to each other.

I ripped the condom package open with my teeth.

Licking her lips, Amelia purred, "In a hurry there, cowboy?"

"I'm not sure how good my resolve is right now, darlin'. My dick is throbbing."

She spread her legs, showing me that sweet pussy that was all mine. Resting over her, I kissed her lips and barely pushed inside. Amelia wrapped her legs around me and pulled me closer, making me slip deeper. Both of us moaned at the heavenly feel of two becoming one.

What started off as frantic and needy turned into slow and beautiful. Like it always did with this amazing woman.

It didn't take long before we were both whispering each other's names and adorations of ecstasy against kiss-swollen lips.

CHAPTER 40

Amelia

I stepped off the elevator holding two containers filled with coffees, trying not to look like I'd just had sex. Wade followed behind me holding two more coffees.

"Lord, thank the stars above! Starbucks!" Aunt Vi said, making a beeline toward me.

The line quickly formed behind us as everyone grabbed coffees. Mitchell and Corina ended up stepping up together. They looked at each other before Mitchell grabbed a coffee and went back to his seat. Corina forced a smile and whispered, "Thank you."

Waylynn was the last one to step up. Lifting her brow, she took the coffee. "So, how was the Holiday Inn Express?"

My cheeks heated under her stare.

"What?"

She leaned in closer. "Oh, please. You have that just-fucked look all over your face. Besides, I saw y'all racing into the hotel, you horny little bitch."

I snarled at her. "You're just jealous because I'm having sex and you're not."

Aunt Vi said, "Honestly, girls, we can all hear you. Who cares where the kids went. They brought coffee."

I stuck my tongue out at Waylynn.

"Really grown up there, Amelia." She leaned closer and whispered so only I could hear. "No wonder Chloe repeats everything you say."

"Shut up!" I said.

"Make me!" Waylynn countered.

"Girls. Will you please stop fighting?" our mother asked.

I went to say something when Steed came into the waiting room and everyone jumped up. Chloe ran over to him. He bent down and captured her in his arms. Giving her a kiss, he whispered what I was guessing was the baby's name. She wrapped her little arms around his neck and started crying.

My heart melted.

"That little girl slays me," Waylynn said, wiping the tears from her face.

Steed cleared his throat. "We have a healthy, beautiful son."

Cheers erupted and I felt my tears fall as I watched my brother crying.

"He's beautiful. Perfect in every way imaginable."

"Congratulations, son," my father said, extending his hand.

"Thanks, Dad."

Everyone took turns congratulating Steed and Chloe and looking at pictures on his phone.

"Wait! What is his name?" Waylynn asked.

Steed looked at Chloe and motioned for her to tell everyone.

"My new baby brother's name is Gage!"

Everyone cheered, and I found myself crying again. My brother looked so incredibly happy.

The rest of the evening was spent taking turns meeting Gage. When it came time for me and Wade to meet the little guy, Chloe was passed out on the sofa in Paxton's room.

I stepped into the room, inhaling deeply and grabbing Wade's hand.

Paxton sat in bed, holding her little bundle of joy in her arms. I'd never seen her look so beautiful.

"Oh, my goodness," I whispered, being careful not to wake up Chloe. "He is beautiful!"

A wide smile formed on Paxton's face. I could see the tears building, but she managed to keep it together. Unlike me.

Sweeping the baby from her arms, I sat down in the chair and stared at him.

"He's perfect."

"I know," Paxton replied. "He's such a good baby, too. All these people in and out and he's not once cried."

"Just wait," April, Paxton's mom, said with a light chuckle. "He's saving it all up for y'all."

"Probably," Paxton said with a grin.

We spent a few minutes visiting before I handed Gage to Steed.

"Paxton, you look exhausted," I said. "I'm sure having the whole family here has been tiring."

She shook her head and went to speak, but yawned instead.

"We're going to leave, as well," April said as she and David kissed Paxton goodbye. "Steed, you let us know if y'all need anything. We'll come back tomorrow to see you and Gage."

After Paxton's parents left, it was only me and Wade. I glanced at Chloe. "How about we take Chloe home with us? We can have a good old-fashioned sleepover. Wade can make hamburgers and the whole works."

Steed's eyes lit up. "Amelia, if you do that, I would owe you big time."

"Nonsense. That's what sisters are for."

When I turned around to say something to Paxton, she was sound asleep. I covered my mouth. "That poor thing," I whispered.

Wade picked up Chloe and tucked her to his chest as we waved goodbye to Steed.

As we walked to the elevator I shook my head. "I know I've already said this once today, but when the time comes, and we have a baby, I'm not letting that dog and pony show go on for hours. Poor Paxton!"

Wade chuckled. "Yeah, I'm going to have to agree. I love your family, but wow."

The drive back to the ranch took over an hour. There was no way Chloe was waking up, so I put her in the guest bedroom next to my room before heading down to the family room. My father and Wade were sitting on the sofa drinking what looked like whiskey.

"I don't think Chloe will be waking up for the rest of the night," I said. "So much for a fun sleepover."

My father grinned. "It's been a big day for her."

Sinking into the oversized chair, I pulled my legs up to my chest. "So, Daddy, are you still gonna give Wade his week off?"

"You never ate lunch with us."

"We spent hours in a waiting room together! That doesn't count?"

He tried to hide his smile, but couldn't. "What would you do with a whole week?"

I peeked over at Wade. "I was thinking a trip to New Orleans."

Wade's eyes lit up, and he sat up a little bit taller. "New Orleans? I've always wanted to go there."

I turned to my father and gave him puppy dog eyes. "See, look at that, Daddy. Wade has come in and literally turned this ranch around! Have you seen the east pasture?"

My father nodded and sipped his whiskey. "I have. Wade's been an invaluable asset to the ranch, there is no doubt about that."

"Thank you, sir. I appreciate that."

"John, for heaven's sake. Let the boy have a week off. Don't you remember what it was like to be young and in love?"

We all turned to see Aunt Vi walking in. Her face was covered in a green facemask.

"What in the world do you have on your face, Vi?" my father asked.

She made her way over to the minibar and poured a straight shot of whiskey. In one gulp, it was gone.

Glancing at us, my father said, "My older sister always could drink me under the table."

"Damn straight, I could. It's a beauty mask, John. Haven't you ever seen Melanie wear one to bed?"

He stared at her like she was an alien. "No, I can honestly say in all my years of marriage, my wife has never come to bed looking like a relative of E.T."

Wade and I chuckled. Aunt Vi gave my father the finger.

"If you get this week off, will you spend part of it slaving over that house?" Vi asked.

I chewed on my lip before slipping out of my seat and sitting next to Wade. "Actually, I was thinking we'd spend the whole time in New Orleans. Do some research for a historical book I'm writing and maybe a little shopping for the new house. I'd love to visit a plantation or two, as well."

Aunt Vi let out a long, loud sigh. "New Orleans. One of the most romantic cities in the south. I have a friend, you can stay with her. I'll make all the arrangements."

I tensed up. "Well, Aunt Vi, I appreciate that, but I was kind of hoping for us to, um…" Peeking over to my father, I added, "Be alone."

She laughed. "Oh, hell, Lou Anne won't be there. She's in New York. She owns a house in the Garden District."

I jumped up and gasped. "What? Aunt Vi, don't play around with me. Are you serious?"

Aunt Vi smiled big. "Five bedroom, five bathroom, over nine-thousand square feet. You could…be alone…all over that house."

"Oh, for Christ's sake," Daddy said, standing up. "It's been a long day. Take the week, Wade, hell, take two if it gets my sister to stop talking."

I jumped up, running to my father to hug him. Wade shook his hand and said, "Thank you, sir, but I'm good with the one."

My father's brow lifted. "Right. Good night, kids… Vi, don't drink all my damn whiskey."

My aunt lifted her hand and waved her long, manicured fingers after my father. "Night, little brother."

When he left the room, she winked at us. "I know he's going to miss me when I move out."

I sat down on the floor in front of her. "Do you think your friend will let us stay in her house?"

She nodded. "Of course, she will. She wouldn't have that house if it wasn't for me. I made the woman millions of dollars years ago when I told her how to invest."

I glanced at Wade. "Are you up for an adventure?"

The smile on his face said it all.

We were going to New Orleans.

CHAPTER 41

Amelia

New Orleans

The taxi pulled up to Lou Anne's house on Prytania Street. The first thing I noticed was the large porch and the huge, white pillars. The black shutters ran the entire length of the windows.

"Wow," Wade and I said at once.

"This is it," the taxi driver said. Wade paid him and headed up the steps that lead to the giant porch with our suitcases.

"This house is amazing."

"And we aren't even through the front door yet," Wade replied with a laugh.

I took the key and unlocked the large front door. I slowly pushed it open and we both stared into the house. The long, yellow corridor was flanked with antique furniture on both sides. An old church pew sat on one side and a large curio cabinet covered the opposite wall.

We stepped inside and Wade shut the door behind us. Making my way in, I marveled at the artwork on the walls.

"Look at this. It's stunning!"

Wade leaned closer to the frames. "Same painter. Looks like it's here in New Orleans."

"Maybe it's a local painter. I'll Google it later."

Wade chuckled. "Okay, let's look around the house."

We walked into the parlor first. The dark blue walls popped against the wood trim and wood ceiling. Not to mention the black fireplace.

"Oh, wow. What a beautiful color. I wonder what it's called," I said, running my hand along the antique furniture.

"Look at the window. Floor to ceiling, like in our house."

My heart skipped a beat when Wade said *our* house. It was clearly his house, but I loved that he thought of it as ours.

"Look at the yellow in the dining room," I said. "And the fireplace!"

Wade walked to the fireplace. "Looks like the original surround. I swear it looks like the one in our master bedroom."

I nodded, taking my phone out and snapping a picture.

We made our way through the formal living room and all the bedrooms. Each had a fireplace that was nicer than the previous one.

Wade pulled me into his arms and said, "Okay, we looked at every bedroom. Which one do you want to sleep in?"

"Well, not the master, that's Lou Anne's. What about the one with the light blue on the walls? It's so romantic, and I bet with the fire going it will be amazing when we make love."

With his dimples on full display, Wade nodded. "Now let's go to the basement. Vi said there was a wine cellar and game room."

Leading us down the stairs, I said, "Aunt Vi was so right about this house. We could have sex in as many rooms as possible and still not get to all of them in the seven days we're here."

"I still can't believe you talked your dad into seven days. You are a negotiator, Amelia Parker."

"Being the baby girl has its advantages, right?"

I stepped into the game room and jumped for joy. "Look at the big-screen TV! We can watch movies down here and feel like we're at the movies!"

Wade agreed. "Yeah, this is pretty amazing."

Wade grabbed a bottle of wine, and we made our way upstairs. We stopped and stared, taking in the massive kitchen.

I ran my fingers along the cold marble island. "Oh, we are so having sex on this."

Pulling me to him, Wade ran his lips along my neck. "Right now I think bending you over this table is what I want to do."

My stomach pulled with instant desire. "I like that idea."

Wade's hand found its way under my dress and inside my panties. He closed his eyes, a low growl slipping from the back of his throat. "Damn, darlin'. You're wet."

"Yes," I gasped as I pushed my hips into his hand. "Take me, Wade. Take me now."

"I need a condom," Wade gasped.

I spun around. "Are you sure?"

He fumbled with his wallet before pulling the little packet out. "Am I sure about what?"

I took the condom with a grin. "I've been on the pill for a while now and with us talking about moving in together, I thought maybe we should move onto fifth base."

Wade's eyes widened. "There's a fifth base? How the fuck was I never told about a fifth base?"

I undid his pants and reached in for his thick cock. "Oh, yes, there is a fifth base. It's called no more condoms."

Groaning, Wade closed his eyes. "I'm going to come the moment I slip inside you."

I laughed. "You better not."

Wade looked into my eyes. "You're sure?"

"Never been more sure of anything in my life. Are you sure?"

"Fuck, yes! Bareback here I come. Literally."

I smiled. "From behind."

Wade spun me around and pushed me onto the table. I loved that we were both still dressed and there was a hint of roughness to our lovemaking. Our first time bare, and I wanted it to be filled with passion. Raw.

Pushing my thong to the side, Wade spread my legs open and pushed his fingers inside. Priming me, he let out a long moan.

"I'm going to bury my face between your legs later, darlin'. I want to taste you so fucking bad."

"Wade, please. Now! I want to feel you."

He slammed into me so fast and hard, I let out a small scream. Wade stopped moving.

"No! I'm okay. Please, don't stop."

"I need a minute. If you move or I move, this show will be over before the opening credits begin, darlin'." Wade took a minute to compose himself from the hedonistic feeling of going commando.

Then he started again, moving in and out building up my orgasm each time he pushed back in. It felt so damn amazing. It wasn't going to take long with the way he was moving. Each thrust was hitting the spot.

Jesus. Why did we wait so long to do this?

Sex without a condom with Wade was my new favorite thing.

"Oh, Amelia. It feels so good. Baby, it feels so good."

"I'm going to come. Oh, God, Wade!"

I could feel myself squeeze his cock. Wade laid across my back and let out a long, low groan as he pushed in deeper.

"Amelia...oh, God."

My body was still trembling as I gripped the table and tried to keep my legs from giving out from under me. The weight of Wade's body on mine felt amazing.

"Jesus, I think that is the fastest I've ever come in my life," Wade gasped as he stood up.

Laughing, I glanced over my shoulder. "As nice as that was, I demand a re-do."

Wade smiled and pulled out of me. The feel of cum running down my leg for the very first time was amazing.

"Damn, darlin'. Let me clean you up really quick."

Wade pulled my panties off, went in search of a washcloth and gently cleaned me between the legs. He slipped my panties back on and stood.

"I love you, darlin'. That was…fuck! I've got no words. It was that damn good."

I reached up on my toes and pressed my lips to his. I pulled back and looked into those beautiful eyes. "It was magical," I said. "I love you, too."

"I'm dying to see New Orleans. Want to head to the French Quarter and find somewhere to eat?"

With a wide grin, I nodded.

Wade and I leaned back in our chairs and grinned.

"I'm freaking full."

With a giggle, I wiped the corners of my mouth and tossed my napkin onto the table. "K Paul's is one of my favorite restaurants. I put it in one of my books and the main characters had their 'dessert' in the bathroom after dinner."

"I can see why it's one of your favorites. The food is amazing."

The waiter brought the check, and Wade tossed some cash down. "Come on, I want to walk around and take it all in."

I stood and took his outstretched hand.

As we strolled the streets of the French Quarter, Wade and I talked about everything. The house, how beautiful Gage was, how well Chloe was adjusting to her new baby brother. Our future.

"Where do you see yourself in five years?" I asked.

Wade shrugged. "I'm not sure. I've never been one who thought too long and hard about things like that. I hope I'm healthy, happy, and waking up every morning next to you."

I stopped walking and faced him. "Do you have any idea how you make me feel? How incredibly romantic you are?"

He grinned and cupped the side of my face with his hand. "It all comes natural when it comes to you. You're so damn easy to love."

He took my hand in his and we continued to walk the amazing streets of New Orleans.

We stepped in and out of bars and stores. My cheeks hurt from laughing as Wade pointed out all the people who were drunk out of their minds.

We found our way to Cat's Meow, where Wade and I danced for an hour straight. The music pulsed through my body as Wade pulled me to him. "Are you having fun, darlin'?"

Tossing my head back, I yelled out, "Yes! Oh, my gosh, this is the best night ever! But I think I need some air."

Wade smiled and guided me out of the bar.

I stepped onto Bourbon Street, took in a deep breath and let it out. I was so happy, my body was buzzing. I spun around and threw myself into Wade's arms.

"This night couldn't be any better!" I said.

Wade gazed into my eyes as he held me in his arms. "I think it could."

Lifting my brows, I asked, "How could it possibly get better?"

Gently setting me down, Wade cupped my face within his hands. The intensity in his eyes made my whole body tremble.

"Marry me, Amelia."

Adrenaline rushed through my body, leaving a tingling sensation in its path.

"W-what?"

Wade searched my face. "Let's get married. Right here, while we're in New Orleans."

I let out a faint laugh. "Wait, are you being serious?"

"Yes! I love you, I want to spend the rest of my life with you. This town is amazing. It's beautiful, fun, crazy, romantic, and perfect! Let's just do it! You and me. No family to deal with. Just us."

My mouth opened, then shut. I'd never felt my heart beat so fast or so loud.

"Seriously? You want to get married? What about my family?"

"If you want a big wedding we'll have one when we go back to Texas, but I want to make you Mrs. Wade Adams now. If you want to keep it a secret, we can, or we can shout it from the rooftops. All I know is I want to marry you before we leave New Orleans."

I glanced around at the people passing us. I knew in my heart this was what I wanted. When I thought of my future, every scenario had Wade in it. This was something I didn't even have to think twice about.

"Yes! Let's get married!"

Wade pulled back to look at me. "Yeah?"

Nodding, I replied, "Yeah! Let's do it!"

CHAPTER 42

Wade

Three days after we filed for a marriage license I stood in Lou Anne's gardens. Her house was the perfect place to get married. It gave me my first impression of New Orleans, it was one of the inspirations for Amelia's historical book...and some day we would walk our kids along this street and say we got married there.

"Mr. Adams?"

I smiled at the pastor Amelia and I had met the other night at a restaurant. When I pulled him to the side and told him we were getting married on a whim, he agreed to perform the ceremony.

"Pastor Miller, I'm so glad you were able to make it."

He smiled and shook my hand. "Are you still keeping all of this a surprise?"

"I am. Amelia's getting ready and thinks we're heading to the Justice of the Peace."

"It's very sweet of you to do all of this."

Lou Anne's caretaker, Louis, walked up to us and cleared his throat. "Mr. Adams, the area is ready."

I watched the florist I'd hired climb down off her ladder. She had covered the entire pergola with flowers.

"Wow," I whispered.

"How stunning," Pastor Miller said.

Lora, the florist, made her way over to us. "Are you happy with it?"

I smiled. "It's perfect. You did an amazing job. Thank you so much."

"You're welcome. Listen, Wade, I was thinking while I was tying up the flowers. Do you have two witnesses?"

My head snapped to the pastor. "I forgot about the witnesses!"

His eyes about bugged out of his head. "We need two witnesses, Mr. Adams."

Lora touched my arm, bringing my attention back to her. "Listen, don't worry, I can stay for the ceremony."

"I can, as well, Mr. Adams," Louis said.

I breathed a sigh of relief. "Are you both sure?"

They nodded and Lora said, "It would be my pleasure. I think this whole thing is utterly romantic. I'd love to bring Amelia her flowers and show her the way out here."

"Really?" I said, my voice a little higher than it should be.

"Yes! Of course."

Glancing to Louis, I asked, "You're sure you don't mind? We're about to start and it shouldn't take long."

Pastor Miller added, "No. Not long at all."

"I do not mind at all, Mr. Adams," Louis said in his thick French accent.

I clapped my hands and looked at my watch. "Then let's get this show on the road."

I adjusted my tie, took a deep breath and headed to the pergola with Pastor Miller and Louis.

"Louis, was that your name?" Pastor Miller asked.

"Yes, sir. That's my name."

"You and the other young lady may stand over here. I'll need you to sign the license after the ceremony."

Louis nodded, a proud smile on his face.

I cracked my neck from side to side.

"Mr. Adams, calm down. Deep breaths in and out." Pastor Miller urged.

Wringing my hands, I nodded. "Right. I'm calming down."

I stared at the side door, waiting for Amelia to walk through it. She'd gone shopping this morning and said she found the perfect dress. I chose to wear jeans, boots, a white button-down shirt and Amelia's favorite blue tie. Of course, I had my black cowboy hat on, as well.

For a brief moment, I panicked as I patted down my shirt for the rings.

Turning to the pastor, I grinned. "I have the rings! They're right here."

He nodded. The guy probably thought I was insane. The back door opened, and Lora walked out first, a huge grin covering her face.

She walked to where Louis was standing. "She's trying to stop crying before she comes out."

My heart squeezed. "Happy tears?" I asked.

"Oh, yes. Very happy tears."

When the door opened again and Amelia stepped out, I felt the ground shake beneath my feet. My breath hitched. I couldn't believe the beautiful sight in front of me.

Amelia stood before us in a white lace gown. Her red hair was pulled up and long curls fell around her face.

She flashed me a beautiful smile that made my stomach do that weird fluttering thing. As she walked closer, I could see her tears. I bit the inside of my cheek, trying like hell not to cry, but it didn't help. The tears flowed openly as my beautiful bride got close to me.

Shaking my head in disbelief at how damn lucky I was, I reached my hand for hers.

"Amelia, you look beautiful. Stunning," I whispered, wanting this last intimate moment of us being Mr. Adams and Ms. Parker locked in my mind forever.

She wiped a tear from her cheek and opened her mouth. Her chin trembled and she closed her mouth and then her eyes.

After a few deep breaths, she opened her eyes again.

"Wade. When did you plan all of this? It's…beyond amazing. It's everything I dreamed of and more."

My eyes swept over her stunning dress. It fell to the ground, and I grinned when I saw she had forgone shoes. Everything about this wedding screamed *us*. Simple, yet romantic.

Taking the hand that wasn't holding her flowers, I said, "I have my ways. I'm sneaky, if you haven't noticed."

She giggled. "I noticed. Boy, did I notice."

Turning to her left, Amelia sucked in a breath. "Pastor Miller? What in the world are you doing here?"

He chuckled. "Mr. Adams pulled me to the side and asked me if I would be a part of your special day. I couldn't turn him down. So, shall we get ready?"

We nodded.

Everything the poor pastor said was an absolute blur. The only thing I could see was Amelia. The only thing I could hear was my heart pounding. And the only thing I cared about was that I was about to be this woman's husband.

"Do you have the rings?"

Pastor Miller's question pulled me from my thoughts. I reached into my pocket and pulled out the wedding bands I had bought while Amelia was shopping for a gown. Amelia's was white gold with a lace rope design on the edge, covered in small diamonds. My band matched hers, minus the diamonds.

"Wade! Oh, my goodness, it's beautiful."

Slipping the band on her finger, I whispered, "I'll let you pick out your engagement ring when we get back to Texas."

Amelia giggled. "A little backwards there, Mr. Adams."

After we exchanged our vows and placed the rings on our fingers, Pastor Miller said, "By the powers vested in me by the state of Louisiana, I now pronounce you Mr. and Mrs. Wade Adams."

Louis and Lora clapped as I slid my hand behind Amelia's neck and leaned down to kiss my wife.

After a few good, solid seconds of kissing, we drew back and gazed into one another's eyes.

"We did it!" Amelia said.

"We sure did."

Making our way to our witnesses, I officially introduced Amelia to Lora. They signed the marriage license and bid their goodbyes, each wishing us the most amazing of futures together.

After we walked Pastor Miller out to his car, I led Amelia back to the spot where we had just gotten married.

"I can't believe we actually did it," she said with a giddy laugh.

I wrapped my arms around her waist and kissed the tip of her nose. "Neither can I."

"Wade, it was perfect. The most amazing day of my life."

"Do you remember you once asked me to sing for you?"

She smiled. "I do. You promised me you would."

I cleared my throat. "I wrote you a song and wanted to sing it to you. It's my first wedding gift."

Amelia's eyes filled with tears. "You wrote me a song?"

"I did. And I've never in my life been nervous to sing, but let me tell you, right now I'm nervous as hell."

She took my hand in hers as a tear trailed down her cheek. "My heart is pounding out of my chest."

We both chuckled.

"I love you, Amelia," I said. "I've never loved anyone like I love you."

I walked her over to the swing and held her hands while she sat down. My guitar was leaning against a chair. I picked it up and sat down. Then I cleared my throat and sang the words I'd written, directly from my heart to hers.

It hadn't taken me long to write the song. Thirty minutes, at the most. But every word I sang had never been truer. She had saved me. She was the light of my world. The love of my life. The dream I had dreamed.

Strumming the last cord, I stared at Amelia. Tears streamed down her face, and I wasn't sure how I'd kept it together while singing.

I stood slowly, setting the guitar down. I studied Amelia's face as she stood, too.

Lifting my brows, I was unable to find the words to ask how she felt. Did she love it? Hate it? I'd have given anything to be able to read her mind.

"This is a moment I will remember for the rest of my life. I've never felt so loved or been so happy."

Letting out the breath I hadn't even realized I was holding in, I took her in my arms.

"I meant every word," I whispered.

She held tight as I wrapped my arms around her.

"Do you know what would be the cherry on top?" she asked, as she pulled her head back to look at me.

"What?"

"Dancing our first dance as a married couple to Frank."

I tossed my head back and laughed. "I can do that."

I took my phone out of my pants pocket and found the song. I set the phone on the chair and pulled Amelia back into my arms.

I looked down into my beautiful bride's eyes while we danced slowly.

"Are you happy, darlin'?"

"So very happy, cowboy."

My heart felt like it would burst. Every ounce of fear, guilt, and sadness that was left melted away. I had said Trevor saved my life, but I was wrong. This woman in my arms was my savior. She was the reason I woke up and fell asleep every single day with a smile on my face.

"Now that we went off and got married, what do we do now to make the rest of our honeymoon exciting?" I asked.

She lifted her brow and tilted her head. "I want to get a tattoo!"

My mouth dropped. "What?"

Nodding, she said, "Yes! You've got that one your arm. I want something to look at that will remind me of this day."

"Seriously?"

"Yes!"

"You want to get a tattoo? Right now?"

"Both of us. Yep!" she said, popping the p.

"There is a tattoo that I've been wanting to get on my side…"

Amelia jumped. "Let's do it, husband!"

"Alright! Let's do it, wife!"

CHAPTER 43

Amelia

I was on cloud nine as I ran into the house for my shoes. My stomach felt like it had been on a crazy thrill ride. With the surprise wedding, Wade singing to me, and a tattoo to mark this day, nothing could bring me down.

"Amelia, are you sure you want to do this?" Wade asked. "Do you even have an idea of what you want to get?"

Nodding, I replied, "Yes, I'm sure, and I'll have to think about what I want. Did you call your friend, Sam, and ask him where we should go?"

Wade had gone to school with a guy who was from New Orleans. "I did. He gave me the address."

I did a little hop and clapped my hands. "I'm staying in my wedding dress! Once we get our tats we can go dancing."

"Tats?" Wade asked with a chuckle.

"My father is going to freak! Oh, my gawd. Cord is going to flip! He's been begging me to get one ever since I turned eighteen.

My father told Cord he forbid it, and if I had it done it would be on my conscience when he fell over dead!"

Wade frowned. "I might be wrong on this, darlin', but it shouldn't make you excited to know that getting a tattoo could cause your dad a heart attack."

I waved him off. "Please! Do you know my father has them? Yep. He tries to hide them, but he has them. And so does my mom! On her ankle!"

"Really? I've never seen it."

"It's a little bitty heart," I said. "But enough about them. Did you call an Uber? Let's go before I change my mind!"

Wade laughed. "Yes, he's almost here."

I grabbed his hand and dragged him out the door. "Let's go!"

As we walked into the tattoo shop, I couldn't stop my hands from shaking. I was really going to do this.

"Hey there," Wade said as he approached the guy behind the counter. "Sam gave me your name."

The guy smiled. "Hell yeah. Wade?"

"That's me."

"Yeah, Sam called and told me you guys were on your way. Perfect timing. We're super slow right now. Do you know what you want?"

Wade faced me. "Do you know?"

I grinned. "I want to get a little giraffe with a heart on my wrist."

"I can do that," Sam said.

Wade smiled hugely.

"And, Wade, I want you to get a little giraffe on your wrist!"

His smile dropped. "Huh?"

The guy behind the counter laughed.

I nodded.

"Wait, you want me to get giraffe on my wrist?"

"With a heart," I added.

Wade stood there with a stunned look. He turned to the guy behind the counter, who lifted his hands and took a few steps back.

"I am not touching that with a ten-foot pole, dude."

Focusing on me, Wade tilted his head and pulled his brows together. He opened his mouth and then shut it.

I slowly pouted. "You don't like my giraffe idea?"

"It's, um, it's a great idea, darlin'. I'm all in."

My heart felt like it would burst knowing that Wade would get the giraffe. But I also wanted to laugh my ass off. The idea that he would go through with it made me realize how much this man truly loved me.

With my hand on his chest, I reached up and kissed him on the lips. "I'm totally kidding. I mean, I'm getting a giraffe, but you don't have to get one."

He closed his eyes and let out a sigh of relief. "Thank God. If your brothers saw it, I'd never live it down."

"Pussy whipped. That's what they'd be calling you," the guy behind the counter said.

Wade lifted his brows. "Yes. That."

"So, who's going first?" I asked.

"I'll do your wrist first. Then we'll do your side, buddy."

Wade and I nodded. I followed him to his station, and we went over all the legal crap and then he showed me how the equipment was sterilized. When he put the design on my wrist I glanced up to Wade and smiled.

"I can't wait!"

He winked and said, "Yeah, me, too."

The second the guy started, my eyes about popped out of my head.

Holy. Fuck.

"That…hurts," I said.

The tattoo artist smiled and kept going. "Let me know if you need a break."

I swallowed hard. "O-okay."

Wade sat on the other side of me and held my hand.

"How's it feel?"

Turning to him, I forced a smile. "G-great. Perfect. Fine. Not really. It hurts like a mother. Oh, my God, why did you let me do this?"

The tattoo guy stopped.

"No! Don't stop! Just keep going!" I cried out.

It didn't take long before he was finished and I was looking down at my cute little giraffe. Wade's name was under it along with today's date in the middle of a heart.

"I love it!" I exclaimed. "It's perfect!"

After he told me how to take care of it, it was Wade's turn. I got lost in a conversation with the other tattoo artist, Bob. He even showed me his garden in the back of the tattoo shop. It was filled with beautiful flowers, herbs, and veggies.

As we walked back in, Bob looked up at me. "All done."

I glanced over to see Wade's side all puffy and red before they bandaged it up. Standing next to the table, I read the tattoo.

DEFEAT IS A STATE OF MIND
NO ONE IS EVER DEFEATED
UNTIL DEFEAT
HAS BEEN ACCEPTED
AS REALITY

Our eyes met, and we smiled.

"I have another wedding gift for you," Wade said.

"Oh, yeah? What is it?" I asked, a goofy grin plastered on my face.

He pulled his pants down to show off the top of his ass. A giraffe was tattooed along with my name and today's wedding date inside the heart.

Snapping my eyes to meet his, I shook my head and covered my mouth. When I tried to speak, I started crying. Bob covered the tattoos and told Wade the same care instructions that he had told me. Wade wasn't listening. He was staring at me while I stood there crying.

This man was everything. My knight in shining armor. The love of my life. The maker of my dreams. The keeper of my heart.

Wade Adams was my happily ever after.

Once we stepped out of the tattoo parlor, Wade cupped my face in his hands.

"What do you want to do now? We got married, I sang to you, and we tatted ourselves up. What can we do to top that?"

The corners of my mouth rose into a sexy smirk. "I'm pretty sure I can come up with an idea or two, Mr. Adams."

Wade's eyes danced with desire as he brushed his lips over mine and whispered, "I have no doubt in my mind about that, Mrs. Adams."

THE END

Enjoy a Sneak Peek from

Tempting Love

The bass rattled against my chest as I danced with Amelia, Paxton, and Jenn. It was Paxton's first night out since the baby, and we were celebrating Amelia's surprise wedding. It was honestly the last place I wanted to be, but the thought of running into Mitchell outweighed my desire to stay in bed with a pint of ice cream and a good movie.

"It feels so good to be able to dance again!" Paxton yelled over the music.

We laughed, and Amelia spun Paxton around a few times.

"Paxton, you look amazing for someone who had a baby not even a month ago!" I yelled.

Her cheeks blushed. "Look at you, Corina! I don't think that dress could hug those curves any tighter! Girl, you are looking hot tonight!"

"Her tits! Look at how freaking perky they are, and you're older than me!" Jenn screamed.

My face heated as a few guys turned, and I instantly regretted my outfit choice.

Of course, the only reason I wore this dress was because I knew Mitchell had tonight off, and Amelia had casually mentioned he would probably be at Cord's Place.

I gave the cowboy who wouldn't stop ogling my breasts the stink eye, and turned away.

I immediately felt someone else staring at me. It only took me two seconds to shift my gaze to the bar and see him.

Mitchell.

My heart raced like it did every time our eyes met. Then it would slowly break when he looked elsewhere and acted like he hadn't seen me.

But tonight he didn't.

Tonight, he kept his gaze on me, and I could practically feel him burning a hole right through the slutty dress that I was *really* wishing I hadn't worn.

"Corina, are you okay?" Paxton yelled.

I nodded. My eyes drifted back to Mitchell, who was still watching us. "I need to use the restroom and splash my face. I'll be right back."

She gave me a concerned look, so I flashed a fake smile. "Honest. I'm hot, that's all. I haven't danced this much in a long time!"

Before I turned to head to the bathroom I peeked at Mitchell again.

Big mistake. He was now talking to the same girl I had seen him dancing with a few months back. He looked to the left and our eyes met again. The girl leaned and whispered something into Mitchell's ear, but he never took his eyes off me.

Spinning on the heel of my boots, I pushed through the crowd. The room felt like it was closing in and I was about to lose the turkey on rye sandwich I had for lunch.

"Hey, beautiful, want to dance?" some cowboy asked.

"No thanks. I feel like I'm going to puke."

He jumped out of my way, allowing me to keep moving forward. Each breath was harder and harder as I tried to get to the hall.

What in the heck is wrong with me? Why can't I forget about him?

Once I broke through the crowd, I dragged in a deep breath while my hand clutched to my chest, trying to calm my racing heart.

I closed my eyes and fought the tears that threatened to spill out. I wasn't sure how much more of this I could take. Seeing Mitchell, not knowing if he left with some whore he would screw in his truck and then never call again.

Maybe that's all I was to him that night. Another notch on his belt.

I wiped my tears and started for the women's bathroom as someone grabbed my arm from behind and pulled me down the hall.

"Hey! Let go of me!" I screamed. Hitting the guy with everything I had, I cried out for him to let me go. I saw the door to Cord's office and panicked.

"Stop! Let me go!"

"Corina, stop fighting me."

It was Mitchell who had taken me by the arm.

He unlocked the door and guided me in as I jerked my arm free.

"Are you crazy, Mitch? You scared the crap out of me. It's dark in that hall, and I had no idea it was you!"

Before I could say another word, his lips were pressed against mine. His hands pushed through my hair and held me gently even as he kissed me urgently.

It was the first time he'd kissed me since that morning he stood at my front door and kissed me goodbye. Leaving me to hope for something that would never be.

My head was telling me to push him away. Argue that he couldn't kiss me like he hadn't ripped my heart out and kicked it to the side all those months ago. But my heart was in control right now, and it loved every moment of Mitchell's kiss and the feel of his hands on my body.

A soft moan slipped from my lips. I grabbed his strong arms while they moved down my body, pulling up my dress.

Stop this, Corina.

He kissed my jaw to my neck, then his lips made their way to the sensitive area behind my ear. His hot breath and hands grabbing my ass had my panties instantly wet.

"Corina."

His whisper sounded so pained that my chest squeezed tightly.

My mouth opened but no words came out. The room spun, and as much as I wanted to tell him to stop, I wanted him to keep going more.

"You look so goddamn sexy in this dress."

I smiled, no longer regretting my decision to wear it. Mitchell's hands pulled me up and my legs wrapped around his waist. He pushed me against the wall, his hard erection pressing against me in the most delicious way.

"Mitch, yes." My breath was needy and rough, but I didn't care. I was in his arms and that was all I cared about.

His breath was hot against my ear. "You drive me crazy. Do you know how much I want you?"

Hope bubbled in my chest. I shook my head, my chest rising and falling while he stared into my eyes.

When I smiled, something in his eyes changed. He dropped his head and buried his face in my neck. He softly kissed me in the most tender way. My skin was on fire after each kiss.

He pulled on my earlobe and whispered, "You're so precious. I'm sorry. I never meant to hurt you."

I closed my eyes and a tear rolled slowly down my cheek. When I felt him pull back, I met his gaze.

I was positive the sadness in his eyes mirrored mine. He slowly let my body slide down his until my feet touched the ground. He wiped my tears with his thumbs, then pulled my dress back down.

He stepped away and dropped his hands to his side. "I can't do this, not like this. You don't deserve to be fucked up against my brother's office door."

My mouth opened while I slowly nodded.

He took another step back and reached for the door. Before he opened it, I grabbed his arm.

"Why are you doing this to me?"

He said nothing, only stared.

Anger raced through my body as I glared at him in disbelief. "Do you have any idea how fucked up this is?"

He winced at my use of *fuck*. Anyone who knew me knew I rarely swore.

"You can't ignore me for months, and then one night haul me into your brother's office, feel me up like some whore for a cheap thrill, then walk away. Were you using me to warm up for the brunette?"

"What? No!"

I hit him as hard as I could on the chest.

"You bastard! How could you?" I cried as tears streamed down my face. I covered my mouth as I stumbled back. "How could you do this to me...again?"

"Corina, I—"

I hit him again as hard as I could. "I hate you, Mitchell Parker. Just go! Go fuck whatever flavor of the month you're into, but don't you dare touch me ever again!"

"It's not like that, sweetheart. Please just wait and let me explain."

He reached out for me, and I screamed, causing him to stop immediately. A look of horror moved across his face.

The door to Cord's office opened, and Amelia and Cord stood there.

"What's going on?" Amelia asked as she glanced between her brother and me.

My chin trembled as I looked at Amelia and Cord, then back to Mitchell.

"Corina," Mitchell said, looking at me with pleading eyes.

I'd never in my life felt so defeated and broken. I'd foolishly believed that Mitchell Parker might actually care about me. Dropping my head, I made my way out of the office.

I stopped in front of Mitchell and didn't bother to look at him as I took in a deep breath and blew it out. "You're right. I deserve someone who actually cares about me and wants to be with me. Someone who will cherish my heart."

When I finally looked at him, my breath caught. There were tears in his eyes. "I'm tired of waiting for something that was never mine in the first place. I'm finished waiting for you, Mitch."

As I walked out, I heard Mitchell call out, "Corina! Wait!"

I tried to hold back my sobs as I pushed through the crowd. I needed air. I needed to leave and get home.

My eyes met Tripp's. His brows drew together as he held out his arms, and I rushed into them.

The little ounce of strength I had left collapsed when he wrapped his arms around me.

"What in the hell happened?" he asked.

"Please, take me home, Tripp. Please."

He lifted my chin and stared at me. "Why are you crying, Corina? Tell me what happened."

His eyes drifted over my shoulder. From the look on his face it was clear Mitchell was standing there.

Tripp looked back down at me and forced a smile. "Let's get you home."

He placed his hand on my lower back and guided me through the bar. The farther I walked, the worse I felt. I could feel Mitchell's eyes boring into me like they had earlier. One glance over my shoulder proved I was right.

If I hadn't known better, I would have sworn I saw a tear slide down his cheek.

Looking straight ahead, I made the decision I should have made months ago.

It was time to move on and forget about Mitchell Parker.

Tempting Love coming January 2018

PLAYLIST

Contains Spoilers

Caroline Jones – "Tough Guys"
Amelia and Waylynn in New York City.

Boyce Avenue – "Scared to Be Lonely"
Amelia and Liam's time in New York City.

Miranda Lambert – "Well Rested"
Amelia and Waylynn on plane after Waylynn leaves Jack.

Frank Sinatra – "Isn't She Lovely"
Wade dancing with Chloe the first time Amelia sees him.

Clint Black – "State of Mind"
Wade doing the cover of "State of Mind" at Aunt Vi's party.

Rascal Flatts – "Banjo"
Wade dancing with Chloe.

Cole Swindell – "No One Left Behind"
Amelia and Wade dancing for the first time.

Brett Eldredge – "Somethin' I'm Good At"
Wade and Amelia dancing.

Adam Sanders - "Thunder"
Wade in pasture when storm is rolling in.

Miranda Lambert – "To Learn Her"
Amelia and Wade dancing at Cord's Place.

David Nail – "Nights on Fire"
Amelia after dancing with Wade at Cord's Place.

Clint Black – "Nothing's News"
Wade at Cord's Place singing the cover of "Nothing's News".

Rascal Flatts – "I'm Moving On"
Wade at Cord's Place singing the cover of "I'm Moving On".

Liam Payne – "Strip That Down"
Trevor's welcome home party for Waylynn.

Miranda Lambert – "Well Rested"
Amelia asking Wade to dance with her at Waylynn's welcome home party.

Miranda Lambert – "Pushin' Time"
Amelia and Wade kissing for the first time.

Michael W Smith – "Do You Dream of Me"
Amelia and Wade at the barn after the great goat incident.

Frank Sinatra – "Witchcraft" and "With Every Breath I Take"

Amelia and Wade dancing on the rooftop of his new house.

Frank Sinatra – "The Last Thing I Do"
Wade making Amelia orgasm for the first time on the roof of the old historical home.

THANK YOU

Thank you to Darrin and Lauren for always being so supportive. This crazy dream called writing steals a lot of my time from the two of you, thank you for always being so understanding.

Thank you to everyone who had a hand in helping with this book. It takes a village and I have an amazing group of folks who help me do what I do! I love you all and couldn't have done this without you.

A HUGE thank you to my readers. If it wasn't for you, I wouldn't be writing out this thank you. I hope that you are enjoying the Parker family!